MR. MIDNIGHT
Allan Leverone

1

Stalking.

Mr. Midnight was stalking.

He trailed along behind his two targets carefully, keeping to the shadows as much as possible, staying a healthy distance away while being sure to keep them in sight at all times. The girls were college students; that much he knew. Whether they attended B.U., Northeastern, Tufts, or any of the dozens of other schools in the Boston area, the predator didn't know and didn't care.

What mattered to Mr. Midnight was that the girls were clearly from out of town, new students still unaware of the lines of demarcation the more experienced students observed automatically, which allowed them to stay safe.

Relatively speaking.

Mr. Midnight had been following the pair for twenty minutes, ever since observing them as they stumbled, drunk, out of a raucous apartment party on Commonwealth Avenue. He had been loitering in the dark recesses of a doorway across the street and gotten a vibe about the girls almost immediately.

Now they were lost, and confused, and just beginning to feel the first tentative twinges of apprehension. Alcohol bravery and the fact that they were together and could count on each other for support had suppressed the panic thus far, but Mr. Midnight knew it was mere minutes away from bubbling to the surface.

He picked up his pace and moved silently closer, now near enough to hear bits and pieces of their conversation. "...think we went in the wrong direction," the one on the left was saying. She had a nice, shapely ass packed into low-rise jeans. Her crop-top blouse didn't come close to reaching her waist and the predator thought he could see the hint of a thong peeking out over the jeans. He smiled with approval.

"...don't recognize anything..." the other one said. She was Asian, a slim, tiny girl poured into a red mini-dress.

"Maybe we should turn around," the first girl said. Mr. Midnight was close enough to them now that he could hear their voices clearly. Both girls sounded near tears and the predator felt himself becoming aroused.

The area was unfamiliar to them.

The streetlights were dim and spaced far apart.

Pedestrian traffic was minimal.

It was time to move.

Mr. Midnight closed the remaining distance between himself and the girls, still unsure of which one he would take, not that it mattered. They were both young and pretty, and he knew he would be more than satisfied with either.

It was almost too easy. The predator wore Nike cross-trainers and moved with a practiced stealth, and the frightened girls were chattering to each other like magpies in an effort to keep their mounting fear at bay.

They were crossing in front of a Catholic grade school, the Victorian-era stone structure looming in the semidarkness behind a padlocked chain-link fence, when the predator struck. He used the butt of his knife to club the girl on the left—he glanced down and discovered he had been right about the thong—in the temple. She let out a low moan and dropped straight down, unconscious before her body hit the concrete sidewalk with a wet *thud*.

The second girl, the tiny Asian in the mini-dress, gasped and froze, trying to process in her alcohol-addled brain what had just happened. A half-second later she drew in a breath to scream, but by then it was much too late. Mr. Midnight slapped a hand over her mouth and lifted the knife to her throat, running its razor-sharp point along her silky skin like a lover's caress. Blood immediately began welling up in the furrow.

The girl stopped struggling, undoubtedly hoping compliance would equate to survival.

She wouldn't find out until much later how wrong she was.

2

The air inside the Super-K Grocerette felt pleasantly cool to Caitlyn Connelly as she waited in line at the register. A low-pressure system had stalled over Tampa, the moisture in the atmosphere combining with the blazing heat to form a mushy tropical blanket over eastern Florida.

Through the plate-glass windows fronting the store, Caitlyn watched as people trudged across the parking lot. They seemed to move in slow motion, as if bogged down by the weather.

The line dragged, Cait inching forward until eventually she stood behind only an elderly woman who had placed her purchases—roughly a fifty-fifty split between food for herself and food for her pets—on the conveyor belt and now reached into a purse approximately the size of a small European car for her wallet.

Cait felt a sensation of pressure inside her skull, a wave rolling over her brain. She blinked twice and her head rocked back slightly. It was the sort of reaction a person might have if confronted with a completely unexpected sight. The image of a tiny kitchen flashed into her head. The room was shabby but spotlessly clean. On top of faded linoleum tiles that had been out of style for half a century, Cait saw a checkbook that had fallen to the floor and now lay against a leg of an ancient kitchen table.

A pair of sleeping cats sprawled on either side of the checkbook, looking like furry bookends, and Cait knew instantly what had happened. The woman had placed her purse at the edge of the table in preparation for her trip to the store—she shopped twice a week, Monday and Thursday—but she had mistakenly left it unclasped. The checkbook had fallen out of the purse when she picked it up, in a hurry because the taxi arrived sooner than expected, and it would simply be wrong to make the poor driver wait.

Caitlyn wasn't guessing about any of it. She knew what had happened because she could see it in her mind as clearly as if it were playing on a high-definition television screen in front of her. She didn't know *how* she could see it in her mind, only that she could. She had been experiencing these visions—"Flickers," she called them, due to their short but intense nature—for as long as she could remember.

The Flickers were, as far as she could tell, completely random occurrences. Sometimes they disappeared for days, the visions going silent for such long stretches of time Cait began to think maybe they had disappeared for good, only to return with a vengeance, dozens of the intense mental movies blasting into her head over the course of a few hours.

More often than not, though, she experienced one or two per day. They seemed normal and natural to Caitlyn because she had been living with them her entire life, but she had years ago given up trying to explain them to anyone else, tired of putting up with the amused smiles or exasperated looks of people who simply did not believe her.

Back in the Super-K, the elderly woman began frantically digging through the gigantic purse, looking for the checkbook she would not find, apologizing for holding up the line. The cashier, a bored teenage girl with purple-dyed hair who demonstrated her annoyance by snapping her bubble gum every few seconds, stood with one hand on her hip. She rolled her eyes at a heavyset woman standing in line behind Cait.

"Oh, dear," the elderly woman said, "I'm so sorry. I know I had my checkbook with me and now it's simply disappeared."

"Listen, lady," the woman behind Cait said, "we all have places to be. How about you step aside while you try to get your act together—not that you'll be able to—so the rest of us,"—she raised her arms like Moses parting the Red Sea—"can pay for our stuff and get the hell out of here."

The elderly woman was now almost in tears, flustered and confused. Cait turned and stared down the woman behind her, locking eyes until the woman turned away impatiently. Cait returned her gaze to Alice—that was the elderly woman's name, the knowledge came to Cait without warning—and said gently, "Do you think you might have forgotten your checkbook at home?"

"I suppose I must have, but I can't imagine how. I always prepare in advance for my trip to the grocery store. I place everything on the table in the morning while drinking my tea. I do it the same way every time to avoid this exact problem. Now, where could that checkbook be?" She began digging through her purse again.

Cait put an arm on her shoulder. "I'll pay for your things."

"Oh, no, I couldn't allow you to do that."

"Of course you can," she answered gently. "I'll pay for your purchases and then this nice young woman behind the counter will give me a slip of paper. I'll write my name and address on it, and when you get home and find your checkbook, you can mail me a check for the cost of your groceries. How does that sound?"

"Well, I don't know..."

The woman behind Cait snorted impatiently and Alice said, "All right, yes, I think that would be fine. Thank you so much, young lady."

Cait paid the cashier for both sets of groceries and then helped the woman load the bags into the trunk of her tiny car, glad to be out of the store. The incident had left a sour taste in her mouth and she felt badly for the old woman, who was obviously alone in the world. She wondered about her history. Was there a husband who had passed, leaving Alice to live out her final years alone? Were there children in the picture who visited once a week, bringing a much-needed break from the loneliness and isolation?

Cait considered the Flickers a normal part of her life. She had long ago stopped thinking of them as strange or unusual, but sometimes they were just so damned frustrating. The mental movies the Flickers provided were almost always incomplete, lacking any sense of context or cohesion—as in Alice's case, where she learned just enough about the woman's life to become curious—leaving her unhappy and upset.

Of course, she thought as she wheeled her bags to her car, *I don't know much more of my own history than I do of Alice's. Someday that will change,* she vowed.

Someday.

Cait loaded her groceries and drove slowly out of the lot. Over Tampa the clouds swirled, becoming thicker and blacker by the minute. A storm was coming, and by all appearances, it was going to be a bad one.

3

Thirty Years Ago
Everett, Massachusetts

Robert Ayers paced relentlessly, unwilling to leave his wife's side but unable to stand still. Back and forth he walked, mopping Virginia's sweaty brow, holding her hand, then marching to the bedroom door before turning on his heel and retracing his steps to her bed.

Shadows crept across the floor as the sun lowered in the late-afternoon sky, the hands on Robert's watch moving simultaneously fast and slow. Virginia moaned and thrashed, screaming at the onset of a contraction, relaxing when the pain eased. Sweat poured down her face.

"This is insane," Robert muttered. "She should be in a hospital. The days of giving birth at home ended decades ago. This is unsafe, especially if something goes wrong."

On the other side of the bed stood a stranger dressed in grubby medical scrubs, a pair of latex gloves pulled over his hands. As far as Robert could discern, the man had done little but observe quietly as Virginia screamed and suffered. The man shot him a dark glance but said nothing.

"She should be in the hospital," Robert repeated. He stopped pacing for a moment and leaned over, stroking his wife's cheek gently with the backs of his fingers. Her eyes were closed and she didn't seem to notice.

"Up to you," the stranger said. "It's your choice. Call an ambulance if you wish, but understand I get paid my full fee regardless of your decision."

Robert Ayers glared at his guest. "You're concerned about your fee? Jesus Christ, you'll get your money, don't worry about that."

"Jesus Christ has nothing to do with this," the stranger shot back, grinning darkly, revealing dual rows of yellowing teeth, irregular stumps thrusting at odd angles out of an unhealthy mouth. For what felt like the hundredth time, Roger wondered where in the hell his wife had found this man, this disgraced medical professional who had been stripped of his license to practice and now skulked about in the night, earning a living providing medical care deep in the shadows outside accepted society.

He called himself "Doctor Jones"—Robert hoped the man was better at doctoring than thinking up aliases—and when Robert had asked Virginia a few days ago where she had found him, she had been unable or unwilling to provide a satisfactory answer.

Locating and hiring "Doctor Jones" was just the latest example of the strange and frightening ability manifested by his wife on occasion. Robert had been completely unaware of her unusual gift until after they married. At times Robert thought "bizarre" would be a better description of Virginia's ability to place herself inside the minds of other people, strangers she had never before met and would never see again.

It was creepy and unsettling.

After their marriage, Virginia had described her unusual talent to Robert to the best of her ability, begging his forgiveness for not telling him sooner but admitting she feared the knowledge might frighten him away. "And I can't live without you," she told him tearfully.

She described the moments of incredible insight—"brain movies," she called them—that came upon her without warning, flashes of thoughts or mental pictures. They represented experiences other people were having, things they might be thinking or plans they might be making.

Suddenly, the strange, thought-provoking scenarios that had occurred over the course of their courtship—none momentous when considered on its own, but all quite disturbing when added together—all made sense. The empathetic connection Virginia seemed sometimes to share with random strangers, her inexplicable flashes of insight into lives and situations of which she should have no knowledge, all of it.

Initially he had been hurt and angry, even frightened. Then, after some time and reflection, Robert had decided it was far from the worst thing that could happen. Quite the opposite, actually, it was in some ways reassuring. Virginia wasn't a freak, she was simply a young woman with an unusual, almost mystical ability; a gift she had not asked for and could not divest herself of even if she wanted to.

Hell, if you really thought about it, the gift was nothing more than a hypersensitivity to the needs of others. And that was a good thing.

That was what Robert told himself.

And he stayed with Virginia.

He assumed Virginia had used her gift to find "Dr. Jones." He assumed she had experienced one of her strange "brain movies" when somewhere near him, maybe at the gas station or while in line at the bank, had uncovered his disgraced standing in the medical community in her mind and then had approached him to deliver her baby.

Virginia had adamantly refused to give birth in the hospital. Her fear of the place was something Robert did not quite understand—he found it illogical and senseless—but his wife would not be dissuaded from her insistence that the delivery occur at home.

Now, with the woman he loved suffering greatly, contractions wracking her body and "Dr. Jones" flippantly unconcerned, Robert began to feel the tug of panic in his gut. Virginia could die in childbirth; it was a very real possibility here in this non-sterile bedroom equipped with only the most rudimentary medical equipment.

Or her baby could die.
Or, God forbid, both things could happen.

4

The tenement was ancient, probably over one hundred fifty years old. Its red brick construction had been worn down by decades of extreme Boston weather until it now sagged and buckled as if the act of defying gravity was becoming simply too much to bear.

The building had been condemned years ago, deemed unfit for human habitation and then ignored, never renovated but never demolished, either. Now it sat, hulking and silent, its interior stripped, everything of value removed, either legally by owners who had long-since disappeared, or illegally by everyone else. Smashed-out windows had been hastily boarded over with sheets of plywood, and the building's exterior doors drooped in proportion with the rest of the structure. The entrances had been secured with locks that were broken off within days, likely within hours, of their installation and the tenement now formed a convenient gathering place for vagrants, drug dealers, users, and the occasional hooker performing a fifty-dollar quickie.

And one other man.

Milo Cain was the only resident of the top floor, having carved rudimentary living quarters out of the empty shell of one of the apartments. In one corner of what at some time in the past had been a living room, Milo had placed an air mattress, which represented a massive improvement over sleeping on the buckling floor. A ratty wool blanket lay over the mattress, one side eaten raggedly away by moths.

In the opposite corner, Milo had placed a Coleman cookstove, offering a way to heat coffee and soup and the occasional canned spaghetti dinner. There was no oven in the kitchen; that appliance had disappeared decades ago along with everything else of value.

Milo sat unmoving, butt on the floor, back against the wall. He stared across the room at nothing in particular. The electricity had been turned off years ago, and candles placed inside grimy old drinking glasses provided uneven lighting, splashing flickering shadows across the wall. A gigantic spider moved slowly and clumsily across the floor in front of Milo, its movements jerky and insectile. He barely noticed and didn't care.

His head lolled, striking the wall behind him as he was assaulted by a series of vivid images, all different but uniformly dark and disturbing. In the first, a man dressed in a stained wife-beater undershirt screamed at a woman, consumed by a white-hot rage that Milo could feel but which was meaningless to him because the vision provided no context. It was simply a scene, picked up at random by his subconscious mind.

The next involved a drug deal going down somewhere near the tenement. Milo watched through his mind's eye, floating high above the illicit meeting, silent and unseen. The participants were nervous, both sides tense and fearful of a double-cross and the potential for deadly violence.

That image seared itself into Milo's brain in an instant, only to be replaced by another, and another. Finally the images came to an end—for now—disappearing as if with the flick of a switch, and Milo sagged against the wall, spent. How long the break would last he had no way of knowing. It might be a precious few minutes, or maybe even a couple of hours if he was extremely lucky, which most of the time he was not. The only thing he knew for certain was that before long the images would return and when they did, they would be uniformly dark and disturbing and exhausting.

But there was one silver lining. When the images returned, maybe they would provide him with information he could use for his own purposes; there was always that possibility.

In the meantime, he would rest while he could. Milo considered crawling to his air mattress and napping while he had the chance, but he was too fucking tired to move. The visions were so goddamned draining.

Instead, he bent down, head hanging between his spread knees, and closed his eyes. God, he was tired. Maybe he would just lie down on his side right there on the floor and nap.

Then the visions exploded into his brain, beginning anew. Milo Cain's head snapped up, smashing against the wall, and once again he stared off into space, lost and dazed.

5

Cait sipped her wine, enjoying the last of the pot roast dinner and reveling in the nearly continuous stream of compliments being lobbed her way by her boyfriend. Kevin Dalton was not a hard guy to please when it came to food, but Cait wasn't about to let that minor detail lessen her appreciation of the moment.

Both worked long hours in the hopes of building their careers, Cait as a real estate attorney and Kevin as a Tampa police officer. But their long-standing tradition was a home-cooked meal every Thursday night, and tonight it had been Cait's turn to cook. She had purchased everything she needed at the Super-K and then spent the next couple hours peeling potatoes and carrots, tossing a salad and cooking the roast, before Kevin's arrival.

"I gotta tell ya," Kevin said, leaning back in his chair with a satisfied sigh, "this might be the best meal I've ever eaten."

Cait smiled. "Like I've never heard that before. I think it may have had more to do with the fact that all you had to eat today was half a cheese sandwich for lunch."

"Duly stipulated. Whew, that was quite the vigorous cross-examination, counselor. You're really getting this lawyer thing down."

Cait laughed and shook her head. "I do real estate law, remember? We don't cross-examine people."

"That's a shame," Kevin answered, "because you'd be really good at it. Anyway, I'll admit it, I was beyond hungry. But I'm still not backing off my testimony. Everything was delicious. I'm stuffed." He patted his belly and grinned.

"If you unbuckle your belt and unsnap the top button of your jeans, you're out of here. And you better have saved a little room for dessert and coffee."

"Note to self," Kevin replied. "No belt unbuckling. At least not until later." He waggled his eyebrows suggestively and Cait laughed. "And as far as dessert is concerned, I've never passed it up yet, and I'm not about to start now. What's on the menu?"

"Nothing. At least, for now."

"Excuse me?"

"You heard me. I'm withholding dessert—it's your favorite, by the way, homemade strawberry shortcake—until I get what I want."

"Ooh, kinky," Kevin said, nodding in appreciation. "If it involves a seductive striptease and grapes being hand-fed to me by a certain sexy young woman, count me in."

"You wish. It involves you letting me in on this big surprise you claimed to have in store for me. No dessert, of the food *or* sexual kind, until you spill the beans."

"Wow, that's cold. Lawyering's changing you, sweetheart." Kevin's eyes narrowed and Cait smacked him on the arm with a laugh.

"Come on," she said. "Give it up."

"All right, all right, I can't take any more. You've worn me down."

"Was there ever any doubt I would?"

"Good point. Okay, you know how you always say you'd like to learn more about your past—the identity of your birth parents, where they live, why they gave you up for adoption, all of that?"

"Sure. I just don't know where to begin. I have no idea where I was born, no idea what my parents' names might be, no clue what agency may have handled the adoption. There's nothing to go on."

"Exactly," Kevin said. "There's nothing for *you* to go on. But a professional could probably handle the job."

"Maybe," Cait answered. "But I don't have the money to hire a professional, you know that."

"You don't have to hire a professional."

"And why's that?"

"Because I already did."

"Uh, Kevin, aren't you forgetting something?"

"What?"

"*You* don't have the money for that, either."

"That's where you're wrong. It just so happens I've been saving up for a while, waiting to surprise you. I have enough cash put aside to at least get started, so I went out yesterday and hired an investigator."

Cait paused at the kitchen sink where she had been rinsing dishes. She stared at Kevin, saying nothing.

"Well?" he prompted.

"Well, what?"

"Are you surprised?"

"Surprised would be an understatement."

Kevin frowned. "What's wrong? I thought you'd be excited."

Cait rinsed her hands under the warm water and dried them on a towel. "It's not that I'm not happy, I am. I guess I just never really thought I would have the opportunity to discover my heritage. It's going to take a little while to get used to the idea that I might be able to learn something after all these years."

"Well," Kevin said, "the guy has a great reputation and all of his references check out. But he told me not to get my hopes up, that it's a long shot at best. He may not be able to find out anything."

"It doesn't matter," Cait said, hanging the dishtowel on a rack. She walked across the kitchen and sat in Kevin's lap.

"It doesn't?"

"No. What matters is that you cared enough to do such a thoughtful thing for me. That was really, really sweet. It's just one more reason why I love you." She put her arms around his neck and nibbled his ear. "Now, about that dessert. Still hungry?"

"I'm suddenly ravenous."

The strawberry shortcake went uneaten.

6

Thirty years ago

 Everett, Massachusetts

 Virginia moaned and thrashed as another contraction struck and Robert's panic bubbled closer to the surface. He decided he could no longer stand the agony of inaction. He had to do something. He just had to. He mopped his wife's forehead with the cool cloth—Christ, she was sweating so much!—and caressed her cheek. Her eyes remained closed.

 "That's it," he announced. "I've had it. This insanity has to end."

 "Dr. Jones" gave no response. It was as if he hadn't even heard Robert speak. He seemed preoccupied and Robert wondered if perhaps he was high on some medication.

 She's going to the hospital," Robert continued. "I'm calling an ambulance."

 He strode across the room.

 Made it to the open door.

 And Virginia screamed, her voice jagged and high-pitched, intense now with anger, not pain. "NO! You will not call an ambulance! I'm having this baby right here. You agreed to this and you will NOT BACK OUT NOW!"

 Robert stopped in his tracks, confused, the certainty of a moment ago gone. At the foot of the bed, he thought he saw a smile flit across "Dr. Jones's" face and disappear.

Then Virginia screamed again as another contraction struck. She sounded like she was being beaten with a baseball bat. The contractions were coming more rapidly now and increasing in intensity.

Robert rushed back to her bedside. He realized it was probably too late for an ambulance now, anyway. Something was going to happen soon, he could feel it. The baby was going to be born in the next few minutes or...well...Robert refused to consider the alternative.

Again Virginia screamed, her voice like a buzz saw ripping through a stubborn plank. She was panting and sweating, screaming constantly now, thrashing on her blood- and sweat-soaked bed.

The unlicensed doctor bent down over Virginia, somehow deciding now was the time to act. "You need to push," he announced softly.

"I can't," she screamed.

"PUSH," Dr. Jones said again, more forcefully this time, grabbing her by the shoulders, and she pushed. She screamed and cried and sweated and swore, but she pushed, and then pushed again, continued pushing when she swore she could not, and then it was over and Virginia Ayers had given birth to a baby girl.

And then to a baby boy.

7

Milo Cain wandered down Washington Street toward Roxbury, moving slowly, randomly. The night was still young, so he was forced to share the sidewalk with plenty of other people. Few took direct notice of him, but, as always, the majority of pedestrians gave him a wide berth, somehow unconsciously sensing menace. Mothers tightened their grips on their children, adults averted their eyes at his approach.

His face was nearly invisible, sunken deep inside the shadows of a hooded grey New England Patriots sweatshirt. Baggy jeans, desperately in need of a washing they would not receive, threatened to slip down his narrow hips, somehow defying the laws of gravity and staying up. Tattered Chuck Taylors flopped on his feet.

A group of three young black males approached, flat-brimmed baseball caps askew, sauntering shoulder-to-shoulder, forcing Milo off the sidewalk and into the gutter. One of them shot him a glance, silent and resentful. They passed and Milo waited for a sign and received nothing, so he continued on.

A small hole-in-the-wall tavern appeared on the right, flickering neon Coors sign illuminating a plate-glass window that probably hadn't been cleaned since the Bush administration. The first one.

Inside the bar, a tired-looking middle-aged waitress schlepped glasses of beer clustered atop a small round tray. As Milo watched, a heavyset drunk lost his footing and stumbled into the waitress, sloshing beer over the sides of the glasses and off the edge of the tray in a golden mini-tsunami. No one paid any attention and the waitress soldiered on.

Two girls, white and young, blonde, clearly college students, too ignorant to realize they had no business being in this area—Milo's favorite kind of girl—rounded the corner and turned in his direction. They chatted quietly, unaware of their surroundings, oblivious to the potential for danger.

The girls passed on his left, quickening their strides, and his head snapped back like he had been struck in the face as an image seared itself into his mind. The girls were students at Northeastern University. Juniors. The one passing closest to Milo was named Angela and she was cheating on her boyfriend, sleeping with her married Philosophy professor for no reason other than it seemed exciting and daring. She had told no one, not even her best friend.

As quickly as it had slammed into his brain, the vision vanished. The two clueless college girls continued on, moving away from Milo, and he paused, stopping in the middle of the sidewalk, analyzing what he had just learned, trying to decide if the information was in any way useful. He glanced at his feet and saw sickly looking weeds struggling through the cracks in the sidewalk.

Then he raised his head and the Northeastern students were instantly forgotten as he locked in on what he now knew he had been waiting for. Across Washington Street, a young Hispanic boy ambled along the sidewalk. The kid was perhaps ten years old, wearing gang colors, MP3 listening buds sprouting from his ears like cancerous growths.

Milo didn't even need a vision to tell him what he needed to know. The kid was a runner, a middleman employed by local gang members to deliver product to customers and cash back to the dealers. It was the oldest scam going. As a minor, if apprehended with illegal drugs, the kid would face nothing more than a slap on the wrist, whereas the older gangbangers could be put away for years, even for life, depending on their arrest records.

What Milo didn't know was whether the kid was carrying drugs or cash; whether he had already made a delivery or was on his way to do so. Milo had no need or desire for drugs, his reality was warped enough from the nearly unending stream of visions he experienced. Cash, however, was another matter entirely. For a man living on the farthest outskirts of society, cash was indispensable.

Milo crossed Washington Street at a jog, moving quickly enough to gain ground on the kid but not so fast he might draw unwanted attention. In this neighborhood, a sprinting young man most often suggested a felony in progress. Behind Milo a cab slammed on its brakes, nearly clipping him as it slewed to the side of the street. The furious cabdriver unleashed a string of broken-English epithets into the muggy night, his anger unacknowledged by Milo or anyone else.

When he reached the opposite sidewalk, Milo slowed. Now roughly twenty feet behind the kid, he maintained his distance. And waited expectantly.

He didn't have to wait long. In seconds a vision sizzled into his fevered brain like a lightning bolt. *It's money,* he thought. *The kid is carrying the proceeds from a drug deal.* It wasn't much, only a couple of hundred bucks, but beggars couldn't be choosers, especially when you took the expression literally. Two hundred dollars would go a long way when you had nothing but a little spare change rattling around in your pocket.

Milo picked up his pace slightly, staying attuned to his surroundings as much as possible while still absorbing the vision. The money was in the right thigh pocket of the kid's cargo shorts, nine twenty-dollar bills and two crumpled tens stuffed next to a throwaway cell phone. Milo could see it in his mind as clear as day. In the left pocket the kid carried a knife, a weapon that would wind up being completely useless to him.

It was perfect.

What was not perfect was the fact that the kid was almost back to the burned-out shell of an abandoned tenement—a building not much different than Milo's—that served as his gang's headquarters, only another block and a half away on the left. Once within sight of that warehouse, the kid would be untouchable, as the gang would have a team of sentries posted, young men who were heavily armed and not likely to approve of their runner being taken down before their very eyes.

Milo knew he had to act now—stealth and surprise would work in his favor. He resumed jogging and wrapped his fingers around the stolen Glock 19 inside the hand-warmer pouch of his sweatshirt.

In seconds he was couple of feet behind the kid, who was still bopping along to the music in his ears, feeling secure in a way he never would again. Milo pulled the Glock from his pocket and in one smooth motion lifted his arm to smash its butt against the side of the kid's head.

The boy had begun to turn at the last moment, some instinct alerting him to the impending attack. His reaction was much too late. He spun around and the gun caught him just above his right eye. He dropped like a felled tree, blood gushing from a jagged gash in his forehead.

This was the critical moment. Time was precious. The kid moaned and clutched at his skull, almost but not quite unconscious. Milo knelt and reached into the left pocket of his victim's cargo shorts, withdrawing the hunting knife still secured in its scabbard and jamming it into his pocket. He didn't really need it, owned plenty of knives already, but he had no desire to find he had misjudged the extent of the kid's injuries by getting shanked as soon as he turned his back.

Milo pulled the wad of cash and the cell phone out of his victim's pants, then stood and began walking briskly away from the tenement building. He made it half a block before the first rough shouts of surprise went up. He didn't turn around, didn't glance behind, didn't do anything. He just kept walking.

In a matter of minutes, Milo had left the scene of the attack behind and was well on his way to the safety of his "apartment." He assumed as a matter of course that he had been seen attacking the kid, but the likelihood of being identified was almost nil between his outfit—the uniform of urban anonymity—and the fact that he rarely spent time in that neighborhood.

To be safe, Milo knew he would have to avoid Washington Street for a good long while, but the prospect didn't concern him. Boston was a big city and there were plenty of areas suitable for hunting. All one needed was the time to seek out victims.

And Milo Cain had plenty of time.

8

The private investigator's name was Arlen Hirschberg and he was hungry. Specifically, he was hungry for a turkey melt with crispy fries and a chocolate shake. Cait knew this because she could see it in her head; the vision exploded into her brain the moment she stepped into Hirschberg's office. It was not exactly the sort of he-man meal Cait would have expected out of a macho private detective, but she had been on the receiving end of Flickers for her entire life and had never known them to be wrong.

Hirschberg had called yesterday and scheduled the appointment, saying only that he had some news to share. When Kevin expressed surprise that the PI had obtained results already, he laughed and said he would be happy to sit on the information for a couple of weeks if it made Kevin happy.

Now, sitting in the PI's office, it occurred to Cait that her expectations of what a private investigator would look like had been inaccurate all around. She had expected to meet a gruff, burly man wearing an ill-fitting suitcoat over a leather shoulder holster into which would be crammed a big handgun. He would have a booming voice and arms like stevedores and his office would be small and Spartan, with a ceiling fan moving the air around and a metal filing cabinet in the corner behind his beat-up desk. He would be the Hollywood noir cliché of a private detective.

The reality was almost the complete opposite. The Hirschberg Investigations office was big and airy, with framed, signed prints of American sports heroes adorning the walls. To Cait's right, Bobby Orr flew through the air, hockey stick held high in triumph, forever celebrating his Stanley Cup-winning overtime goal for the Boston Bruins in 1970. To her left, a young Michael Jordan slammed down a dunk, tongue wagging out of his mouth. Behind her, some NFL kicker she didn't recognize was booting a football into a raging blizzard.

Instead of a clichéd cheap suit, the private detective was dressed casually but crisply in tan Dockers and a midnight blue golf shirt. His weapon, if he was sporting one, was nowhere to be seen. There was no ceiling fan, and the filing cabinets weren't even in this office, they were located behind Hirschberg's receptionist in the waiting area. Behind his desk, the glass wall offered a breathtaking view of the Tampa cityscape, with the greenish-blue waters of the Gulf of Mexico beyond.

In short, Caitlyn realized this was no down-on-his-luck Hollywood PI. Everything about Arlen Hirschberg screamed competence and success, and Cait supposed that was exactly the point. She wondered how much money Kevin had had to shell out to secure this man's services. She had asked him that very question on the way over but he refused even to discuss the issue.

"So," Hirschberg said after introducing himself and seating them, "can I get you something to drink? Coffee? Tea? Sparkling water?"

"I'm fine, thanks," Cait replied, smiling. If she had held on to any remaining stereotypes about Arlen Hirschberg, the offer of sparkling water pretty much destroyed them. Her adopted father had been a devoted fan of the 1970s TV series *The Rockford Files*, in which James Garner played a down-on-his-luck private detective. As a child, Cait had watched just about every episode with him on TV Land and she was almost certain he had never once offered sparkling water to anyone.

"Okay, then, let's get right to it. You have quite the unusual history, young lady," Hirschberg said with a smile. "In most cases, when an adopted child wishes to unearth her history, the official records may have been sealed to protect the privacy of the birth mother and thus are not accessible, but there *are* records."

Cait nodded. "I understand. But that's not the case with me, is it?"

"No, Ms. Connelly, it's not. In your case, there *were* no official records, accessible or otherwise. You weren't born in the Tampa area, I'm sure you are aware of that much. Do you have any idea where you were born?"

"The only information I ever got from my adoptive parents regarding my birth history was that I was born somewhere in the northeastern United States. That's as specific as they would ever get. I got the impression that even they didn't know exactly where I came from."

"And your adoptive parents are now deceased, is that correct?"

"Yes, that's right."

Hirschberg crossed his arms and cupped his chin in one hand. "What do you know about the black market baby trade, Ms. Connelly?"

The question caught her by surprise. She paused and then shook her head. "Um, nothing, really."

"You're not alone. It's not a subject that gets a lot of media attention. But it should. There is a flourishing market in this country for people who want babies but are not able to have their own and, for whatever reason, cannot or will not go through the normal and accepted—and legal—channels of adoption. This market has existed for decades, centuries probably, and continues to this day. It will likely continue long into the future."

"Are you saying I was a black market baby?"

"It would seem logical, wouldn't it, given the lack of official documentation regarding the circumstances of your birth?"

Cait nodded and Hirschberg continued. "This would explain why there seems to be no way to trace your adoption through legal channels. There *are* no legal channels to speak of."

"But you said you had news for me. If there's no way to trace my history, why am I here?"

Hirschberg held up a finger. "I didn't say there was no way to trace your history. I said there was no way to do it through legal channels. I've worked in law enforcement my entire adult life and over the course of my career have served as a patrol officer, a homicide detective and federal agent, among other things.

"Over time I developed a fairly extensive network of contacts, as you might imagine. In your case, mining those contacts was problematic due to the fact that three decades has passed since the adoption occurred. Many people who might have been familiar with the circumstances of your case are now dead or moved on years ago and cannot be found. However, 'problematic' does not mean 'impossible,' and I was able eventually to secure the information you wanted."

Cait shook her head, confused. "How in the world could you do that if there are no records?"

"Oh there are records, Ms. Connelly. There are always records, at least in these sorts of cases. They may not be official government records, all neat and clean and notarized and legally binding, but they do exist. And those records are accurate, certainly accurate enough for your purposes."

"So..." After years of dealing with the pain that came from assuming she would never learn the specifics of her familial background, Cait discovered that being on the verge of getting that information was more than a little daunting.

She took a deep breath and started again. "So, where am I from, Mr. Hirschberg?"

9

The visions pounded through Milo Cain's head, one after the other, like movie trailers playing non-stop on some cursed screen in his brain. These trailers, though, often made no sense. They were mostly short snippets of lives being lived by anonymous people Milo would never meet. Pointless visions of ordinary actions, like a woman washing the dinner dishes or a man making plans to play basketball the next day. Their very pointlessness made Milo Cain's torture even more difficult to bear.

He sat in the tiny shell of an apartment, back propped against the wall—his usual method for riding out the storm of visions—waiting for them to take a break. They always did, eventually, just as they always came roaring back eventually as well. When they finally, mercifully, came to an end, an exhausted Milo Cain considered how to spend his evening.

It wasn't supposed to be like this. Milo had survived a traumatic early childhood involving physical and mental abuse, had survived and moved on and deserved better. Up until the age of five, he had lived in suburban Austin, Texas, with his adoptive parents, both executives in the nuclear power industry.

Normal.

Respected.

Abusive to Milo.

He didn't remember much of anything about Texas, but one thing he *did* know was that while living there he could not recall so much as a single episode involving visions blasting into his head.

Milo remembered with crystal clarity the first time he had ever experienced a vision. When he was five years old, the Cain family moved to Amesbury, Massachusetts, a seaside community on Boston's North Shore. His mother and father had both received promotions involving higher pay and additional responsibilities to work at the Seabrook nuclear plant located up Interstate 95 in Portsmouth, New Hampshire.

The incident occurred at the end of the family's first day in Massachusetts. Everyone was exhausted from the move, hunkered down in a motel for the night, in bed early because the following day was to be spent conducting a lengthy house-hunting search. Milo lay in the room with his father and mother, almost asleep in his rollaway bed despite the discomfort of the lumpy mattress, when into his head blasted a strange, frightening vision, almost, but not quite a dream.

In the vision, his parents were lying in bed, and his father was doing something to his mother; it almost looked as though he was attacking her, hurting her somehow. And she must have been getting hurt, because she was moaning, her head thrashing back and forth on the pillow. It was horrifying, and not just because the young Milo Cain didn't understand what it meant. What made it all the more frightening was that he had no idea where it had come from.

The disturbing vision had all the qualities of the dream state, the vivid colors and the hyper-reality, but it could not be a dream because Milo was not yet asleep. Even five-year-olds know you have to be asleep to dream, and the moment the vision began, Milo opened his eyes wide in mute, helpless terror, mouth agape, waiting for the scene to end.

When the vision did end—thankfully, this first one was short and to the point, even if Milo didn't understand the point—his head lolled to the side, and he found himself simultaneously comforted and horrified by the sight of the sleeping forms of his parents in the bed across the semi-dark motel room.

That long-ago night in Massachusetts represented the beginning of the visions for young Milo Cain. The family found a home and remained on the North Shore, and as Milo grew, the visions became more and more pronounced, growing ever darker and more disturbed even as his treatment at the hands of his parents became more and more twisted.

For a short time he tried to describe the horror of the visions to his mother and father, eventually coming to the realization they didn't believe him, would never believe him, and would not care even if they *did* believe him.

After that, Milo simply gave up. He stopped telling his parents about the strange scenes exploding into his head, the visions that now populated more and more of his waking hours. And he began to fall behind in school. His teachers assumed he was daydreaming and uninterested when his features slackened and his eyes glazed over and he stared at the blackboard or out the window, not disturbing anyone or causing trouble but clearly not paying attention, either.

He became withdrawn and sullen at home, spending all his time in his room, stretched out on the bed staring at the wall, unwilling to discuss his problem but unable to make it stop. Soon after, neighborhood pets began disappearing, mostly cats and a couple of small dogs, the occasional mutilated small-animal carcass thrown carelessly into the woods along the side of the road.

One morning in midsummer 2001, when Milo Cain was not quite eighteen years old, he walked out of his parents' Amesbury home and never returned. Over the next decade, Milo wandered throughout New England, traveling as far south as Bridgeport, Connecticut, and as far north as Jonesport, Maine, at times gaining temporary respites from the torture as the visions receded, at other times suffering mightily as they attacked with renewed fervor.

But they never completely disappeared, and Milo found it easiest to survive inside the sprawling Boston metropolitan complex, where he could disappear, losing himself in the crowds of down-on-their-luck vagrants who, like himself, fit in nowhere.

There was another advantage to living in Boston. Milo's compulsion to *do* things, bad things, horrible, twisted things, had blossomed as the visions increased in frequency and intensity. His need to injure, to destroy, to tear apart based on the information contained in those visions was often overwhelming, and this compulsion was fed most easily in the city. The atrocities he committed were not invisible in Boston, of course, but they were much easier to get away with in the teeming metropolis than in the wide-open spaces of a small town like Amesbury, where everyone had known him and seen him as a freak.

After years of restless wandering, Milo moved to the city permanently at the age of twenty-two, never staying in one place too long, moving around obsessively. When his compulsions began to attract the attention of the wrong people, he would simply pick up stakes and wander to another neighborhood, from Dorchester to Roxbury to Mattapan to Back Bay, thrilled that by traveling just a few blocks he could begin fresh.

There was the occasional brush with the law; it was almost impossible to be a vagrant, even in a city as large as Boston, and not catch the eye of the authorities every so often. But to Milo's continuing amazement, most of the suspicion involved his appearance, his dirty clothes and unkempt hair, those superficial things that made the good citizens of Massachusetts uncomfortable.

The things that *should* have been of interest to the police—the abductions, the torture, now of humans rather than animals—never seemed to find their way back to him, despite the fact he rarely made more than a token attempt at disguising his activities, and despite the fact that the media had begun playing up the horrifying exploits of "Mr. Midnight," the tag a clever television news reporter had hung on him a few months ago, when a trash bag filled with decaying body parts had been discovered behind a restaurant in Chinatown.

He supposed his visions were largely responsible for his invincibility. Thanks to the images flashing into his head, he was able to select as victims only people who would pose no more than a minor threat to him. The irony of being insulated and protected by the very visions that tortured him day after day and made his life a living hell was not lost on Milo; he appreciated it in the way an entomologist might appreciate being bitten by a particularly poisonous insect: the experience was painful and rewarding at the same time.

All of this ran through Milo Cain's mind as he leaned against the bleak apartment wall. He savored the clarity of thought that accompanied his brief respites from the visions. The damned images spent so much time bouncing around inside his brain that when they finally subsided, his head felt large and airy, like a penthouse apartment that has been cleared of all furniture.

He considered the long night ahead, stretching dark and empty before him. His skin was beginning to feel tight and hot, and his breathing felt ragged and constricted. His obsessions were beckoning again. It was time to play.

Tonight he would find a streetwalker. Playing with hookers was especially enjoyable. Milo loved taking the hardened, streetwise bitches, with their garish makeup and their superior, sneering attitudes and turning them into helpless victims, begging and pleading for their worthless lives, suspecting but never knowing for certain until the very end what their fate was going to be.

With hookers, the risk of getting caught was minimal. Dealing with pros meant dealing with people who, like himself, spent their days and nights on the fringes of accepted society. Their pimps would miss them, but that would be it. There would likely be no worried husbands or boyfriends to report them missing, no concerned coworkers to alert the authorities when they didn't report to the office Monday morning.

They would simply vanish.

So that was it, then. He would take a walk tonight and let the visions lead him to the perfect victim. The visions would be there to guide him. They always were.

10

Thirty years ago

Everett, Massachusetts

The sun had by now descended below the horizon, and the room was enveloped in a gloom Robert thought most appropriate for the occasion. Virginia dozed and Robert sat next to her, holding their children, one in each arm, fighting a sadness that threatened to overwhelm him. What should have been one of the happiest days of his life was turning into one of the most horrifying.

"Dr. Jones" had departed, collecting his fee in cash as previously agreed upon and promising to stop by tomorrow to look in on Virginia. By then the babies would be gone, not that Dr. Jones would care one way or the other. He had been contracted to provide medical services to Virginia Ayers during the delivery, and that was all. The infants were not a part of that contract and thus not Dr. Jones's concern.

Virginia had refused to hold either of the babies when offered. She simply moaned softly and rolled onto her side, refusing to answer Robert's questions, refusing even to meet his eyes. Eventually she had slipped into a restless slumber.

The doorbell rang and Robert sat up with a start, shocked to discover he too had fallen asleep. How he had managed that feat while holding two newborn babies he did not know, but he felt fortunate not to have dropped either of them.

"Christ," he mumbled disgustedly, "maybe it's a good thing we have to give them away." Then he glanced at his children and immediately changed his mind.

He stood and turned toward the front of the house, stopping to glance at Virginia before leaving the room. He was surprised to see her staring steadily back at him.

"It's time," Robert said simply, and she nodded. "Would you like to..."

"No," she interrupted. "I don't want to say good-bye to them. I can't bear to do it. I'm sorry to put this on you, my love, but could you please handle this?"

Robert looked at the floor and scuffed the carpet with the toe of his shoe. "Of course."

He left the bedroom and trudged through the small house. He thought he now knew how an inmate might feel making the walk to the gas chamber. He stopped and took a deep, shaking breath. Opened the door. On the landing stood a stranger dressed head to toe in black. Black watch cap, black trench coat, black trousers and shoes. The man even wore a solid black necktie over a black Oxford shirt.

The stranger eyed Robert for a long moment, not speaking. Then he inclined his head at the babies. "Are they ready?"

Robert nodded. "Come in," he said.

The stranger—Robert didn't know his name and didn't want to know—entered without another word. Next to the door sat a small duffel bag, packed earlier in the evening. Inside it were two outfits for each infant, a small supply of diapers and baby formula, and a pair of blankets, all items that had been agreed upon weeks ago.

Robert picked up the bag and handed it to the stranger, who hesitated a moment. It seemed as though the man wanted to say something, but decided against it. The stranger shrugged and carried the bag to a car idling at the end of the driveway. He dumped the bag into the trunk.

A darkness unlike anything he had ever felt filled Robert's heart. He had never seen the man in black before and knew he would never see him again. He knew nothing about the stranger, only that he was to hand over his two children, his own flesh and blood, to the man and allow the man to disappear with them forever.

He couldn't do it.

He wouldn't do it.

11

Cait leaned back in her seat and tried to relax as the half-empty airplane carved the sky northbound over the Atlantic coast. Kevin dozed next to her, as did most of the other passengers on the late-night flight, but Cait was far too keyed up to sleep. She was on her way—hopefully—to meet her biological mother, and it was all she could think about.

After a lifetime of wondering where she came from and who she was, and having resigned herself years ago to never learning her personal history, the speed with which the investigator, Arlen Hirschberg, had uncovered the clues to her past was astonishing. It took less than a week for Hirschberg to determine that she had been born June 15, 1983, in a suburb of Boston, Massachusetts, to a young couple named Robert and Virginia Ayers.

There was no record of the birth in any of the local hospitals—not surprising, Hirschberg said, given the Ayers's subsequent release of the infant into the illegal baby market—so it was reasonable to assume she had been born inside the Ayers home. Tiny Caitlyn had spent just a few hours in her birthplace before being spirited away in the middle of the night by a nameless representative of a faceless black market adoption ring.

She had been raised by a young married couple living outside Tampa and had grown up on the west coast of Florida, wondering

Why? every time she thought about her biological parents. It was not that she didn't love and appreciate her adoptive family. Margery and Walt Connelly had showered her with love and attention, raising a strong and caring young woman. To Caitlyn, they would always be her real parents, and both had gone to their graves knowing how much they were loved by their only child.

But none of that changed the fact that Caitlyn Connelly needed to plug the hole she felt in her heart every time one of her friends would say something like, "Oh, my grandfather came over from Verona, Italy, in 1935, and started his own plumbing business." Caitlyn wanted—*needed*—to be able to relate her own family history. She wanted—*needed*—to understand where her *own* grandfather had come from and what *he* had done for work. Was he a plumber, carpenter, doctor, lawyer?

For all of the excitement she felt as the airplane hummed its way north, though, Cait knew there was every possibility this trip would end in disappointment. Arlen Hirschberg had contacted Cait's birth mother, Virginia Ayers, now widowed and in ill health, living in her longtime home outside Boston, and the woman had flatly refused to see her daughter. According to the investigator, she was shocked at being tracked down after all this time and had seemed somehow frightened at the prospect of meeting her now thirty-year-old child.

Caitlyn knew how she felt. The idea of seeing the woman who had given her up so long ago caused a snake made of nerves and fear to twist through her belly, and she knew that snake would never slither away as long as the questions she had been carrying around for so long remained unasked.

So, despite the fact that Virginia Ayers had turned down Hirschberg's request for a face-to-face meeting, Cait and Kevin bought the cheapest red-eye tickets they could find to Boston, determined to see the woman in person and convince her to share just a few minutes of her time.

Cait didn't intend to bully the woman. She just had to know.

She gazed out the tiny window, watching the lights blink on the tips of the wings as they swayed hypnotically, buffeted by the wind resistance created by an aluminum tube shooting through the air at hundreds of miles per hour. Cait tried to imagine the circumstances that might have forced her mother to abandon her. Her fantasy had always been of a young teen, pregnant and terrified, the father unwilling or unable to support her, hiding her pregnancy in shame and then ridding herself of her baby immediately following its birth.

But she knew now that fantasy was far from accurate. Hirschberg said she had been born to a married couple. Maybe there was mental illness involved—that certainly seemed possible, given the existence of the Flickers Cait had experienced her entire life—or maybe her parents had been on the run, fleeing some unknown threat, unwilling to subject their newborn baby to the danger in their lives.

Cait sighed. She was being ridiculous and she knew it. Her birth mother hadn't been fleeing from some shadowy Hollywood B-movie assassin. Virginia Ayers had lived in the same area, under the same name, for decades, maybe for her whole life. The reality of the situation was clearly different than anything Cait had spent a lifetime imagining, so it was pointless to speculate. Better to simply wait for the meeting, pray she could convince the woman to talk to her, and then try to get as much of the full story as possible.

But relaxing was out of the question. Kevin snored softly next to her and then without warning the Flickers began, crashing into her brain like an out-of-control freight train. Her head jerked once, almost imperceptibly, as it always did when the Flickers began, and then the images invaded her mind, random scenes of random people, all of whom were sitting quietly on this airplane.

A little girl hugged her stuffed bear close to her chest as she tried to sleep. She had to go to the bathroom but was trying to ignore it because she didn't want to wake her sleeping mother.

A man experiencing money problems could not stop worrying how in the hell he was going to make his next mortgage payment, and how long he might be able to stall foreclosure when that payment was missed, as he knew it inevitably would be.

A young woman, newly engaged, was traveling to meet her fiancé's parents for the first time, nervous about the meeting and fearing she was making a mistake. She worried that she didn't truly love her husband-to-be, and that he wasn't the one for her. Should she back out of the wedding, and if so, how would she tell her fiancé?

Cait reached over and took Kevin's hand gently in hers. It was large and it enveloped her smaller one like a big, warm glove. His eyes blinked open and he looked up at her sleepily. He squeezed her hand once and then dozed off again. She had told him she could make the trip herself, that it wasn't necessary for him to babysit her, that she was a big girl and could handle meeting her mother alone, but he had just smiled and nodded and gotten the time off from work anyway.

"You don't get to have all the fun," he had said. "I could use a little mini-vacation, too."

But Cait knew why he had really tagged along. He was afraid that she would arrive at Virginia Ayers's home and the woman would simply send her away, or, worse, she would agree to talk but would be caustic and nasty, and Cait would be devastated. He was coming along because he wanted to be there in case it became necessary to pick up the pieces.

Cait wondered what she had done to deserve Kevin. How had she gotten so lucky? She knew there was nothing so horrible in the world that you couldn't face it head-on if you had the right partner. And she had the right partner.

Outside, the lights on the wing continued to wink, the plane moving steadily north over the dark ocean far below, vast and silent and ghostly. The Flickers continued for a while longer, flashing into Cait Connelly's brain at random intervals, imprinting themselves on her consciousness and then disappearing like scenes picked up by a flashbulb popping in a dark room.

They didn't bother Cait. Not really. She was used to them.

12

The problem with hunting at night in the neighborhoods Milo liked to frequent was that there were too damned many potential victims. In addition to the usual suspects—prostitutes, pimps, gang members, petty criminals—there were always plenty of clueless ordinary citizens who somehow felt comfortable walking the streets of a dangerous city alone after dark.

These fools were the people Milo tried his best to stay away from. He wasn't always successful, but he tried. Ordinary citizens were the ones most likely to cause problems when they vanished. They were the ones with money, with pull, with worried families only too willing to make tearful appearances on the TV news and beg for their loved one's return. Their cases were the ones the police spent most of their time and efforts trying to solve, and therefore Milo considered them, with rare exceptions, off limits.

Milo was much more interested in the hunt and in the subsequent pleasure he could get out of his victim than in any cat-and-mouse game he might play with the authorities. He wanted to satisfy his cravings in anonymity, not have to spend precious time and effort avoiding capture. That goal had vanished when Carrie Collins of Channel Seven news had coined the term, "Mr. Midnight," but it was nevertheless still good practice to stay away from publicity. To that end, the people of the night—lost souls similar to himself—made much more logical targets.

And there were plenty of them.

Tonight, having decided upon a hooker as his prey, Milo took his time, stalking the streets patiently. A light drizzle cloaked the scene in an eerie glow, indistinct yellow halos surrounding the streetlights, making the city look more like nineteenth-century London than twenty-first-century Boston.

Cars cruised past, some low-slung and sporty, successful horny middle-aged businessmen with more money than sense out for taboo satisfaction, others boxy and utilitarian, less successful horny middle-aged businessmen out for their own taboo satisfaction. The parade seemed endless. Milo paid them little attention.

The girls, however, were a different story. His tastes weren't overly particular, but if he was going to go to the trouble of selecting a companion, he wanted to take his time and do it right. There was no point grabbing the first girl he saw and then being disappointed; having to kill her and dump the body and then begin his search all over again.

So the girls he paid attention to. He wandered along the sidewalk, scrutinizing them as they stood in the shadows in groups of two and three. Most often they were bored, passing the time by chatting and joking with each other as they waited for potential customers. When a car containing a john drove by slowly and deliberately, the occupant's intentions clear, the girls would emerge from the shadows like modern-day vampires, strutting and posturing, offering up the most favorable view of the merchandise.

Sometimes the car would pull to the curb and stop, the driver rolling down a window, chatting nervously with his favorite, negotiating terms. Other times the car would accelerate away, the shopper unimpressed, continuing his search elsewhere, and the girls would retreat into the alley or doorway, resuming their wait for the next potential customer. They never had to wait long.

Milo glided through the night, haunting the streets, occasionally catching a vision as he passed the hookers. Here was an aging pro, prematurely hardened by years on the street, worried about getting beaten by her pimp—again—because her earnings were slipping.

Here was a younger girl, prettier and less hardened but still a veteran of several years, snapping gum, strutting for customers, but in her mind thinking she was going to have to take the next few days off. She felt bloated. Her period was about to start, and that was exactly what she didn't need. Taking time off would cut into her income stream. She was pissed.

Milo continued, unimpressed with the pickings. He hated the visions, wished for the millionth time in his miserable life he could be a normal guy with a normal brain, unencumbered by the unending onslaught of mental pictures and snippets of the thoughts and conversations of strangers. Then maybe this compulsion to hunt and torture and kill would disappear. Maybe he could finally achieve some peace. Maybe.

But it didn't matter, because it was never going to happen.

He rounded a corner and saw her. A pretty young thing, new to the game. You didn't have to be the recipient of inexplicable mental images to see that. The girl stood off by herself, awkward and uncomfortable, differentiated from her peers by the approach she was taking to lure business. Her contemporaries were dressed as provocatively as possible, decked out in micro-minis, fishnet stockings, tight crop-tops, four-inch heels.

They looked like sluts, in other words, and why wouldn't they? They *were* sluts. Professional sluts.

But this girl had taken a different approach. Her chestnut hair, straight and lush and shiny in the drizzle, was split into two long ponytails, cascading over her shoulders and down her back over a tight sweater. A short plaid skirt barely covered her ass, and long bare legs, adorned only with white striped knee socks worn over patent leather shoes, drew the eye like yesterday's trash draws flies.

The schoolgirl look.

Most pros, especially low-rent ones like the girls in this neighborhood, simply couldn't pull off the look. They were too old, or too hard, or too used up, and weren't able to effect the appearance of innocent sexuality it required.

But this girl was different. There was no telling how long she could manage it—the girls around here hardened quickly and permanently—but for now her freshness was unmistakable, and a welcome counterpoint to the cynical carnal excess on display everywhere else.

She was the one.

He had to have her.

Milo approached as slowly as he could manage without drawing undue attention to himself. He had been moving at a leisurely pace before and now scuffled along even more deliberately, dragging his feet and doing his best to make it appear he was paying no attention to the schoolgirl when, in reality, his entire being was focused upon her.

He passed a convenience store, one of the franchises known for being open twenty-four/seven. Not this location. This place was closed up tight, the owners having apparently decided the convenience to customers of a twenty-four-hour operation was not worth the constant threat of armed robbery. Metal shutters, the kind that could be levered up inside a steel awning during business hours, covered the windows, preventing entry from anything short of a military assault vehicle.

In the store's recessed entryway stood a cluster of girls, three of them, chirping to one another like birds on crack as they waited for business to pick up. Their conversation died off as Milo wandered past and they watched him with a suspicion that caught him by surprise. He was used to being ignored, not scrutinized. Somehow, concentrating so hard on the girl he wanted had made him more noticeable.

He cursed softly. This was the sort of thing that they would remember. Not right away, but when their little schoolgirl compatriot disappeared and her pimp and/or the police started asking questions, sooner or later one of them would recall the strange man walking all alone in this neighborhood, the man who showed up just before she checked out.

Milo knew he should just forget about this one, cut his losses; walk away and continue the search. It wasn't like he wouldn't be able to find another suitable playmate before the end of the night. But something about this girl really stoked his fire. Maybe it was nothing more than the fact that she represented an interesting challenge, but Milo wanted her. Only her. And he was goddamned well going to have her, the consequences be damned.

What would these drugged-up witnesses remember, anyway? He was just another anonymous guy in anonymous clothing. And he would disappear like smoke. There was nothing to worry about.

Milo walked past the hookers, ignoring them even as they eyed him with a mixture of curiosity and resentment. They seemed to realize he wasn't a customer, and if he wasn't planning to drop some cash on any of them, they wanted him away as fast as possible, so as not to scare off the next potential sale.

He didn't care. He wasn't going to hurry things along just to please a couple of skank hookers. He stared them down as he passed, knowing he shouldn't do it but unable to stop himself. Who the hell did they think they were? He blinked as an image of a knife flashed into his head. One of them had a knife hidden inside her boot and she was thinking about it, grateful she was protected against...whatever the danger was. She wasn't even sure. She only knew that she felt uneasy and concerned for her safety.

Then the vision passed and Milo was able to refocus his concentration on his target, the little faux schoolgirl standing off by herself on the sidewalk ahead. This novice streetwalker apparently had not yet developed whatever sixth sense the pros in front of the convenience store had that warned them of the menace inherent in Milo Cain. She looked ill at ease, but didn't seem to feel she was in any danger.

The girl twirled a finger through a stray lock of hair, gazing across the misty street at nothing in particular that Milo could see, so totally oblivious to her surroundings that he was able to move up right next to her, invading her personal space, before she even realized anyone was standing there. She turned and almost bumped into him, jumping back with a tiny yelp.

Milo arranged his face into what he hoped was his most ingratiating smile, aiming to look like just another pathetic horny bastard out for a little professional action on a Friday night. His nerves were thrumming and the tension in his gut was building as he approached the point of no return.

The hooker returned his smile hesitantly and said, "Hey, baby. Can I borrow some lunch money?"

The question was so unexpected that Milo laughed out loud in spite of the circumstances. "You don't even have to borrow it," he told her. "I've got money and it's all yours. Of course, there are a few strings attached."

"There always are," she answered with a wistful smile. "What can I help you with tonight?"

"Oh, we're going to do all kinds of fun stuff," Milo said, thrilled that he didn't even have to lie. Of course, she might disagree with his definition of fun, but that was her problem, not his. "Follow me."

"Follow you? Where are we going?"

"My car's right around the corner," he said. "Let's get out of this rain." He began walking away without looking back.

He knew the hooker would follow him. He was right.

13

Thirty years ago

Everett, Massachusetts

The stranger dressed all in black dumped the canvas bag into the truck of his idling car and returned to the doorway. Virginia had warned Robert this moment would be stressful, had told him to steel his heart, to avoid forming even the slightest attachment to the babies. She had said that to do so would only make the moment of parting that much more difficult. But how could it possibly be more difficult than this?

She had explained, clearly and patiently, that this parting was a necessary step. It represented the only way to protect the children, to ensure them of a fair chance at a happy life, and, more importantly, at a safe life. It had to be this way.

And Robert understood, at least as much as was possible. He had listened without judgment to her dispassionate recitation of her strange and terrifying family history, their discussions lasting hours at a time, deep into the night, for weeks on end. He trusted his wife, had complete faith in her, accepted the words she told him without reservation. He knew she would never suggest abandoning her own children unless there was simply no other way.

So he had agreed.

And it had all led to tonight. He had thought he was ready; had believed he had constructed a wall around his heart, impenetrable and thick.

But he had been wrong, because the moment he laid eyes on the two tiny newborns, helpless and innocent and entirely dependent upon others for their survival, Robert had fallen hopelessly in love.

He could not do it. He could not give them up.

The stranger cleared his throat respectfully, then reached out and gently plucked the baby girl from Robert's left arm. He tucked her away exactly as Robert had done, and then lifted the baby boy from his other arm. Robert did nothing to stop him.

Then the stranger looked at Robert and nodded. He said nothing. There was nothing to say. The man turned and walked back to his car, seeming to dissolve into the inky night thanks to his black clothing. He fastened the babies expertly into identical car seats, positioned side-by-side in the rear of the vehicle.

The man walked to the front seat and climbed in, his feet crunching gravel. He backed out of Robert and Virginia Ayers's driveway and accelerated smoothly forward. He turned left at the end of the lonely road and was gone.

14

The Parkman Hotel was short and squat and had at one time been considered high-end, if not quite luxurious. It had been built in the late 1800s and in its day it had been the equal of any surrounding construction, according to the research Kevin had done on the Internet. The problem was, its day had passed decades ago and the building now appeared overwhelmed by the modern steel and glass high-rises surrounding it.

The room was clean, but the furnishings were dowdy and out of style, not that Cait cared. This wasn't a vacation or a pleasure trip, but a fact-finding mission with a specific goal—to unearth as much of her family history as possible.

The trip from Logan Airport to the hotel in a Boston cab had been like some crazy amusement park ride, the driver whipping between lanes at will, driving one-handed, sometimes one-fingered, gleefully cutting off other vehicles like the fate of the free world rested upon his passengers arriving at their destination in the absolute minimum time possible. This vehicular insanity had elicited honks and angry gestures, but to Cait's surprise most of the other drivers' reactions seemed perfunctory, as if they had fully anticipated being cut off in traffic and were only responding because they knew it was expected of them.

"Christ," Kevin muttered as he dropped their bags on the hallway floor and unlocked the door to their room. "I'm sure glad we didn't tell him to step on it."

Cait smiled her agreement. She trudged to the queen-sized bed in the middle of the small room and flopped down on it, too tired to unpack, surprised to discover the bed was fairly comfortable.

She patted the blanket next to her. "Let's get some sleep, I want to get up first thing in the morning and get an early start."

Kevin grimaced. "It's *already* first thing in the morning."

"No rest for the weary," Cait said, and as she did, a Flicker struck with such force her head was thrown backward, bouncing off the hotel room wall with a thud. She moaned and her eyes glazed over before her eyelids fluttered madly. In the Flicker, she was looking through someone else's eyes, gazing at a schoolgirl standing on a drizzly Boston sidewalk. Upon closer inspection the girl turned out to be a young woman acting out what she thought might be a man's schoolgirl fantasy. She stood on a wet sidewalk covered by a shroud of heavy mist, and whoever this Flicker belonged to was gazing at her with a predatory lust that was shocking in its intensity.

He—Cait knew it was a he, although she couldn't have said *how* she knew—was talking with the young woman, joking, keeping the conversation light, but there was no real humor behind the words; they were a put-on, designed to keep the woman (the VICTIM) at ease until he could get her alone. He was tense and high-strung, not exactly nervous, more like excited, anxious to begin playing with (TORTURING) her.

The woman was a prostitute, that was obvious, but the man wasn't interested in sex; at least not primarily, not right now. He wanted to hurt her, to do things to her, bad things; the evil oozed out of him, rolling off his body in waves like heat off a rapidly accelerating fire.

Cait wanted to shout at the girl, to tell her to run, to sprint in the other direction and scream at the top of her lungs, to alert everyone in this grimy neighborhood to the fact that there was a monster in their midst. But of course she couldn't yell, she couldn't warn anyone of anything, she wasn't even really there. She was a mute witness to a random event occurring somewhere nearby.

The young prostitute was uneasy, but she allowed herself to be convinced to accompany the monster. He said something about his car being around the corner, which was patently stupid. It was raining and no one else was around, and there was no good reason in the world why any john would park out of sight and negotiate with a prostitute on foot before bringing her to his car. It was clear the prostitute knew something was not quite right, even the man (MONSTER) could see that, but he knew she would follow him anyway, and she did.

His thoughts were swirling and violent. He was picturing pliers and knives and what he would do with them, how he would use them to elicit shrieks of terror from the girl. He would taunt her with them, pinching her nipple lightly, just enough to cause her to gasp in shock and fear and a little pain; then he would move down her body and stroke the skin of her inner thigh with the back edge of a knife-blade, barely touching her but demonstrating his evil intent with crystal clarity.

Then he would get down to business in earnest. He would open the jaws of the pliers wide and he would—

—and then the Flicker was gone and Cait's eyes snapped into focus to see a worried Kevin leaning over her. Concern was written on his face as he held her hand and stroked her arm gently.

She bolted upright and pushed him out of the way, sliding off the bed and rushing into the tiny bathroom where she puked, her partially digested dinner of chicken parmesan with rice and vegetables searing her throat on the way out.

Kevin followed her and rubbed her back wordlessly until she had finished. She relaxed and then abruptly dry-heaved into the bowl in a kind of horrible exclamation point. Sweat rolled down her face and Cait felt jittery and washed-out, like a marathoner who had run an entire twenty-six-mile race without drinking any water.

She struggled to her feet and staggered to the sink, dizzy and woozy, thankful for Kevin's strong hands supporting her. Cait splashed cold water on her face and then shuffled out of the bathroom and sat down on the bed, her shoulders slumped and her head resting on her chest. She thought she might get sick again and clamped her jaws shut, swallowing hard.

"What was that all about?" Kevin asked quietly.

She shook her head, instantly regretting it, clenching her teeth until another wave of dizziness and nausea passed. "I'm not sure."

"Is it something you ate? Maybe you're just overtired and stressed out about seeing your biological mother for the first time."

"No," Cait said, her voice shaky and reed-thin. "It's nothing like that. I'm nervous about seeing my mother, that's true, but this was unrelated to that. It was the Flicker."

"I don't know," Kevin answered, clearly skeptical. "I've seen you have Flickers plenty of times but you've never reacted to one like this before."

"That's because this was different from a normal Flicker, if there even is such a thing. Usually I see random events or occurrences that have no value judgment attached to them. Like yesterday in the grocery store when I saw the little old lady had dropped her checkbook on her kitchen floor. It wasn't anything good or bad, it just *was*. Do you understand what I mean?"

Kevin shrugged. "I guess so." He was still watching her closely and Cait knew he was worried she might toss her cookies again.

"Well, this Flicker wasn't like that. This was evil personified. I was in a man's head, and the man was looking at a woman—a prostitute—and he was planning to do things to her."

"Well," Kevin said, "I'm sure you realize that's the whole point of prostitution."

"No." Cait shook her head again, firmly this time, ignoring the wave of nausea that accompanied the gesture. "That's not what I mean. He wasn't thinking about sexual things, at least not the usual sexual things a normal man might do with a prostitute. He was planning to do awful things to her; to torture her, to injure her. Badly. Kevin, I could feel the evil inside this man and it was overwhelming. It was like a black cloud roiling in his body waiting to explode out of him."

He stared at her for a long time, saying nothing. It was as if he was no longer her boyfriend but was on duty, his cop eyes probing. "I've never seen you go into such a deep trancelike state before when you had a Flicker. Usually you just sort of stare off into space like you're thinking really hard about something. If I talk to you, you are still able to hear and answer me. But this time, you were gone."

"That's what I'm trying to tell you," Cait said. "This was *not* a typical Flicker. It was terrifying. I don't know what it was all about, and I sure hope it doesn't happen again, but Kevin, that's not the point. We have to call the police. We have to alert them to what's happening out there."

Kevin shook his head and Cait said, "What?"

"We can't call the police."

"Didn't you hear what I just said? This man is going to hurt a young girl, badly, maybe he's going to kill her. We have to do something to stop him!"

"How?"

"Excuse me?"

"How are we going to stop him? Do you know who he is, or even *where* he is? Do you know who the girl is? Do you know where he's taking her? Do you know—"

"Okay, okay," she interrupted. "You've made your point. We don't have any specific information. Why can't we just call them and at least alert them to the fact there's a homicidal maniac roaming the streets of their city?"

"Because they're not going to pay any attention to you, that's why."

"What are you talking about?"

"Unless you have a name or a location, the Boston police are going to listen to you, politely at first, then not so politely if you go on for too long, and when you're done, they're going to send you on your way—or hang up, if you call—and blow you off. They will assume you're just some lonely nut job desperate for a little attention."

She stared up at him, her face drawn and pale, and he said, as gently as he could, "This is a big city, Cait. The cops here deal with crazies every single day. If you start telling them about Flickers and seeing things in your head, you're going to be just another crazy to them. There's nothing we can do unless you have more information."

"But that poor girl..."

"I know, but maybe it's not as bad as you think. Maybe you misinterpreted what you saw. Maybe it's a case of some bored married couple playacting, trying to spice up their lives a little by pretending to be a hooker and a john."

Cait shook her head. By now the resulting nausea didn't surprise her. "I didn't misinterpret anything. This was no kinky married couple. This man was evil, and he was ruthless. He was an animal, a predator stalking his prey, and he is going to hurt her, maybe kill her."

Kevin sat on the bed next to her and wrapped an arm around her shoulder. "You know, if you're still planning on getting up early tomorrow—I mean, today—we should really get some rest. You look like hell."

Cait laughed in spite of herself. "Thanks for the compliment. How do you always know the just-right thing to say to a girl?"

"It's a gift."

She crawled under the covers, still dressed in her jeans and T-shirt. She had been tired when they arrived, thanks to the red-eye flight from Tampa. Now she was beyond exhausted, she felt as though she had been run over by a truck. A truck being driven by a homicidal lunatic.

Kevin was right, of course. If they were going accomplish anything in the morning, rest was critical. But how was she supposed to sleep after experiencing that terrible Flicker? Cait Connelly was thirty years old and had been dealing with Flickers for as long as she could remember. They had long since gotten to the point where she viewed them as nothing more than an annoyance, a small part of her personality that she had learned to live with, like some people live with migraines or the occasional terrifying nightmare.

But tonight's Flicker was different than anything she had ever experienced. This wasn't a mental image of an old lady forgetting to bring her checkbook on her twice-weekly trips to the grocery store. This was a blackness so complete it was stifling, a thirst for violence and depravity that dwarfed anything Cait had ever imagined.

This was true evil.

How can I sleep after experiencing something like that? Cait wondered. She knew she would lie awake all night, tossing and turning, listening to Kevin snoring softly beside her, jealous of him for not having to experience the Flickers, for not having to feel the rage and corruption of a monster somewhere in this city who was even now doing twisted things to a helpless young woman.

But she didn't stay awake all night. Her head hit the pillow and within minutes she was asleep. And she didn't dream at all.

15

Getting the girl into his third-floor apartment unseen was simple. The back of the old tenement's ground floor had at one time—a century ago or more—housed some sort of business enterprise. Perhaps a bakery, or maybe a small shoe-repair shop. A service entrance had been built on the back corner with a narrow hallway running behind the first-floor apartments to a seldom-used secondary staircase providing access to the second and third floors.

The service entrance had of course been locked up years ago, but those locks had been removed at the same time, and with as little difficulty as the locks on the front door. With access in the front of the building, there was no reason for any of the itinerants and vagrants using the location as a flophouse to bother traipsing down the trash-littered alley on the north side, risking being mugged for their booze or drugs, just to enter from the rear when they would end up in exactly the same place.

By the time the schoolgirl—"My name is Rae Ann," she told Milo in a frightened voice—discovered what Milo knew she had suspected all along, that he was not your typical horny man anxious for a quickie, it was much too late. She had followed him down the sidewalk and around a corner, where she learned the ugly truth: there was no car. There was also no streetlight—he had conveniently smashed it out—and the area was deserted.

Milo pulled a freshly sharpened carving knife out of his pocket, the stainless steel blade dripping water in the steady drizzle. Rae Ann had backed up a step or two in fear and confusion and he covered that distance before she could react further, wrapping an arm around her waist like some arduous suitor. He placed the tip of the wicked-looking knife lightly against her throat, just under her jawline.

"I—I don't have any money on me," she stammered. "Big Daddy—he's my pimp—he took it just before you saw me. If I had any cash, I would give it to you, all of it, I promise, but I don't have any."

Milo smiled. The dangerous part was over and he was in his element now, completely at ease and under control. "I'm not after money. If it was money I wanted, I wouldn't have chosen the newest girl on the block to play with. I would have grabbed someone with more experience." He was excited, aroused as always by the prospect of impending humiliation and torture, and he pressed his crotch against her butt.

"Is it sex, then? I'll give you a freebie if you want. I'm not supposed to, Big Daddy will kick my ass if he finds out, but I'll do it for you. What do you like, baby?"

"Right now I'd like you to shut your mouth and come with me. We're going to take a short walk and if you scream or cry or make so much as one second's eye contact with anyone, anyone at all, the last thing you will ever feel will be me cutting open your chest and ripping your heart out with my bare hands. Do you understand me?" Despite the fact that Milo was whispering—or maybe because of it—the implied menace inherent in his words was real and terrifying.

They walked the seven blocks to Milo's building in silence. He draped his right arm casually around her shoulders like a possessive boyfriend, the knife held in his left hand, pressed against the leg of his jeans.

Rae Ann walked with her head down, subservient. Milo knew she was afraid even to look around for fear her kidnapper would misinterpret the action and begin stabbing and slicing her. He could feel her shivering and shaking under his arm, the terror building inside her but the fear transparent to anyone besides the man causing it.

They shuffled along slowly, Milo in no hurry. At last they reached his block. Through various rounds of urban redevelopment conducted over the last half-century, this neighborhood had been unaffected, steadfastly ignored by politicians and do-gooders alike. It resembled a war zone, a United States version of Baghdad after a suicide bombing. Burned-out apartment houses stood empty and silent, graffiti covering every square inch, dandelions fighting grimly for life, growing through gaping holes in the sidewalk, the cement smashed and gutted and crumbling.

Activity was virtually nonexistent, due in part to the lateness of the hour, but also to the fact that this was one of the most dangerous places in the city. The few people moving about were, like Milo himself, ghosts, wraiths skittering through the shadows, invisible and unnoticed by the rest of society.

Milo turned off the sidewalk, pulling his terrified young victim across a tiny weed-infested yard, the original lawn long dead, random tufts of crabgrass sticking up crazily in all directions, trash covering the ground. A rusted chain-link fence lurched at an angle, pulled partway to the ground by vandals before being abandoned as not worth the effort.

He released his prize just long enough to reach out with his right hand and pull a length of fencing toward them. The metal links had been cut away from the post, and Milo indicated to Rae Ann with a flourish that she should proceed through the opening.

She bent down and squeezed through the small space, and for maybe two seconds was actually free of her captor. Had she known exactly what was coming, and exactly when she would be pushed through, she might have been able to make a break for it, to sprint away across the desolate yard in a headlong dash to freedom.

But Milo knew she wouldn't run and she didn't. She was terrified and in shock, and long experience had taught him that by the time his victim recognized the possibility of escape it would be too late.

He was right. He squeezed through the opening right behind her and then once again grabbed her possessively.

They turned down an alley, skirting a tenement similar in style and condition to his own, and within seconds were on the back side of the block, invisible to the other occupants of his building. At this hour, any witnesses would likely be so drunk or so wasted on meth or crack or LSD or bath salts that they wouldn't even notice, much less remember, him bringing the girl into the building, but Milo wasn't about to take any unnecessary chances. He had gone to a lot of trouble and risk to secure this playmate; he wasn't going to let her slip though his grasp before he had had an opportunity to fully enjoy her.

They approached the ancient service entrance, the wooden dormer constructed over the door mostly rotted away by time and neglect. Rae Ann sobbed steadily, great silent heaves wracking her shoulders. Milo knew she was afraid that once she entered this building, she would never leave it alive.

He had to give her credit. She was a perceptive young lady.

He lifted his knife and pressed it against her throat in the identical spot he had used before. He placed just enough pressure on the razor-sharp tip to draw blood. A drop welled up like a tiny black marble and then rolled down her neck, disappearing under the collar of her sweater.

"Do you remember what I said about screaming?" he whispered, his mouth caressing her ear like a wanton lover.

Rae Ann nodded, still sobbing but indicating she had not forgotten.

"Good," he said, removing the knife from her throat and licking her blood, his tongue caressing the bulge of her collarbone and up toward her ear. She shivered in fear but stood still.

He smiled. He couldn't help it. He was just about there. Once inside his little den of iniquity, this sweet thing would be all his to enjoy in any way he wanted. Keeping her quiet while he played his games could be a problem, but Milo Cain was nothing if not creative. He would be able to handle that issue with no trouble at all.

He pushed open the service entrance door and the bizarre-looking couple disappeared into the darkness of the condemned building. The pitch-black darkness of the narrow hallway was all encompassing, but it didn't matter. Milo knew exactly where he was going.

16

The alley behind the condemned tenement was uncomfortable, garbage-strewn and rat-infested, but it had one thing going for it—it was secluded. And seclusion was exactly what Franklin Marchand was looking for when it came to sleeping off a bender.

Never one to keep a tight grip on his wallet even in the best of times, the last economic downturn had seen Franklin lose everything—his job, his self-respect and, perhaps inevitably, his family. Anna had called him a drunken, shiftless bum during their final blowout, then concluded the festivities by kicking him out of their home and screaming "And don't ever come back!" through the closed front door.

Franklin had never gone back.

But even though he had forfeited most of his self-respect, Franklin had no desire to advertise to the rest of the world the depths to which he had plummeted, transitioning from successful banker to out-of-work banker to homeless, drunken ex-banker in just a few short months. So Franklin's routine was to panhandle enough cash to buy a cheap bottle, get trashed in this nice, secluded alley he had found, and then pass out and sleep off his buzz on a pile of moth-eaten wool blankets he had stolen from another drunken bum a few blocks away while *that* guy was passed out cold.

Every once in a while that strange dude from the third floor of the tenement across the alley would pass by in the middle of the night, unaware of Franklin huddled behind the wooden latticework falling off a rusting iron fire escape in the darkest corner of the alley. When he did, often it was with a young girl in tow. A different young girl every time.

There was something wrong with the dude, Franklin could deduce that much even in his near-constant state of bleary-eyed drunkenness. The man carried a weapon—a knife—and almost always displayed it conspicuously for his female companion's benefit while they shuffled past, causing Franklin to reach the obvious conclusion that this parade of reluctant young women was not accompanying the strange dude voluntarily.

And that bothered Franklin.

He was no prude, and certainly no shining beacon of righteousness. Franklin Marchand had done plenty of things he was not proud of, some of them before his fall from grace, while still making a living in the banking industry, and some after, as witnessed by the blanket thievery of recent vintage.

But Franklin was no rapist. He had a daughter of his own, pretty close to the approximate ages of the girls Strange Dude liked to parade past him at knifepoint. Granted, he hadn't seen his daughter in a while—she'd sided with Anna in their parting of the ways and hadn't even spoken to him since—but nevertheless she was still his child. His flesh and blood. And the thought of his little girl potentially falling prey to Strange Dude or someone like him gnawed at Franklin.

What else could the guy be but a rapist? Franklin had never actually *seen* Strange Dude rape anyone, had never heard a scream or a cry of protest floating through the thin walls of the dilapidated building across the alleyway, but, really, what else could the guy be doing in there but raping the girls? A man goes out at night and returns under cover of darkness, sneaking a reluctant companion into his condemned building via the seldom-used service entrance in the rear, and always with the aid of a knife to provide proper motivation.

Even worse, Franklin had never seen any of the girls leave the building afterward. It was a fact he had not given much thought to until recently, because Strange Dude invariably brought the girls into the building in the middle of the night, three a.m. or later, and by that time Franklin had usually finished guzzling his nightly bottle of Mad Dog and was ready to pass out on his stolen wool blankets. So it stood to reason he wouldn't be conscious by the time the girls exited the tenement.

But then another thought occurred to Franklin. A terrifying thought. Why would Strange Dude run the risk of using his own place to rape the girls? Wouldn't he be concerned that he might eventually grab one who possessed enough self-respect to go to the police afterward? And if she did, wouldn't she then know exactly where to lead them?

Of course she would.

Unless, of course, the victims never left Strange Dude's pad. Unless, of course, he kidnapped them and raped them and then, holy shit, *killed* them.

Was that really possible? Could the strange man living on the third floor of the building across the alley really be not just a rapist but a murderer as well? Franklin decided he had to find out. Because if that was the case, and Franklin didn't do something about it, he knew he couldn't live with himself.

Franklin slammed down the last of the MD and belched as it crash-landed in his belly. He felt good about himself, better than he had in a long time. He would figure out just exactly what was going on in Strange Dude's third-floor love nest. And if the situation was as he feared, he would goddamn well go to the cops. Not in person, of course, Franklin hated the cops almost as much as he hated himself, but via anonymous phone tip, which would work just as well and represent less personal risk.

And that's exactly what he would do.

Tomorrow.

Because tonight Franklin was so fucking drunk he doubted he could stand up, and he *knew* he couldn't punch the numbers on a phone with any degree of accuracy. What Franklin needed to do tonight was sleep. He rolled the empty bottle along the pavement of the trash-littered alley and watched as it skittered and bounced, eventually coming to rest against the side of Strange Dude's building.

Then Franklin stretched out on his blankets, determined to take action, proud he was still capable of doing some good in this world. In a matter of seconds, Franklin Marchand was fast asleep.

17

"What do you suppose the chances are that my mother will actually agree to see us?" Cait clutched the taxi's worn vinyl door handle with one hand and held tightly to Kevin's forearm with the other. They had just left the hotel for the cab ride to the address Arlen Hirschberg had supplied for Virginia Ayers, and the driver seemed intent on performing the same vehicular ballet as last night's cabbie, changing lanes frequently and shooting in and out of gaps in the heavy traffic that seemed too small for a motorcycle, much less a full-sized sedan.

Kevin seemed unruffled and grinned, enjoying her obvious discomfort. He pried her index finger off his forearm and she chuckled uneasily.

"Sorry about the death grip," she whispered. "Do you think any of these guys actually, you know, have a real driver's license?"

"Think of this as a little bonus. Along with a scenic trip through Boston we get a free amusement park thrill ride."

"Free?" she said. "Obviously you don't have a clear view of the meter."

"Okay, maybe not free, but you get my point. Relax and enjoy the roller-coaster ride. This cabbie's gotta be at least fifty, which means he's been driving for close to thirty-five years and hasn't been killed yet. How likely is it that this will be the exact moment he suffers his fatal accident?"

Cait punched her boyfriend in the arm and he laughed. The driver glowered at them through the rearview mirror and said nothing.

"Anyway," Kevin continued, "to answer your first question, I think it's a toss-up. This woman"—he glanced at a small wire-ring notebook containing the information given to them by Arlen Hirschberg—"Virginia Ayers, turned Hirschberg down flat when he requested an interview, so it seems unlikely she will have changed her mind in the last twenty-four hours. I think our only realistic chance is to get her face-to-face and somehow convince her to share a few minutes of her time. Hopefully once she catches sight of you, once she gets an actual view of her long-lost child, she'll have second thoughts about her refusal.

"So I don't know, babe," he said again, giving her hand a squeeze. "I wouldn't give it any better than fifty-fifty, and even that might be a pipe dream."

The ride continued in silence. Cait tried to push last night's horrific Flicker to the back of her mind. She stared out the window and watched the cityscape roll by, the cab moving past tall steel and glass skyscrapers, past men and women in business suits carrying briefcases and walking briskly between buildings, through narrow one-way streets, some barely wider than alleyways, past restaurants and bars and universities and apartments, block after block of four-hundred-year-old city.

Finally the taxi left the skyscrapers of Boston behind, entering the smaller city of Everett. They drove a few minutes, the traffic still nearly as heavy, and eventually made a right turn at a weathered sign reading, "Riverfront Acres." The driver cruised into a small neighborhood consisting of a half-dozen tiny cape-style homes huddled in a cluster around a narrow cul-de-sac. The pavement was cracked, desperately in need of repair, and the taxi bounced along crazily. All of the homes looked nearly identical except for their paint color. Cait couldn't see any water and wondered where the river advertised on the sign might be.

The cab rolled slowly into a driveway barely long enough to accommodate its length. Cait and Kevin exited and while Kevin paid the cabbie, Cait examined the outside of her mother's house, doing her best to ignore the nervous tension building inside her. At one time it appeared the house had been painted a deep ocean blue, but that had been years ago. Decades of New England weather and salty Atlantic Ocean air had rendered the siding a dull monochromatic gray, and the once-white trim had long since given way to encroaching mold and mildew.

In the picture window the curtains had been drawn against the morning sun, and it was impossible to tell whether anyone was even home. The place felt still, abandoned, and Cait supposed the same could be said for the entire neighborhood. No children played in any of the fenced-in front yards, no barking dogs marked their arrival. Nothing moved.

The cab backed out of the driveway and accelerated slowly down the street toward Everett and the land of the living.

Cait grabbed Kevin's hand and held on for dear life. "Am I making a mistake?" she asked in a small voice as they approached the front steps.

"Ever since I met you, you've had questions about your past," Kevin said. "Now you finally have an opportunity to get some of those questions answered. Of course you're not making a mistake. You're just nervous. Settle down and let's see what happens."

"What if she slams the door in our faces?"

"Then we try to convince her to open it up again. If she refuses, we get that cab back here and enjoy another thrill ride back to the hotel, where we'll get our things together and then fly back to Florida. Even if that happens, you're no worse off than you were before, so you have nothing to lose," he said, returning her hand squeeze.

He rang the doorbell. Cait could hear it reverberate through the house, loud and jarring, and she jumped.

For a moment nothing happened and then as Kevin was reaching out to ring the bell again, the heavy wooden door swung open and Cait's mother peered through the screen at them, dressed in a thread-bare robe and holding a cup of tea. Cait knew she was in her mid-sixties, Arlen Hirschberg had told them her age, but she looked much older. Deep creases lined her haggard face, and her hair, although the same auburn color as Cait's, had somewhere along the line lost its luster and now looked dried out and brittle, as though it might snap off and clatter away in a stiff breeze.

The woman blinked twice, staring uncomprehendingly for what felt to Cait like hours but was undoubtedly only a second or two. Then she clapped her left hand to her mouth and took a step back, her eyes filling with tears. "Oh, my God," she mumbled through her fingers. "Oh, my God. Oh, my God."

Tears rolled down Virginia Ayers's cheeks and Cait felt her own eyes fill and the three people stood motionless, one inside the house and two outside.

Finally, Kevin said, "This is Caitlyn Connelly, Mrs. Ayers. This is your daughter."

* * *

The inside of Virginia Ayers's kitchen looked exactly as Cait had pictured it since learning she was going to meet her birth mother. A gas stove, decades old, sat against the far wall, its ceramic finish worn and chipped. Next to the stove and of the same vintage stood a small refrigerator with rounded corners, originally white but now yellowed with age.

The threesome sat awkwardly around a Formica kitchen table that had probably been new in the 1950s. The surface featured an unidentifiable pattern that looked a bit like spilled ice cubes and had been dulled by age and use. The same was true of the wooden chairs upon which they sat. The finish had been worn completely off the seats but the chairs were solid and sturdy and surprisingly comfortable.

The kitchen was impeccably clean, spotless, and Cait thought she could probably eat off the floor's ancient linoleum tiles, which, although worn and faded like everything else, sparkled as though they received a thorough mopping once a day. Maybe twice.

"You shouldn't be here," Virginia Ayers said softly, blowing on the steam curling into the air out of her teacup. Identical cups had been placed on the table in front of Cait and Kevin. Both had so far been ignored.

After her initial shocked reaction at the door, Virginia Ayers recovered quickly, and instead of having the door slammed in her face as Cait had feared might happen, the woman had bustled forward, crying, and ushered them inside. She led them down a short hallway to the kitchen where introductions were made again; then she invited her guests to sit while she busied herself boiling water for tea. Cait and Kevin sat silently.

Now Cait picked up her tea and blew away the steam like her mother had done. The delicate porcelain cup was bone-colored with a silver plated rim, clearly reserved for special guests.

"Why did you invite us in if you don't want to see me?" she asked timidly. "After hearing your response to Mr. Hirschberg's request for a meeting, we almost didn't even bother flying up here."

"Oh, child, I never said I didn't want to see you. I've wanted to see you for the last thirty years. I've wanted nothing more than to lay eyes on you myself, even if for just a few precious minutes. This might be the happiest day of my life. I only wish your father had lived to see you, too."

Cait sipped her tea and shook her head in confusion. "Then I don't understand..."

Her mother's face darkened. It was as if a storm cloud had rolled in and taken a position directly over her head. "This is so difficult," she said. "It's very complicated, in ways you may not be able to understand. I'm not sure even I understand completely. I...I don't even know where to begin."

"I do," Cait interrupted gently. "Begin at the point that matters the most, at least to me. Why did you give me up? No matter what hardships you were facing in your life—money problems, job woes, personal issues, whatever—how could you believe they would be solved by giving up your newborn baby?"

Virginia held her tea in two hands, elbows on the table, looking into the cup like it was a crystal ball.

She shook her head. "I *never* wanted to give you up," she whispered. "Neither did your father. My God, we were never the same after the night we...watched you leave. Before you were born, we were a normal couple, at least as normal as possible. But after that horrible evening..."

Cait waited, spellbound. She glanced at Kevin and he was riveted as well. Virginia Ayers's eyes were red-rimmed, tortured.

She said nothing for a moment, composing herself, and then continued. "You were born in this very house, you know, and then taken from it just a few hours later. After that cursed night, your father and I never looked at each other the same way again. We blamed ourselves, we blamed each other, we blamed fate, we blamed God. We laid blame everywhere, even though we both knew we were doing the right thing by giving you up."

Virginia looked at Cait bleakly. "Eventually your father couldn't take the guilt. He hanged himself in a men's bathroom at South Station a few years later."

Cait gasped and even Kevin seemed startled. "But I don't understand. If you both wanted me...*why?*" There seemed to be no need to finish the question.

"As I told you before, it's very complicated. More to the point, it's dangerous. It's bad enough that you're here, but the more you learn, the worse the situation becomes."

"Well, it's too late now," Cait said. "The genie is out of the bottle. How bad could it be? Please tell me; you owe me that much after making me wonder about my history for the last thirty years, making me wonder what a tiny baby could possibly have done that was so horrible her own mother had to abandon her. Please."

Virginia Ayers shook her head in mute protest at the words coming from her daughter's mouth. She had begun crying again and the tears ran down her gaunt cheeks, dropping off her jaw and splashing on to the table around her teacup like a tiny rain shower.

"I'm so sorry," she sobbed. "It wasn't your fault; none of it was your fault. Of course you didn't do anything wrong. But we simply had to separate you from your twin, we had no choice in the matter."

Cait froze, teacup halfway to her mouth, staring at her mother in astonishment. She set her cup down on the table with a clatter and tea sloshed over the side unnoticed.

For a long moment, no one moved.

Then Cait said, slowly, "I have a twin?"

18

The chair occupied a position of honor, placed by Milo Cain squarely in the middle of the mostly unfurnished room. Dust bunnies surrounded it like tiny sentries on the scarred hardwood floor. Occasionally a stray breeze would catch one, sending it skittering through the accumulated trash into a corner, only to be blown back to the center of the room with the next air current. The chair looked like a bare-bones throne for a deposed king.

Atop it lay the disheveled body of the prize Milo had won last night. Rae Ann dozed fitfully, her head lolling to the right, resting precariously on her bony shoulder. Her ponytails had been removed and now messy hair partially obscured her face, a clump sticking to her cheek, glued to her flesh by last night's dried sweat and tears.

Her sweater and short skirt—and her panties—remained undisturbed for the moment. Milo had every intention of relieving the girl of her clothing—eventually—but for now occupied himself by indulging in one of his favorite fantasies. He played with the handle of the long-nose pliers absently, snapping the jaws open and closed while he watched his guest sleep.

Snap...Snap...Snap...

Thick strips of silver duct tape secured Rae Ann's forearms to the chair's sturdy armrests, slapped down tightly by Milo to eliminate any possibility of escape. Her ankles were secured in a similar manner at the base of the front legs. Her torso he had left intentionally unencumbered. Years of perfecting his hobby had taught Milo that if tied up in this manner, his subject's natural reaction to the pain he was inflicting would be to thrust her hips up and down over and over in an obscene parody of sex—fear and desperation driving her body in a vain attempt to escape the torture—while he played his games. This was what he lived for.

Duct-taped to Rae Ann's right hand as she dozed was a dingy white dishtowel. Milo had fastened a makeshift cotton mitten last night when he finished playing with her, placing the towel over her hand and then winding a long strip of the tape tightly around her wrist. A tinge of light-pink stain was just visible, indicating the blood had continued dribbling out of her missing fingernails, soaking into the terry cloth for quite some time.

It was no wonder she had thrashed around on her throne, moaning into her duct-tape gag, long after Milo went to bed on his air mattress. He had implored the girl to sleep while she had the chance but had been largely ignored. Eventually he had drifted off to a contented slumber, tuning out her pathetic noises, and slept soundly, as he always did after beginning a new adventure with a new girl.

Now he stepped forward. He slid the pliers into the right rear pocket of his jeans and then cradled Rae Ann's head in his hands. She groaned and blinked rapidly, her eyes dazed and sleepy. Then they snapped into focus, widening in terror as she awoke fully and the reality of her predicament struck like a sledgehammer.

Milo smiled paternally. "Welcome back from dreamland, darling. Did you sleep well?"

Rae Ann turned her head to the side, avoiding his probing eyes. She began begging into her duct-tape gag, the words indecipherable but their meaning clear.

He shook his head. "We're not done playing yet, so you may as well forget about being released. It's not happening. Now, back to my question: Did you sleep well?"

The girl ignored him and kept her eyes glued to the corner of the room, looking at nothing, refusing to give him the satisfaction of returning his gaze.

Milo squeezed her head between his hands. "Answer me."

Still she refused to look. He sighed. He had chosen a strong-willed one this time, which in many ways represented an exciting challenge but in others was just plain frustrating. He removed his left hand from her head and flicked it out casually, smacking it against the bloody towel covering her right hand. The contact was minimal, barely more than a light tap, but his prisoner screamed into her gag, her head snapping back and forth as she tried desperately and unsuccessfully to move her injured hand out of harm's way.

Milo tried again. "Did you sleep well?"

This time he was rewarded with an enthusiastic nodding of his prisoner's head even as she whimpered and tears streamed down her now-filthy face. A snot bubble blew out of her nose and Milo shook his head, disgusted. He crossed the room and retrieved a tissue, then held it under Rae Ann's nose and she blew with gusto.

"Now," he said softly. "What you need to understand is that I expect you to answer promptly when I speak to you. Things will proceed much more smoothly between us if you do. Is that understood?"

This time there was no hesitation. The young hooker again nodded enthusiastically.

"Much better," Milo said, reaching into his left rear pocket and withdrawing an X-Acto knife. "See? We're getting along beautifully now."

At the sight of the knife, Rae Ann's eyes widened again in panic and she began breathing heavily, nearly panting.

Milo said, "Relax, before you give yourself a stroke," and then he leaned down and deftly sliced the duct tape holding the blood-soaked towel in place over her right hand. The towel unwound and fell to the floor, revealing a hand featuring three hideously misshapen digits.

The nails were missing from Rae Ann's first three fingers. They were gone, torn out last night with Milo's pliers, and the tips of all three fingers were now swollen and purple, twice their normal size. The blood had more or less clotted overnight but still oozed sluggishly, pooling on her fingertips now that the towel had been removed, then dripping onto the clear plastic tarp covering the floor in fat blackish-red globules.

Milo felt a surge of excitement as he viewed his handiwork. "What have you done to yourself?" he asked with false concern, removing the pliers from his pocket and snapping them in front of Rae Ann's face to observe her reaction. He wasn't disappointed. Just as she had done when she saw the knife, she panicked. Her eyes widened and her head thrashed and she whimpered desperately into her gag, her terror complete.

"I'm just teasing you," he said. "We'll play again, don't you worry about that, but the fun will begin later. I'd hate to get the reputation around town of being a poor host, so how does a little breakfast sound?"

His victim gazed up disbelievingly. Her desperate whining noises stopped but her tears continued to fall as she waited to see what would happen next.

"Silly me," Milo continued. "You probably have to go to the bathroom. It's been a long night, hasn't it?"

He waited for a response and got none. The girl sat completely still, as if confused by this unexpected turn of events, her eyes locked on his. He bent down without another word and retrieved his X-Acto knife. He sliced the rest of the duct tape from the girl's limbs and helped her to her feet. He led her unsteadily across the room and down a short hallway, turning into a grungy bathroom. He indicat-ed the tiny stand-up shower with a flourish, like a Realtor showing a mansion to a prospective buyer, turning to her with a smile and say-ing, "Play your cards right and maybe you'll get to clean up later. For now, though, just do your business and come back out. I'm going to show a little trust and give you some privacy. Fuck with me at all, even a little bit, and the next time you'll be peeing in front of me, probably into your clothes."

He turned and paused at the door of the bathroom. "Oh, by the way," he said. "Before you get any bright ideas, everything that could possibly be used as a weapon has been removed from this room, as has the toilet, as you have undoubtedly noticed. Just squat over the hole in the floor, do your business and come out. Are we on the same page here?" The duct-tape gag remained in place so she nodded, the seemingly unending supply of tears still flowing down her face.

"One more thing," he added with an impish smile. "Just kidding about the shower. The water hasn't worked in this building since be-fore you were born, probably." Milo stepped through the doorway and pulled the flimsy wooden door shut behind him, waiting on the other side. Moments later the door swung open and his guest ap-peared, eyes downcast. He took her by the elbow and led her back to her chair where he picked up his roll of duct tape and expertly re-se-cured her in a matter of seconds.

After taping her ankles to the chair, he said, still crouched on the floor, "Now, back to my original question: What would you like for breakfast? I don't have a lot of choices but I might be able to find something that would be acceptable, unless of course you're one of those chicks that eat nuts and berries like a frigging squirrel—"

His eyes rolled up into his head and he slumped sideways, his forehead thumping against the arm of his prisoner's chair. He fell to the floor on his side and then staggered to his feet, stumbling blind-ly toward the shell of a kitchen, trying desperately to maintain consciousness as a vivid image invaded his skull. It was a vision similar to the ones he had been cursed with his entire life but much, much stronger.

More lifelike.

More real.

A young woman and a man roughly the same age sat at a table in the kitchen of a small house talking with an older woman. The house was near here but not too near; it was definitely farther away than was typical for his visions. He knew this because through the kitchen window he could see none of the tall buildings or warehouses or city hustle and bustle that he should see at any location in Boston. The scene was more pastoral; still bleak and run-down, as if the area—wherever it was—had seen its best days decades ago and had been sinking into a state of neglect ever since.

At the table, the conversation revolved around a painful shared personal history. The two women were related. They were discussing details of a baby given up for adoption. The younger woman was the baby and the older woman her mother. The younger woman was asking questions; she could not understand why she had been abandoned so long ago.

Milo chuckled, lost in the vision blasting through his head. He leaned against the wall in a state of semi-consciousness. He could tell the young woman a thing or two about abandonment and loss. The older woman struggled to explain her rationale for giving up her child but the daughter seemed skeptical of the explanation.

As he watched the scene unfold, Milo felt a sense of rage begin to envelop him, a blackness of spirit much stronger even than he normally felt. He wouldn't have imagined it possible. The sensation was directed at the young woman. He wanted to reach through the vision and strangle the stupid little bitch with his bare hands, to choke the life out of her and cut her up into tiny slivers of bone and flesh and then throw the pieces around the room.

He hated her.

He more than hated her. He wanted to destroy her.

The vision wavered in his mind and then faded as his rage increased, becoming all-encompassing. He could no longer make out the conversation at the table, not that he cared. All he wanted was to get at the young woman, to make her suffer. It wasn't a sexual thing or even a power thing, like the sensation he felt toward Rae Ann and the other girls he had tortured and killed over the years. This was something deeper, more elemental, originating in the depths of his soulless existence. The intensity was frightening, even to Milo Cain, who had long ago reached the conclusion he was incapable of feeling anything.

Then the vision was gone, disappearing from his skull as quickly and unexpectedly as it had come. Milo moaned and dropped to his knees. His head ached uncomfortably and he could feel an egg rising on his forehead where it had impacted the chair. He looked across the room to see Rae Ann staring back at him fearfully. He ignored her.

He was confused and even a little scared. This was a vision totally different than anything he had ever experienced. In the normal ones, he observed random slices of other people's lives, scenes with no emotions or value judgments attached to them. He had no feelings about them, they just *were*.

But in this vision, Milo had wanted nothing more than to destroy the young woman, to rip and rend and kill. And it was just the younger woman. The other two people who had appeared in the vision he couldn't give a shit less about. He walked unsteadily into the bathroom, leaning over the hole where the toilet used to be, feeling like he was going to puke, but nothing came up. He rested his head lightly on the dirty floor.

Finally he stood again, exhausted. He had been extremely lucky in one way. If the vision had invaded—and that's exactly what it felt like, an invasion—his brain a couple of minutes earlier, while his guest had been alone in the bathroom, she might have been able to rush past him and out the door as he struggled to avoid blacking out. She could have been down the stairs in seconds, screaming at the top of her lungs as soon as she hit the street. Even in this neighborhood, that scenario would have spelled the end for Milo Cain.

He looked at the bathroom wall, bare where a mirror used to be. Instead of his face staring back at him, Milo saw faded plaster with a hairline crack spidering diagonally toward the ceiling. That was probably for the best. He doubted he was looking too steady at the moment. He certainly didn't feel steady.

Milo straightened slowly and returned to the living room. Rae Ann was watching him closely, the terror written on her features even more intensely now than at any time since he had brought her here.

Milo didn't care. He continued to ignore her for the time being. She wasn't going anywhere. He dragged himself to his air mattress and tumbled onto it. He was exhausted. He fell asleep and didn't dream.

19

Cait's question hung in the air like an accusation. She supposed it probably was. Of all the things she had expected to hear from the woman who gave her up in an illegal adoption three decades ago, "You have a twin" had never even entered her mind. Yet there it was.

For a brief moment, she thought maybe she hadn't heard the woman correctly. Maybe her mother had said something like, "Separating you from us was a sin," not, "We had to separate you from your twin."

But that was patently ridiculous. The room was so quiet you could hear a pin drop, and Virginia Ayers was sitting less than three feet away at the same table. Of course she had heard her mother correctly.

"I have a twin?" she repeated for the third time.

The woman sighed deeply, the sound filled with longing and regret and, it seemed to Cait, perhaps a touch of fear.

"This is a mistake," Virginia said, but before Cait could say a word in response, she disregarded her own statement and began telling the story Cait had waited her entire life to hear.

"As you've undoubtedly concluded, your family history is more than a little unusual. And yes," she added hastily, sensing Cait's impatience, "you heard me correctly. You have a twin. A brother, actually. He was born minutes after you."

"A brother," Cait said wonderingly. "Where is he?"

Virginia shook her head. "I don't know."

"You don't know? You gave him up, too? Why in God's name would you do that?"

Tears welled in Virginia's eyes and Kevin laid his hand gently on Cait's arm. "Maybe you should let her tell the story in her own way," he suggested. "I'm sure she'll get to that when she's ready."

Cait looked the distraught woman in the eyes and she nodded gratefully. "Thank you," she said.

She took a shuddering breath and continued. "Incidences of twin births run throughout our family's genealogy, as far back as can be traced. Lots of twins, twins born roughly two of every three generations; a statistically impossible number of twins. For many families, twin births are a burden due to the fact that they require twice as much food, twice as much clothing, twice as much attention, twice as much of everything. For a young family without a lot of money, having twins can be stressful and difficult—"

"You gave up your children because it might be *difficult?*" Cait interrupted. Kevin stroked her arm and she closed her mouth reluctantly. She could feel her face flush and her mouth was set in an angry line.

"No," Virginia answered simply. "That's not why we gave you up. I mention these issues as examples of the many problems faced by the typical family with twins. To provide a little perspective. For your father and me, the problem was a far different one." She gazed into Cait's eyes and Cait felt her mother reaching into her very soul.

"You can sense things, see things in your mind, can't you?" Virginia asked suddenly, changing the subject, catching Cait off guard.

She blinked in surprise. "How—how did you know?"

"I know because I have the same gift. Or the same curse, depending upon how you look at it. I know because this gift, or this curse, has been passed down through our ancestry for generations. For hundreds of years, maybe thousands.

"If this gift is similar to my own—and I have no doubt it is—you receive occasional flashes of insight into the lives of the people around you, often trivial, meaningless things, always at random and always in the form of mental pictures or images." She paused and looked at Cait, waiting for confirmation.

For a moment Cait simply stared, unable to speak, shocked into silence at the turn the conversation had taken. Then she nodded.

Virginia nodded back absently, lost in her thoughts, and continued. "You've been able to do this little parlor trick since your earliest days, it's a part of your personality that you once questioned but have long since learned to live with. You usually ignore the mental pictures—"

"Flickers," Cait interrupted.

"Excuse me?"

"Those mental pictures. I call them Flickers."

"Flickers," Virginia responded, pronouncing the word slowly, trying it out, rolling it around on her tongue, savoring it like a coffee aficionado might savor a particularly flavorful sip of dark roast. "I like it. It fits. Anyway, as I was saying, you usually ignore these 'Flickers,' as most of the time they mean nothing. Occasionally, however, you will receive a Flicker of significance. When that happens, you will attempt to put the mental image to use to help someone, to do a good deed, the clairvoyant's version of helping an old lady across the street."

Cait nodded again, unconsciously this time, as she flashed back to the elderly woman at the grocery store who had dropped her checkbook on her kitchen floor. She looked up to see Virginia Ayers—her mother—watching her with a tiny smile on her face. The smile seemed out of place; the rest of her face looked as though she might break into tears again at any moment.

"I've always been curious about my ability," Cait said, "about whether it was a genetic thing or if I was just some weird freak of nature. But you're right about one thing: for the most part, I don't give the Flickers a whole lot of thought anymore."

"Now that you know you are not alone, you shouldn't be surprised to learn that your twin brother possesses the same ability. He also receives these Flickers, as you call them."

"How do you know that?"

"What do you mean?"

"I mean if you gave my brother and me up as newborns, how could you possibly know he has the ability as well? Have you been keeping track of him? Do you know where he is? Can I see him?"

Virginia shook her head firmly. "No, honey, it's nothing like that. Your father and I *did* surrender both of you as infants. You were only hours old when you disappeared out of our lives forever. Or so I thought, until I heard from that private detective down in Tampa."

"Then, how? How do you know?"

"Because that's the way it works with twins in this bloodline. It's the root of the whole problem. There is no doubt that your brother had—has—the same ability as you. It's why we had no choice but to give you up in an illegal adoption, surrendering you to a group that promised to place the two of you as far apart geographically as possible. It was the only way we could think of to keep you safe, to give you any chance of having a normal life. Or a life, period."

Cait shrugged, bewildered. "We had to be taken from our parents and placed hundreds, maybe thousands of miles apart simply because we both had the ability to receive Flickers? That doesn't even make any sense."

"It doesn't make sense because you don't know the whole story."

"Then tell me the whole story."

Virginia stared at the surface of the small table and took a delicate sip of tea. Cait's tea sat in front of her, forgotten.

Finally the older woman shook her head, a tiny movement filled with resignation and defeat. "I suppose there's no stopping you. As you said yourself, the genie is out of the bottle now, isn't it?"

"If you're asking whether I plan to forget about the fact that I have a twin brother and stop digging into this family's supposedly mysterious past, if that's what you're asking, then no, there's no stopping me."

"I didn't think so," Virginia said, and placed her teacup onto the table with a clatter. Cait looked down and saw the woman's hand shaking as if palsied. She tried to recall if it had been doing that earlier and could not. "Then I suppose there's not much point beating around the bush."

"None."

"All right. We gave up our only children in an illegal adoption as the only means of protecting you from your twin brother. Had we not done so, you would be long dead by now. He would have murdered you years ago."

20

Milo awoke from his nap feeling groggy, tossing and turning on his air mattress before finally abandoning the idea of sleep and rising bleary-eyed and exhausted. It had been a couple of hours since the disturbingly strong vision of...whatever the hell it had been...had knocked him on his ass like never before.

He sat up, rubbed his eyes with the heels of his palms, and glanced toward the middle of the room where his terrified house-guest remained securely fastened to her chair. From this angle Milo couldn't be sure, but the hooker appeared to be dozing. Her head tilted forward as if her chin was resting on her breastbone and she sat unmoving.

He rolled off the mattress and stood, and Rae Ann snapped awake at the sound of the old floorboards creaking underfoot. She shook her head once as if to clear the cobwebs and then looked around, obviously trying to locate her captor.

Milo smiled. "I'm behind you," he said playfully, "so you can't see me." She whimpered into her duct-tape gag and he stepped into her field of view.

The entire day's schedule had been thrown off by the earlier un-planned interruption, that disturbingly strong vision of the three people sitting around a kitchen table. He stretched, trying to choose between eating breakfast—it was so late now, he supposed, that it could more appropriately be described as lunch—or getting on with the day's entertainment.

Entertainment won out. Sure, he was hungry, but he could eat anytime. His chances to play with a fresh victim were distressingly infrequent. He gazed down at the schoolgirl hooker appraisingly and saw her staring back at him with eyes wide and fearful. In the harsh light of midday, after the first round of play last night and without an opportunity to shower or apply makeup, the girl didn't look quite so youthful after all—certainly not an age to justify her ridiculous outfit. Streaks of mascara ran down her cheeks like tiny canals and traces of crow's feet were beginning to radiate outward from her blue eyes.

Milo didn't care. She was still relatively young and sexy and, best of all, she was his. His to use in the manner of his choosing for as long as he elected to do so, before tossing her corpse into a Dumpster when the pleasure he received from torturing her was no longer worth the effort of keeping her alive. He smiled and instantly the girl began thrashing about in her chair, her efforts pointless but enthusiastic, somehow apparently tipped off to his intentions solely by the look in his eyes.

He watched her struggle, aroused by her reaction, his predator eyes locked onto her body, determined not to miss a moment of the fun. Eventually she tired and slumped back, her slim form shaking either from exertion or fear. Milo wasn't sure which and didn't care. She had graduated from whimpering to moaning, the sounds still muffled by the thick silver duct tape layered over her mouth. He wished he could remove the gag to fully enjoy her terror, but unfortunately, even in this neighborhood, the screams she would immediately unleash would not go unnoticed.

It was a damned shame. Furthermore, it was completely unfair. Milo had found her and lured her here fair and square; he should be permitted the luxury of enjoying her in whatever manner he pleased. He sighed deeply. Someday he would get his own home way out in the country, a place with no pesky neighbors, a place where not only could he play with his victims without having to gag them, he could hook them up to a loudspeaker if he wanted to and still not have to worry.

In the meantime, he would make do with what he had. No one ever said life would be easy.

Or fair.

Now, on to the business at hand. How did he want to play today? He fingered the pliers in his pocket and came to a quick decision. It wasn't all that difficult. "What do you say we take a look at those fingers you injured last night? Maybe I can fix them up for you."

"Mmmph mmmph mmmph mmmmmph," Rae Ann replied, resuming her impressive routine of head-shaking and body-thrashing. It occurred to Milo that his little deception had not fooled her. She knew she was in for pain. There just wasn't anything she could do about it.

He displayed his pliers for her with a flourish, holding them in front of her eyes, which she had squeezed tightly shut as though she might be able to make the whole nightmare disappear. Eventually, though, Milo knew she would become curious and reopen them, and eventually she did. The terror in them blossomed at the sight of the small hand tool.

The pliers seemed relatively benign to Milo, grey steel pincers with curved handles covered in red rubberized plastic for a firm grip. Rae Ann didn't see them as benign, though, probably thanks to her slightly different perspective. She was clearly terrified.

In a quick motion, he fell to his knees in front of his guest. To anyone entering the shabby apartment at that exact moment, he might have looked like a nervous suitor proposing marriage to his young girlfriend. Except, of course, that the bride-to-be had been duct-taped to her chair and blood was dripping steadily from three ruined fingers.

But no one walked into the apartment. Milo reached forward, grabbing Rae Ann's badly injured right hand with his left, holding it steady, waiting patiently for her to calm down.

She never did, and when he got tired of waiting, Milo opened the jaws of the pliers as widely as he could, placed the tempered steel between the first and second knuckles of her swollen pinky finger, and deftly twisted his wrist, snapping the delicate bone with an audible and satisfying *Crack!* She screamed in agony, the sound muffled almost to the point of inaudibility. Milo removed the pliers and the tip of the finger tilted at nearly a ninety-degree angle, pointing toward the floor, blood dripping more steadily now onto the makeshift plastic tarp.

Rae Ann continued to scream into her gag; she was panting and hyperventilating, and Milo came in his pants without even touching himself. He never tired of the sexual gratification he received from the suffering of his guests. He knew this made him different from most, but was bothered by that fact only inasmuch as it wasn't always easy to avail himself of a young girl to torture. And now that he had one, he certainly wasn't about to let her go to waste.

After maybe thirty seconds of what must have been some of the most intense pain the young woman had ever endured—although it was nothing compared to what Milo had in store for her—Rae Ann passed out, her head slumping to the side, her face streaked with tears and snot and drool. It was disgusting

Milo didn't care. He rose from the floor and went into the bathroom to clean himself up with a dirty towel.

* * *

The girl was still unconscious when he came out of the bathroom, so Milo sat on the floor with his back against the wall, watching her and thinking about nothing in particular while waiting for her to wake up so they could have more fun together. She looked so peaceful, nothing like the panicked animal she had been prior to blacking out.

His mind wandered back to the mysterious vision he had experienced earlier in the morning. He was certain he had never seen the young woman from that vision before and wondered why she had inspired such a vile, hate-filled reaction, the intensity of which still surprised and troubled him. As an antisocial personality, undoubtedly diagnosable as a sociopath—Milo Cain had issues with mental stability, he knew that, but he wasn't stupid—he was used to viewing the world through a lens of anger and mistrust, but his reaction to the girl in the vision had been off the charts, even for him.

What did that mean? Even now, sitting here recalling the vision, he could feel the hate bubbling up inside him like a rapidly filling well, causing his pulse to race and his breathing to quicken. Even now, hours later, the mere thought of the bitch—it was only the young woman, the other two people in the room inspired nothing more in him than his usual disgust and loathing—caused a blackness to fill his already-corrupted soul and thoughts of murder and mayhem to swell in his consciousness, almost to the exclusion of everything else.

The girl in the vision was young and pretty, roughly his own age, and she radiated *goodness* and *decency,* two things he hated, despite the fact he wished he could have them. But it was more than that. There were plenty of people, even in his shabby orbit, who were good and decent and who didn't make him feel as though he wanted to rip them apart with his bare hands, who didn't inspire this single-minded desire to rend and destroy and kill.

In the vision, the girl had been discussing her heritage, mostly listening while the older woman held court, occasionally asking questions, occasionally displaying flashes of anger. It was righteous anger, Milo could tell, and that was another thing that pissed him off. Who the hell did she think she was, the goddamned righteous beautiful bitch?

Another wave of bilious rage swept over him and he went with it, closing his eyes and envisioning what he would do if (when) he ever caught up with her. He would hurt her, he would torture her, he would make her wish she had never been born, he would do things to her that would make this pliers activity with Rae Ann the School-girl Hooker seem like child's play, like Arts and Crafts time for a preschooler.

Milo realized his eyes were screwed tightly shut and water was leaking from them. He was crying like a fucking baby while picturing all of the things he would do to the unknown and unnamed girl from his vision. He sniffled and wiped his eyes with the back of his hand and realized he needed to blow his nose.

That realization made him think of his houseguest and her snot-covered face. He was going to have to clean her up before he could play with her again. He glanced across the room and saw that she had awakened and was watching him. Her eyes were filled with the fear he had come to expect, as well as with the terrible pain that must be ra-diating outward from her yanked-out fingernails and especially from her broken, mangled pinky finger.

But there was something else as well, Milo thought. In her eyes a hint of laughter shone through, a hidden smile, a mocking contempt for the weakness she had caught him displaying. It was like the time his mother had caught him jerking off in bed when he was twelve. She had been shocked and angry, there was no doubt about that, but Milo had also glimpsed the same barely masked contempt he was see-ing here.

There had been nothing he could do back then. He was twelve and his mother was...well...something, he wasn't really sure how old she was, but she had been a hell of a lot older than he, and had held all the power along with his asshole father.

That was not the case now, though. Milo Cain was in charge now, and if this Rae Ann the Schoolgirl Hooker bitch thought she could get away with mocking him, he would make good and goddamn certain she would never make that error in judgment again.

He rose to his feet with renewed vigor. As much as he was going to enjoy the upcoming session with Rae Ann, it would now have a little added meaning thanks to her arrogant disregard of the power structure in their burgeoning relationship. He reached into his pocket and pulled out his trusty pliers, *snap, snap, snapping* them absently as he approached her chair.

21

Cait stared at her mother, again rendered speechless by a statement that had taken her completely by surprise. She realized her mouth was hanging open and she closed it. "I must not have heard you correctly. I thought you said my twin brother would have murdered me by now if we had grown up together."

"You heard me," Virginia countered. Now that she had come out with the words that had obviously been eating away at her, she seemed calmer, more in control of herself and her emotions.

Cait, on the other hand, felt much less so. She stood suddenly, her calves shoving the wooden chair back on the ancient floor with a loud squeal. She began pacing in the tiny kitchen. Kevin started to rise and she motioned him back down in his seat.

"I have to tell you," Cait said, choosing her words carefully. "If you thought that statement was somehow going to clear everything up, to answer all of my questions, you were very much mistaken. Why would my own brother—my own *twin!*—murder me? What possible reason would he have? And furthermore, how can you say such a thing when you only knew us for a couple of hours years ago? When we were only infants?"

Virginia seemed unruffled by the outburst. "You remember what I told you about the frequency of twin births occurring throughout this family's history, and how it is a statistical impossibility?"

Cait nodded, saying nothing.

"Well, in every instance of twin births into this bloodline—and when I say 'every instance,' I'm talking about a history going back hundreds of years—one of the twins has wound up dead at the hands of the other. *Every single instance. Bar none.*"

Nobody moved and the kitchen was silent.

"What? Why? How is that possible?" The questions sounded hopelessly insufficient to Cait as she asked them. She trudged back to her chair and sat, stunned and confused.

"I believe, and your father believed as well, that the cause of this tragic history is related directly to the quirk of genetics that allows you to see the flashes—Flickers, as you call them—into the lives of others. When a single child is born with the gift, as I was, for example, the normal notions of right and wrong—what we know as 'conscience,' for lack of a better term—are as fully developed as they would be with any other human being. This is important, because it means that each time I, for example, receive a Flicker, there is no natural inclination to use the information gained from the vision in a destructive way."

"You make a choice to behave in an acceptable manner."

"Exactly. It's like walking into a candy store and seeing no one behind the counter, but all the candy is placed out in the open where it is easily accessible. You are faced with the choice of doing the right thing or the wrong thing—waiting for the proprietor and paying for the candy, or shoving it into your pocket and leaving the store."

"I understand the concept of conscience and choosing to do the right thing," Cait said, realizing she sounded harsher than she intended but not caring. "I just don't see what all this has to do with twins and the ability to receive Flickers."

"I'm getting to that," Virginia said patiently. "So you agree that we all face situations in our lives where we must choose between right and wrong?"

"Of course," Cait replied with a shrug. "We face those choices daily, both large and small."

Virginia nodded. "Yes, we do. Now, let me ask you a question. Can you ever recall a time in your life when you received a Flicker and were tempted to use the information you received in a destructive way? With malicious intent?"

"Well, often the Flicker is pretty nonspecific. A lot of the time, the information isn't anything that could be used for good *or* bad."

"Understood. But there *are* times when the opposite is true, and you see things in your head that *could* be used either in a positive or a negative way, correct?"

"Of course."

"Well, in those instances, have you ever been tempted, even a little bit, to use the Flicker in a negative way, to turn the information to your advantage somehow?"

"Of course not!" Cait flushed and drew her head back as if she had been slapped. "That would be wrong!"

Virginia smiled. "It's never occurred to you that even though you face the same struggles with right and wrong—good and evil, so to speak—as everyone else in the world, every day, you've never once had to do the same thing with a Flicker?"

Cait furrowed her brow, her indignant reaction of a moment ago suddenly forgotten. She was silent for a long moment. "I—I guess I've never thought about it in that way."

"Of course you haven't, dear, because doing the right thing when you receive a Flicker is the most natural thing in the world to you. It's like breathing, or blinking. When was the last time you gave either one of those things a conscious thought?"

"Never."

"Exactly. And that's my point. It goes against your very nature to use a Flicker negatively or destructively." Virginia stopped talking and

Cait sat unmoving, absorbing this strange revelation. Kevin sat next to her, saying nothing, spellbound by the entire bizarre conversation.

"Then my twin brother..." Cait's voice drifted off as she digested the implications of what she had just learned. A sense of dawning horror wormed through her.

"That's right, your twin—in this case it's a brother, by the way, but it didn't necessarily have to be, you could just as easily have been born the same sex—has undoubtedly been receiving Flickers his entire life, just like you. But in his case, the natural reaction is to *mis*use the information he receives. Seeking a negative, destructive outcome with Flickers comes as naturally to him as taking a positive path does to you."

Cait sat back in her chair, thunderstruck. She felt like Alice after falling through the rabbit hole. Suddenly reality was warped and reflected in ways she would never have imagined just an hour ago. It was like looking at life through a fun house mirror.

"But...*why?*"

"Well, as I said before—and keep in mind, this is only conjecture, the best theory your father and I could come up with after spending months thinking about it once we discovered I was pregnant with twins—we theorized this dichotomy is somehow related to whatever psychic ability we possess that allows us to receive these Flickers. Or maybe everyone has the ability, but the average person is unaware of it. In any event, your father and I guessed that this psychic ability must be somehow incompatible with twin fetuses as they develop in the womb, that the sense of morality that accompanies the deciphering of Flickers cannot be split. Thus—"

"One of the twins reacts to Flickers as good and one as evil," Cait interrupted, so caught up in following her mother's chain of logic that she was unable to stop herself from blurting it out.

"That's the conclusion we came to."

"But it still doesn't explain why one twin would *murder* the other."

Virginia smiled. "You're quite the sharp cookie."

Cait said nothing, concentrating on trying to puzzle out the mystery.

"Now we've descended into a realm so far removed from normal behavior patterns that it becomes difficult even to hazard a guess, but the best theory we could come up with is that the psychic ability that allows us to receive Flickers is similar in some strange way to the positive and negative polarity of a magnet. If you place the two oppositely polarized sides of a magnet together, they cling to one another, but if you place the two similarly polarized sides together, they reject one another, making it impossible for them to occupy the same space."

"You're saying I'm the same as some maniac who wants to kill me."

"Only in the sense that you have the same psychic ability, an ability containing a moral component that is impossible to split equally, so one side—the good—receives the morality gene, if you will, while the other side—the evil—gets, unfortunately, passed over. Through no fault of his own."

"So, my brother—the one I've never met and wasn't even aware existed until this morning—and I are similarly polarized psychic magnets. We can't coexist in the same space."

"That was the theory your father and I were working with, a theory backed up by centuries of real-world history. That was why we knew we had to surrender the two of you for adoption. We had literally no choice."

"But why do it illegally?"

"Because it was the only way to ensure the two of you would end up in different areas of the country, thousands of miles apart. We never knew where either of you went after leaving our house that horrible night—that was part of the agreement—but we were promised you would be separated by a minimum of one thousand miles, so the odds of you ever settling down close enough to each other to put you at risk were infinitesimal."

The conversation dragged to a halt, three people lost in their own thoughts. Cait felt overwhelmed, like she had been exposed to Einstein's theory of relativity in one grueling session and now had to figure out how to absorb and understand it. She glanced at Virginia Ayers, the mother she had spent a lifetime wondering about, and the woman appeared lost in a sea of regret. She also seemed to have aged appreciably during the conversation, which clearly had taken a heavy toll on her.

Cait didn't remember having sat back down and wondered how long ago *that* had happened. She lifted the ceramic cup to her lips automatically, more to occupy her time than because she was thirsty, and was surprised to discover the tea had grown stone cold.

Virginia stood and bustled around the kitchen in a false display of energy. She lifted the teacups off the table and carried them to the sink, where she made a show of rinsing them out in one basin and dropping them in the other with a clatter.

Cait realized the woman's hospitality had reached its end as Virginia said, "Well then, I don't believe I can be of any more help to you. I've answered all of your questions and undoubtedly raised many more in your mind. Unfortunately, the questions you are left with are ones you will have to puzzle out for yourself."

Cait and Kevin stood and began walking down the short hallway toward the front door. She grabbed his arm and held on tightly as he punched the cab company's number into his cell phone. They reached the door and turned around to discover Virginia Ayers had followed and was now standing right behind them.

"I have just one more question," Cait said.

Virginia said nothing so she continued. "How did you know when we showed up here today that I was the twin that had been blessed with the good polarity and not the evil?"

Virginia laughed out loud, despite appearing ready to break out in tears. Her eyes watered and she blinked hard. "It's as plain as day, sweetheart. Your goodness is written all over your face. I could see it the moment I laid eyes on you. You are no more capable of evil than I am of running the Boston Marathon."

Cait had no idea how to respond, so she took half a step forward and wrapped her arms around her mother's frail body, holding on tightly and squeezing until she was afraid one of the older woman's ribs might snap.

After a second's hesitation, the hug was returned fiercely and in that moment Cait knew everything she had learned today was true. This was a woman who had torn her family apart and lived with an overwhelming sense of sadness and regret every day for the past thirty years, but she had done it to preserve the lives of her two children the only way she could think of. She had sacrificed everything for two people she barely knew.

As she pulled away after an instant and a lifetime, Cait realized she was crying soundlessly, tears running down her face. She looked up at Kevin and he was crying as well. So was Virginia.

"Well," she said with an awkward laugh. "Aren't we a cheerful bunch."

They opened the door and walked onto the tiny front landing. The door closed behind them and through the screen Virginia sniffled and said, "I have one request before you go."

"Anything," Cait said.

"You see this number?" she asked, pointing at a tarnished, brass-plated "7" screwed into the faded vinyl siding next to the front door.

"Of course, it's the address of your home—Seven Granite Circle."

"That's right," Virginia answered. "Now please forget you ever saw it. Forget you were here and don't ever come back. I don't think I could survive if I had to go through this again."

Cait opened her mouth to reply, with no idea what words might come out. Her face flushed and tears filled her eyes again and before she could say anything, the storm door closed and she was left listening to the sound of her mother's footsteps moving slowly down the hallway. They faded and then disappeared. She looked at Kevin in utter brokenhearted bewilderment as their taxi pulled to a stop at the end of the driveway.

22

The amount of blood that could spill out of a relatively small injury was impressive, Milo thought. He had seen it before, but it never ceased to amaze him. He stood next to his homemade torture chair watching Rae Ann squirm and cry and beg for mercy into her duct-tape gag. Her words were indistinguishable, of course, but their intent was clear, as was the desperation behind them.

Just for fun, Milo had taken his pliers and smacked their heavy metal jaws against the backs of the fingertips on her right hand, where the nails would be if she still had any. The freshly crusted scabs had broken open immediately, and the blood once again began to flow, dripping in thick globs off her hand.

Each time he introduced himself to a new girl, he celebrated the occasion by using a fresh tarp, unstained by the blood and bodily fluids of another. It was an expense he couldn't really afford, but certain rituals demanded observance and this was one of them.

He watched the small dark maroon rivulets spread slowly across the clear plastic and contemplated his next move. Breaking fingers and tearing off nails was enjoyable—he could do it all day long and on more than one memorable occasion had done exactly that—but he felt in this case it was time to move on. There were incisions to be made, flesh to be torn, impromptu surgeries to be performed on his cute little friend, and it would be nice to accomplish some of those things before she was so far gone from the pain she was unable to participate satisfactorily in the process.

Removing one of her pert little breasts might be nice. It would be a relatively simple procedure, not terribly time-consuming either, and would allow him to get his feet wet, so to speak, before moving on to more complex surgeries either tonight or tomorrow.

Rae Ann whimpered quietly, still recovering from the most recent explosion of pain in her mangled fingers, and she watched him with fearful eyes as he wandered into the kitchen to retrieve his surgical supplies. It was almost as if she could read his thoughts. Or maybe she had already reached the conclusion that all of his guests eventually tumbled to: Milo Cain was one crazy motherfucker, not to be trusted, and it behooved you to keep a close eye on him at all times.

Whatever the reason, her eyes were still trained on the kitchen door when he returned, clutching his supplies. He had assumed she would fail to immediately grasp the significance of the tools he was holding, but he was wrong. The moment he reentered the living room she began the now-familiar process of thrashing in her chair, straining against her duct-tape bindings and screaming—if it could be called that—into her gag.

Milo was impressed. This girl was sharp, especially for someone who made a living selling her body to strangers. He almost wished he could get to know her better before killing her and dumping her body, but realistically, knew that would not happen. Impulse control had never been one of his strong points, especially where his unique hobbies were concerned. His enjoyment of Rae Ann the Schoolgirl Hooker would proceed at its own pace, more or less regardless of his intentions.

He had crossed roughly half the distance from the kitchen to her chair when another intense vision, similar to the one he had experienced earlier this morning, crashed into his head with a vengeance, walloping him like a baseball bat to the skull. He crumpled to his knees, this time managing to avoid smacking his forehead on the wooden chair. His surgical supplies—knives, bandages, more pliers, clamps—fell from his hands, scattering around him like snowflakes during the first winter storm.

Milo's eyelids blinked rapidly as he struggled to maintain consciousness, the vision pounding in his brain. In it were the same group of three people he had observed earlier, except now they stood clustered at a doorway, presumably the front door of the same house. The two younger people—probably a couple but it was impossible to say for sure—were outside the house standing on the landing, while the older woman, the one who had done most of the talking in the first vision, remained inside in the foyer, speaking to them through the screen door.

And once again his attention was drawn to the younger woman like metal to a magnet. Now that she was standing, he could see her more clearly and, as he had thought earlier, she was breathtakingly beautiful. Milo Cain had a keen eye for the female form and even in this moment of pain and confusion, could not help but admire the young woman's physical gifts.

But despite her beauty, or perhaps partially because of it, he hated her. As with the first vision, the very sight of the woman caused an instant, visceral rage to well up inside him, a pulsing to begin behind his eyeballs, a feeling like his optic nerve was going to explode, which of course was ridiculous because he wasn't really "seeing" her, at least not with his eyes. A blood-red shadow seemed to outline her form as she stood on the landing, a development new to this vision and one that did not extend to the other two people in it.

Milo watched her and hated her. The animosity he felt toward this young woman he had never met was far beyond anything he had ever experienced. He wanted to reach through his brain, fasten his hands around her pretty neck, and choke her and slam her to the ground. Then he would kick her and stab her and slice her, do the sorts of things he had planned for Rae Ann the Schoolgirl Hooker, only in the case of this unknown woman it would not be to achieve any kind of satisfaction, sexual or otherwise; it would be for one purpose only: to destroy her, to tear her apart and stomp on her and crush her delicate bones and watch her blood spurt and her flesh rip, to turn her into a rotting dead shell of a human being and then spit on the carcass.

He watched closely—not that he had a choice—as the trio interacted. He forced himself to bring his roiling emotions under control, at least enough to pay attention to the conversation. It was as if he was standing on the stoop next to the young couple, inches away from them, but completely invisible to them. He was close enough that had he actually been there in a physical sense, he could have reached out and begun strangling the girl at whom all his hate was directed without even fully extending his arms.

But of course he *wasn't* there physically, so he watched and listened, drinking it all in, already having come to the conclusion he would not rest until he had hunted this girl down and snuffed the life out of her, and in the most painful manner possible. Somewhere in the back of Milo Cain's racing mind—he kneeled unmoving on the filthy floor of his shabby hovel, eyes glazed over, tongue lolling, drool oozing from the side of his mouth, yet he had never felt so alert, so *alive* in his entire life—he wondered why this beautiful woman he had never met generated such incredible animosity inside him. But it was a detached curiosity, similar to how a scientist might wonder as he performed experiments on an animal how much pain he was causing: the question was there, but the answer didn't really matter.

Milo observed the conversation with rapt fascination. None of the people were happy, that much was clear immediately. A sense of despair enveloped the older woman like a cloak, like she had been living with whatever heartbreak was eating away at her for so long it was second nature, like she would not know how to get through her daily routine without it.

The man seemed agitated. It appeared he wanted to protect the young woman from something that he knew was bothering her but had no clue how to do so.

But the young woman was without a doubt the most miserable of the strange trio, and it seemed to Milo that he wouldn't have needed any strange psychic ability to sense it. Her eyes were red and swollen from crying and her face was bloated and puffy and she seemed unable to stand still.

Good, Milo thought. *Serves you right, you stupid fucking little whore. Wait until I get ahold of you, then you'll find out what it really means to cry.*

He tamped down on his once-again rising tide of anger and forced himself to pay attention. Whatever drama was playing out here seemed to be drawing to a close. The older woman was talking, albeit reluctantly. In a voice choked with emotion she said, "You see this number?" She pointed next to the door.

"Of course, it's the address of your home—7 Granite Circle."

"That's right. Now please forget you ever saw it. Forget you were here and don't ever come back. I don't think I could handle it again."

The young woman looked like she had been kicked in the teeth by a mule and Milo felt a sense of vicious satisfaction spread through his body. *Yes,* he thought. *Give it to her good, make her suffer! Get her ready for me!*

And then, as quickly as it had thundered into his head, the vision disappeared and the three people vanished. His eyes cleared and he found himself back in his ratty condemned tenement, crouched on the dirty floor three feet from the torture chair, Rae Ann the Schoolgirl Hooker watching him closely, a mixture of fear and curiosity in her eyes. He wiped the drool off his cheek absently with the back of his hand, lost in thought.

7 Granite Circle.

Interesting.

He had no idea in what city or town 7 Granite Circle might be located, but that minor point didn't concern him. Milo Cain was nothing if not resourceful. He searched around on the floor until finding a scrap of thin cardboard, a packaging insert for the chocolate snack cakes that so often made up his dinner. Grease and stale chocolate cake crumbs crusted one side of the cardboard, but the other side seemed relatively dirt-free.

He rose to his feet and wandered into the barren kitchen and rooted around in a drawer, eventually locating a pen. He jotted the address down on the clean side of the paper. It seemed important and he didn't want to forget it.

Then Milo returned to the living room and began gathering his surgical supplies off the floor, his interest in Rae Ann waning, his mind on other things.

23

"What the heck was that all about?" Kevin shook his head in bewilderment inside the dirty yellow taxi as they braced for another thrill ride back to their hotel. "Is it just me or does it feel like we just spent the last two hours inside some bizarre LSD trip?"

Cait was silent for a long time, her head turned away from Kevin as she watched the traffic roll by. Finally she said, "Do you think she really meant what she said about never coming back? Could it really be possible that I've finally found my mother after thirty years, only to lose her again forever?"

"Try to look at it from her point of view for a minute," Kevin said. "For the last three decades she has dealt with what was obviously a very traumatic event—giving her children up in an illegal adoption just hours after their birth—by pushing the painful memories away and locking them up in some rarely visited corner of her brain. When we showed up on her doorstep today, those feelings of guilt and loss came rushing back."

"But still," Cait persisted. "How can I simply forget my mother when it took so long just to find her?"

"You can't force yourself upon her, and if what she truly wants is to be left alone, you're going to have to respect those wishes. But that might not necessarily be the case. Maybe what she needs right now is some time to absorb this new reality, where she suddenly has the potential for a relationship with her daughter. Maybe after a few weeks or months she'll be able to open herself up to that reality."

The cab driver made a quick lane-change, accelerating past a slow-moving produce truck and then cutting the wheel sharply back to the right. The car crowded into the nearly nonexistent space inches in front of the truck's bumper. The momentum pushed Cait against her seat belt. She unsnapped the buckle and slid over, leaning into Kevin's bulky body. He wrapped an arm around her shoulder.

"And that's another thing," she continued as the cab rocked on its springs. "I have a brother! Not just a brother, but a *twin* brother! How am I going to go about finding him?"

"Well," Kevin answered. "We can go back to Arlen Hirschberg in Tampa. He's a little pricey, but he was able to locate your birth mother quickly and without too much trouble. He can probably do the same thing for your brother. The problem is..."

"I know," Cait said. "Bad things will happen if the two of us get together. Are you really buying that mumbo-jumbo? Does it make any sense to you?"

"It's more than just a question of 'bad things happening,'" Kevin said firmly. "You heard your mother. Bad things will happen *to you.* Really bad things, like you getting killed."

Cait waved her hand as if shooing away a pesky mosquito and Kevin said, "No, no, you're not allowed to disregard what she said just because you don't like it or it's inconvenient for you. You know me, I'm naturally skeptical. Suspicious, even. All cops are. But this woman *knew,* before you ever brought it up, about your Flickers. She described them perfectly, even admitting to possessing exactly the same ability.

"That being the case," he continued, "I think we have to give credence to what she said about how much danger you would be in if you found your brother. We may not understand what's going on yet, but that doesn't mean we should ignore your mother's concerns."

"But none of it makes any sense. Why would twins, each of whom have inherited the same unusual genetic ability, be somehow incompatible based solely upon their geographic proximity to each other?"

"How the hell do I know?" Kevin answered, exasperated. "I just found out about all of this, too! But there is so much we don't understand—so much that *no one* seems to understand—about these Flickers, that I think you should assume, until proven otherwise, that what your mother said is true. Maybe it's like blood transfusions, somehow."

"What? You've lost me."

"Yeah, you know, blood transfusions," Kevin said excitedly, becoming more animated as he warmed to the subject. "You know how, if you receive a blood transfusion from someone who is not the same blood type, your body will reject the blood? Maybe it's something like that."

"But we're twins," Cait replied. "Twins share the same blood type, don't they? That scenario would be impossible with my brother and me."

Kevin shook his head. "I'm not trying to suggest this Flicker thing is *exactly* the same as rejected blood transfusions. I'm just saying that there are plenty of scenarios where two seemingly compatible people are found to be medically *in*compatible, for reasons that may not be readily apparent. Organ transplants would be another example. Sometimes the human body rejects a donated organ for reasons the experts don't even understand.

"Let's face it," he continued. "As far as we know, nobody outside your own bloodline even knows these Flickers exist, so it's not like they've been the subject of any scientific research. We have no idea what sorts of personality traits might be associated with them. Until we learn otherwise, I think we have to treat everything Virginia Ayers just told you as being true, if for no other reason than the risk of assuming otherwise is so extreme. I don't want to see you put in danger."

"There's still no proof," Cait mumbled stubbornly. "Where's the proof? How can I just take her word for it?"

"Where's the proof?" Kevin asked incredulously. "Did you really just say that? Her story *is* the proof. The proof is in the fact that this woman turned her life upside down and destroyed her marriage—Christ, her husband was so devastated he ended up killing himself—to protect her newborn children. The proof is in the hundreds of years of family history she related. That's all the proof I need, and it damn well should be all the proof you need, as well."

"But still..."

"There is no 'but still.' You can't pick and choose what you want to believe, especially when it's so important. If you accept that Flickers are real—and you *know* they are—and if you accept that your birth mother has the same ability—and you *know* now that she does—then you have to accept what she said about your twin brother also, at least until you see proof otherwise.

"But," he continued, holding his hand up to stop her from interrupting. "When we get back to Tampa, we can sit down and do an Internet search on your family history. If what Virginia told you is true, there should be plenty of archival evidence, in the form of newspaper reports and the like, of the murders to back up her story. Don't you agree?"

"Probably," Cait admitted grudgingly.

"Not probably, definitely. So let's make a deal." The taxi turned a corner and pulled to a stop in front of their hotel. "If we find out through these online searches that there *is* a history of twin deaths in your family, then you forget you ever learned of the existence of your twin brother. If it turns out the whole thing is some bizarre tale concocted by your long-lost mother because she's just loony, I will help you do everything possible to locate your brother. That seems reasonable, don't you think?"

Cait sighed deeply and opened her door. "I suppose."

"Hey, look on the bright side," Kevin said with a smile.

"There's a bright side?"

"Of course. We've been so wrapped up in trying to figure out what the hell went on at your mother's house that you didn't even notice we almost got killed six or seven times on the ride back here. That's something, right?"

The cab driver fixed Kevin with a stare, but his scowl turned to a tight-lipped smile when he received his tip. Apparently in Boston insults were forgivable if the price was right. Kevin slammed the door and the taxi pulled out into the heavy traffic almost immediately, serenaded by a chorus of angry horns.

Cait watched the car pull away, standing in the middle of the sidewalk, lost in her thoughts. Kevin took her gently by the elbow and led her inside.

24

Milo squinted at the computer keyboard, typing carefully into the search engine, anxious to see the results for his entry: "Granite Circle, Massachusetts." He had jotted down the address to be sure he didn't forget it, but it was burned into his mind like it had been put there with a branding iron. He was determined to find the fucking little bitch from his strange vision and teach her a much-needed lesson.

Milo knew there was no logical reason for the burning hatred he felt every time he thought about the pretty young woman roughly his own age. As far as he knew, she had never done a thing to him and, in fact, they had never met. He was certain of that. The only two times he had ever seen her were inside his own head.

But he could not help how he felt, and he was determined to place everything else in his life—including his current project, Rae Ann the Schoolgirl Hooker—on the back burner until he could settle this mysterious score with the beautiful unknown woman.

To that end he sat in a utilitarian plastic chair in the Boston Public Library, perched in front of a gigantic desktop computer that had probably been brand-new sometime around the turn of the century, checking search engine results for "Granite Circle, Massachusetts." Milo couldn't afford a computer of his own, and in any event, had no need for one. The World Wide Web was of little interest to a man who spent the majority of his time in the shadows, moving from dark alley to dark alley, living his life outside the realm of so-called "normal" society.

Milo felt uncomfortably exposed in the library. The lighting seemed harsh and unnaturally bright, causing the shadows cast by his body to stretch away at odd angles, their edges knife-blade-sharp on the chocolate brown of the worn carpet. The soft murmur of muted voices should have been soothing and reassuring, but instead seemed fraught with danger, as if at any moment someone would leap from between rows of hardcover volumes and point accusingly, shouting, "That's him! That's the man who mutilated and murdered my wife/girlfriend/daughter/top-earning prostitute!"

But this was the only way to accomplish what needed to be done, short of traveling through the state checking telephone books to see if any of the towns in their coverage areas contained a street named Granite Circle, so it was the library or nothing.

He looked around nervously. No one was paying any attention to him. He relaxed slightly and ran the second vision through his mind again, concentrating with particular emphasis on the young woman's recitation of the address. "7 Granite Circle." He had replayed it a hundred times in his head, each time willing the stupid bitch to recite the *name of the town or city* as well, each time infuriated when she did not. She was fucking worthless, and this was just more proof of that fact.

The search results popped onto the monitor's screen after a length of time so absurdly short it seemed impossible the damned computer could have done its job. In just .22 seconds, less than a quarter of a second, Google claimed to have examined its entire database and returned over six million results. Ridiculous.

Milo made a conscious effort to tamp down his frustration and anger. Focus. That was the watchword for today. Focus, get the answers he was looking for, and then he could get the hell out of Dodge, also known as the Boston Public Library, and escape the smothering sensation of claustrophobia threatening to overwhelm him.

He wiped his face with the back of his hand and examined the search engine results. Six million, two hundred sixty thousand results for "Granite Circle, Massachusetts"? When he started clicking links, though, Milo relaxed, even managing a tiny smile.

The first link provided the answer he was seeking: there were two.

Two towns in the Commonwealth of Massachusetts contained streets named "Granite Circle." How the search engine managed to bombard him with more than six million other things it claimed might be a match for "Granite Circle, Massachusetts" Milo had no idea, nor did he care.

The town of Sandwich contained a Granite Circle, and so did the city of Everett. *Now we're getting somewhere,* Milo thought. This was going to be easy, almost absurdly so. Sandwich was a sleepy little village on Cape Cod, east of Buzzard's Bay and south of the Mid-Cape Highway, roughly in the vicinity of the bicep on the crooked arm forming the cape's outline on a map.

Everett was the polar opposite of Sandwich. Located just north of Boston—not far from the neighborhood housing Milo's current residence, in fact—Everett was a hardscrabble, blue-collar city filled with traffic and people, aging factories and mills, high unemployment and a kind of determined refusal to knuckle under to an economy that had left the city behind years, if not decades, ago. If Sandwich was latte, Everett was black coffee left on the burner too long, with muddy grounds lining the bottom of the cup.

And that was all. Out of 351 cities and towns making up the Commonwealth of Massachusetts, only two contained streets with the name, "Granite Circle." Milo sat back and replayed the two visions in his mind yet again, hoping to unearth some detail he could use to ascertain which Granite Circle he was interested in. His line of sight during the second vision, the one that took place outside the older woman's home, had been toward the three people having their strained conversation and away from any neighborhood landmarks or other characteristics he might have been able to use for easy identification.

Still, there had to be something. The house itself had seemed worn and bedraggled, old. It appeared beaten down by decades of neglect, maintenance delayed either by lack of funds or lack of interest, more likely a product of the bleak environs of Everett than the leafy suburbia of Sandwich.

And there was something else. Although Milo had not been able to *see* anything of interest during the vision, that did not mean he hadn't been able to *hear* anything. As he caressed the second vision in his mind like a lover stroking his partner's skin, Milo began to recall sounds, almost unnoticed by the long-time city dweller; things that told him the meeting had taken place in an area surrounded by people. A lot of people. Thousands upon thousands of people, all packed into a steaming concrete jungle.

The honk of a horn from a frustrated driver, the rumble of a big diesel engine, the constant white noise of city life that was curiously absent in the suburbs. It was all there in the vision, just waiting to be noticed.

And now Milo had noticed it.

And he knew. Everett it was.

He picked up the small notebook he had brought on the mistaken assumption that he was going to have multiple cities and towns to remember, pushed the chair back on the carpet, and stood to leave. He relaxed, feeling almost normal for once, thankful he had not been observed despite the fact he might have been the worst dressed person in the library. Scratch that. He *definitely was* the worst dressed person in the library.

He took one step toward the door when it hit.

His eyes rolled up into his head and he stumbled forward, crashing face-first to the floor like an Olympic diver hitting the pool. His nose mashed the thin carpet and he rolled onto his side, the motion accomplished more by momentum than by planning. He struggled to his knees, blood cascading down his face, and fought hard to maintain his equilibrium.

Milo Cain was caught in the grip of another disturbingly intense vision, his third within the last eight hours.

* * *

This time when it finally faded, Milo was prepared. The overwhelming feeling of lethargy he had experienced following the first two visions was there this time, too, but he was ready and tried to fight through it. It seemed unlikely the Boston Public Library would allow him to nap on their floor. He blinked a few times to ease the watering in his eyes brought on by the throbbing in his nose, then wearily pushed himself upright, using his sleeve to stanch the flow of blood.

And a hand grabbed his elbow. It was a small hand but one with a surprisingly firm grip. Milo turned to see a fussy-looking bespectacled man pulling him back into the chair he had so recently vacated. The man was chubby, not overweight, exactly. The word "portly" sprang into Milo's head unbidden. A vague suggestion of a mustache colored the man's upper lip and his thinning salt-and-pepper hair had been combed meticulously across his head, the act serving no real purpose other than to alert everyone around to the fact he was going bald.

"Please have a seat, sir," the man insisted, his voice high-pitched and nasally. He sounded exactly like he looked. "You nearly fainted," he explained, apparently on the off chance Milo was somehow unaware of that fact.

Milo allowed himself to be eased to a sitting position. He had to admit it felt pretty fucking good to get off his feet. Goddammit, he was tired.

The nasally man continued. "Don't worry, the EMT's have been called and will be here soon." His faced wrinkled in an unconscious display of disgust, clearly displeased at having to touch Milo, his manner belying the caring tone of his words.

Milo jerked his elbow out of the man's grip. "EMT's?" he said as if he didn't quite understand the meaning of the word. "I don't need any freaking EMT's, I'm just fine."

He knew exactly what the fussy little man was thinking: drugs. This street bum had come into the library seeking a comfortable place to enjoy his high and had suffered a bad reaction. The call for medical assistance had undoubtedly been made more to get the bum with the dirty, smelly clothes the hell out of the Boston Public Library than out of any real concern on the fussy man's part for the bum's welfare.

"They're on their way," the fussy man said as if he hadn't heard Milo. "Don't worry, you're going to be fine." The man turned and walked across the spacious lobby to the glass front door, clearly hoping to look out and to see an ambulance with flashing red lights screeching to a halt in front of the building, followed immediately by two competent professionals rushing into the library to take control of the situation.

The moment the guy reached the front door, Milo lifted himself off the chair and followed. He shouldered past the smaller man, juked left when he sensed a hand snaking out to grab his arm, and was gone, bounding down the granite steps with an energy he did not feel.

Behind him the man sputtered and complained to no one in particular. "You need medical attention, do you hear me? Get back here, the EMT's will be along any second. Hey! Do you hear me?"

On the sidewalk the pedestrians paid no attention to him. He might as well have been invisible. Every head turned toward the fussy little man—presumably the curator, or head librarian, or whatever the hell the guy in charge of the library was called. Milo was grateful for the distraction.

In the distance an ambulance raced straight at him, the sound of the siren growing steadily louder. It blew past and then turned toward the library. *Might as well slow down,* Milo thought. *You're going to have nothing to do when you get there, unless of course the fussy little man strokes out.* He smiled. It seemed like at least a decent possibility.

At the end of the block, Milo turned and melted into the crowd, anxious to get home. He had work to do.

25

Rae Ann the Schoolgirl Hooker was turning into a problem. Milo had had such ambitious plans for her, but now, with all of his attention focused on the mysterious bitch in Everett, Rae Ann had become nothing more than a risky loose end.

He supposed he could leave her tied up—or, more accurately, *taped* up—in her chair, immobilized in the middle of his living space while he went away and took care of business. That was the obvious choice.

But doing so came with some serious downsides. He had no idea how long it would take to accomplish the things he wanted so badly to do to the Everett bitch. That in itself wasn't a problem, but every hour he was away was an hour the unattended Rae Ann could potentially wriggle free of her bonds and either escape or remove her gag and begin screaming for help.

And if that happened, everything would fall apart. Rae Ann would be rescued and the police would come and stake out the tenement. They would wait for him. The police weren't terribly bright but they could be very patient. When he returned, no matter how long it took, he would be captured and arrested, and after that all of his previous murders would fall into place like dominoes.

Milo had no doubt about how it would go down, even if he kept his mouth firmly closed and admitted to nothing. The pigs would search the tenement with a fine-tooth comb, evidence would be discovered that would lead the authorities to the remains of one or more of his previous playthings, and DNA or some equally inconvenient piece of scientific mumbo-jumbo would lead to life imprisonment or worse. Milo didn't think guys like him got the death penalty in Massachusetts, but he wasn't certain and damned sure didn't want to find out.

So leaving Rae Ann alive was just too risky.

Milo knew what he had to do: eliminate the risk.

It was a goddamned shame. He had worked hard to get Rae Ann here, and had only just begun to enjoy her. But Milo Cain was nothing if not a big-picture type of guy. The annoying little bitch who had suddenly begun haunting his visions was more important than Rae Ann the Schoolgirl Hooker, Milo knew that as surely as he knew his own name, and as long as he concluded his business with Rae Ann properly, Milo reasoned he could always find another hooker to play with later.

Milo sighed. Life was so unfair sometimes. He could still enjoy himself while eliminating the risk Rae Ann represented, but the days and days of bliss he had been anticipating were not going to happen; at least not right now and not with Rae Ann.

He glanced up at his guest from the corner of the room where he sat leaning against the wall, legs crossed in a modified lotus position. Her pretty eyes returned his gaze skittishly. He wondered what she was thinking, and whether she knew her fate had just been decided.

Probably not. As far as Milo knew, he was the only person in the world gifted—cursed?—with this strange psychic ability to experience random slices of people's lives served up in his head like the devil's home movies.

More to the point, if Rae Ann realized her life span was down to minutes, a couple of hours at the most, she would most likely not be sitting there in relative calm. Milo had learned enough about his guest by now to know she would be doing that amusing writhing, complaining thing he enjoyed so much.

In fact, with that pleasant picture foremost in his mind, Milo decided it was time to get to work. The sooner he finished this little sideshow, the sooner he could begin the main event.

He rose, stretched, and playfully said, "Hey, schoolgirl, guess what the principal has in store for you now?"

He waited and when no response was forthcoming, said, "This is where you say, 'I don't know, Principal Milo, what do you have in store for me now?'"

Milo lifted his pliers from his pocket and began snapping the steel jaws for emphasis. *Snap, snap, snap.* The tactic was effective, the response immediate. Rae Ann's eyes opened wide in panic and she immediately began chanting, "I don't know, Principal Milo, what do you have in store for me now?"

At least Milo assumed that was what she was saying. It was hard to be sure, thanks to the muffling effect of the duct tape, which Milo sorely wished he could remove but didn't dare.

He smiled in appreciation. "That's more like it. You have the potential to be my best student ever, my little teacher's pet. Would you like to be my teacher's pet?"

Rae Ann paused, her confusion evident. She had no idea how to answer the question and Milo could see the wheels turning in her head: Would it be a good thing or a bad thing to be the monster's teacher's pet?

He took pity on her, saving her from having to decide. "It doesn't matter, unfortunately. Something has come up and class is going to have to be cancelled. Permanently, in your case. I would have loved to explore pain management in-depth with you, but the principal has been called away on an emergency—a home tutoring session, you might say—and that means this classroom must be evacuated. Do you understand where I'm going with this? I hope so; you *are* one of my best students, after all."

Rae Ann's expression had become more and more horrified during Milo's short soliloquy, and now sheer panic took over. She bucked and writhed and tried to scream into her gag, still not accepting after all this time that nothing of any value was going to come from any of it.

Milo concluded that the response meant, yes, she did understand where he was going with this. In fact, he decided she now knew *exactly* how her short but eventful attendance at Milo University was going to end. And he loved it. The utter, naked terror in her eyes and indeed in her entire *body* was the biggest turn-on imaginable. He could not understand how everyone else in the world could not be excited by this type of display.

It had to be a classic case of people not realizing what they were missing. If they could see for themselves how enjoyable torturing a helpless victim was, there would be a run on prostitutes not seen in this country since the national conventions of the major political parties, Milo was sure of it.

He readjusted his jeans to provide a little breathing room for his massive erection and got to work, lining up his tools on the floor in the order he expected to use them. The last thing he wanted was to be in the middle of the session and have to bring the slicing and dicing to a grinding halt in order to search out the proper tool. Preparation was essential.

During prep time, Rae Ann provided the most enjoyable background music imaginable. She bucked and she moaned and she begged and all the while, Milo whistled happily, like a man who truly enjoyed his work. Because, of course, he did.

Finally, he was ready. So was Rae Ann, judging from the looks of things. Red splotches covered her face. Tears tracked down her cheeks. Another of those fucking snot bubbles had appeared in her right nostril. Milo decided she must have medical issues, nasally speaking, perhaps a deviated septum from snorting coke.

No matter. The snot problem was easily remedied, and soon Rae Ann the Schoolgirl Hooker would have much bigger things to worry about than hygiene, anyway.

In fact, she already did.

Milo grabbed a tissue and patiently cleaned her face. It was the least he could do, considering the pleasure she was giving him. Besides, what was to come would be much more enjoyable if his guest didn't look like a disgusting pig.

Wrinkling his own nose, Milo tossed the tissue onto the floor and got started. Soon he was lost in his work, tearing and ripping and stabbing and cutting. Blood flowed and limbs cracked and muffled screams continued with renewed frenzy for a short time, and Milo was glad he had not surrendered to his misguided desire to remove the gag.

Then the screaming died away, and a few minutes after that so did Rae Ann the Schoolgirl Hooker. It was a long time before Milo noticed, and when he did, he didn't care.

26

Cait tossed clothes into her bag, not bothering to fold them, barely even looking at them. On the bed next to her, Kevin did the same. They had taken some time to play tourist before heading back to Tampa, walking the Freedom Trail and taking a Duck Boat excursion around the city.

"We might as well enjoy the sights," Kevin had said. "Who knows when we'll be back here again, if ever?"

For Cait, though, the sightseeing had felt forced and unnatural. Her focus was still solidly on Virginia Ayers and the strange story her long-lost mother had related before politely asking her daughter to butt the hell out of her life and never return.

The whole situation was bizarre. Even if everything she said was true, why kick Cait to the curb now, just hours after meeting her? Virginia claimed she hadn't seen Cait's twin brother in thirty years, and as long as he stayed in Seattle or Minnesota or New Mexico or wherever he had ended up, there was no danger anyway.

And if the danger was long past, why couldn't Virginia have welcomed Cait with open arms? Why reject her outright?

The pain throbbed and pulsed inside her like an infection. If she had known this was how she was going to feel after finally meeting her mother, Cait thought she might have decided to forget about learning her family history. Just let the whole thing drop and go on living in ignorance in Tampa.

But of course she would never have done that. It simply wasn't in her nature. Cait Connelly had more than once been compared favorably to a bulldog by her fellow lawyers: relentless, unstoppable, moving resolutely forward until either achieving her goal or exhausting every last possibility. It was that personality trait that made the current scenario—packing her bags and returning home before learning her brother's identity or establishing a relationship with her birth mother—so objectionable.

"Maybe I could..." she began, only to lapse into silence.

"Or what about..."

She realized she had stopped packing and resumed with renewed vigor, taking her frustrations out on her clothing, slamming the offending outfits into the suitcase. Kevin was right. There was no way to force herself on her mother, and if the woman wanted to live in fear of an unrealistic and paranoid scenario, there was nothing she could do about it. Maybe someday the woman would come to her senses. Maybe someday—

—Cait dropped straight down, landing face-first on the bed, falling onto a silk blouse before rolling sideways and crashing to the floor. Her eyes rolled up into her head. She was vaguely aware of Kevin picking her up and cradling her in his arms, calling her name, his panicked voice sounding much too far away, but she was incapable of answering him, incapable even of acknowledging him.

The Flicker roared into her head like a runaway freight train and it was terrifying. The vision was of the man she had seen in yesterday's awful Flicker. It was the man whose predatory lust had frightened her so badly, the man who had daydreamed about doing twisted, evil, hurtful things to an unsuspecting prostitute with his trusty pair of pliers. It was the man Cait had wanted to notify the police about, but had not done so because she had no proof.

And this Flicker was one hundred times worse. The man was getting down to business.

Bad business.

The young girl was being held prisoner in what appeared to be a small, nearly empty apartment. The place was dingy and threadbare and littered with trash.

The girl had been immobilized, her arms and legs duct-taped securely to a solid, blocky wooden chair. Several strips of the silver duct tape circled her head and covered her mouth, preventing her from crying out, although it was not for lack of trying.

The girl was being tortured. The man had been fantasizing about using his pliers in the previous Flicker, and now he was doing it. And he was using other implements of torture, too. The scene was horrifying. The girl was naked and covered in blood; it flowed from wounds in at least a dozen different places.

Her captor studied her appraisingly, looking exactly like an artist examining his canvas. He tilted his head sideways. Took a step back. Then he advanced, plunging the pliers into his victim, wielding them like some demented sex toy, ripping and tearing the soft flesh of her inner thighs as she bucked and thrashed. Fresh blood flew, splattering the man's hands and wrists, dripping down the insides of her legs in thick trails.

Cait wanted to avert her eyes, she *tried* to avert her eyes, tried to close her eyes to the horror, but she couldn't, because her eyes didn't matter. She was seeing the ghastly sight with her mind, and there was no shutting down her mind, no closing her mind to a Flicker. She had no choice but to experience it until it ran its course.

She tried to scream, to cry out for help, but she could not. She wondered if she was going mad, sinking into her own personal hell, where she would live out her days doomed to watching this depraved horror show inside her head.

In the Flicker the man continued his torture. He was relentless, stabbing and slicing. The suffering girl's head whipped back and forth, her face puffy from crying and blotchy from fear and pain. On the floor her clothes had been scattered like wrapping paper around a toddler's gifts on Christmas morning. Wounds covered her, large and small, all of them red and raw and angry and weeping blood. There was barely a spot on the girl's entire body that had not been attacked with the awful pliers or with razor-sharp knives.

Finally the suffering victim's eyes opened widely in an obscene parody of disbelief, as though it had only now occurred to her that something awful was happening to her. She blinked several times, rapidly, as spasms wracked her body. Her muscles contracted and released and contracted and released again, and then her head lolled to the side and back, eyes closed, mouth agape.

And then she was gone.

And so was the Flicker.

And Cait was back. She opened her eyes and saw Kevin, sweet, considerate Kevin, his worried face staring down at her. She was stretched out on the hotel room floor, next to the bed where she had fallen when the Flicker started, lying flat on her back, legs splayed. Kevin crouched next to her, cradling her head in his arms.

She shuddered. Opened her mouth. Tried to speak. All that came out was a terrified husky squeak. She shook her head and realized she was panting, hyperventilating, and tried to slow her breathing but could not. She burst into tears and Kevin lifted her easily in his arms. He kicked the open suitcases to the floor, one after the other. Clothes burst out of them and formed small fluffy hills around the luggage. Then he set her down on the bed and held her as she cried.

After a while—Cait couldn't say how long; maybe five minutes, maybe thirty—the terror began to abate, and the vision of what she had seen dimmed enough to allow her to concentrate on the here and now. Kevin stroked her hair rhythmically, caressing it, saying nothing, waiting for her, endlessly patient.

"Oh, God," she whispered. She sobbed deeply and she thought she might scream but didn't.

"Where were you?" Kevin asked.

"I don't know. It looked like it might at one time have been an apartment. It was messy and dirty and in the middle of the room was a chair with a naked girl strapped to it. It was the girl from last night and she was being tortured horribly. I...I think I watched her die..."

Cait squeezed her eyes closed as if to ward off the vision, just as she had done during the Flicker, but she was no more successful now than she had been then.

"Oh God," she said again.

27

The streets were relatively traffic-free—at least as traffic-free as they ever got in this metropolitan jungle—as Milo cruised toward Everett. Following his play time with the now-deceased Rae Ann the Schoolgirl Hooker, he had wiped the bloodstains off his hands and arms as best he could using a series of dirty towels, then slept fitfully for a short while.

Following the invigorating nap, he clambered up off his air mattress and changed his clothes. Then he walked to the YMCA a few blocks away and showered with the hottest water he could stand, scrubbing the filthy stench of dead prostitute off his body.

Normally Milo could sleep like a baby for twelve to fourteen hours after one of his play sessions, but today was different. Today was special. Rae Ann had become nothing more than the first act, the warm-up band for the rock concert of torture that would soon follow. Milo was determined to introduce himself to the arrogant little bitch who had so recently begun haunting his visions.

His routine—and, in fact, his entire life—had been completely disrupted thanks to the mysterious young woman, and that made Milo nervous. Uncomfortable.

Usually, when entertaining one of his special guests, he was able to make the fun last much longer than it had with Rae Ann, although never as long as he wanted. He inevitably began a session with the best of intentions: to keep the girl alive for as long as possible. Not because he gave a damn about the girl, but rather because his surgical procedures only served to stimulate him while the victim was alive and conscious and thus able to appreciate what was happening to her. Once she was dead or even just passed out, the entire affair was instantly rendered pointless.

So his goal was always to do enough to provide for his own stimulation while not going so far that his guest slipped into unconsciousness, either from pain or blood loss. Eventually, of course, it would always happen. It was inevitable. And often when it did occur, the girl wasn't just unconscious but dead. Unfortunately, and despite Milo's best efforts at controlling his urges, he had a habit of becoming so engrossed in his work he was unable to hold back. He would pass the point of no return and lose his victim to eternal darkness.

Today that moment arrived even faster than usual, for the very reason that today Milo did not *want* to make the fun last. Today he had other business to attend to. He was only playing with Rae Ann because...well...because she was *there,* and it would be unacceptable to leave home without getting at least a small taste of such a succulent morsel.

So he had hurried things along. The session had still been immensely enjoyable, but varying his routine had taken him outside his comfort zone and had made him feel anxious and upset, like he was trying to keep a secret and was afraid someone else might have learned it.

And he had varied his routine in other ways too; ways that represented infinitely more risk to Milo than simply making him feel anxious. Typically, when finished with a girl, he would dispose of the body immediately, even before allowing himself to slip into the comforting cocoon of a good night's sleep. Normally he played his games in the middle of the night, in part because it added a certain delicious ambiance to the proceedings, but also for the practical reason that it made corpse disposal much easier. He would simply hack off his victim's arms and legs and stuff everything into garbage bags. Then he would take a midnight stroll, toting the bags to various restaurant Dumpsters around the city.

The only inherent risk was of being stopped by a patrolman while making his "deliveries," but Milo had long ago discovered that law-enforcement presence in the neighborhoods he haunted was minimal in the middle of the night. Even the cops who did patrol were not inclined to step outside the safety of their cruisers for anything short of a murder in progress. Milo had more than once been given the stink-eye by a passing cop, but he had never yet come close to being questioned while in possession of body parts.

Thus, the plan was nearly foolproof, if a bit labor-intensive. Restaurant Dumpsters always smelled of rotting food and the addition of one more piece of decomposing garbage would never even be noticed. Plus, they were emptied on a regular basis, meaning the evidence never lingered in the same location for long before being trucked away to wherever the hell restaurant trash went, probably an incinerator somewhere, which served Milo's purposes perfectly.

That was how it was normally done.

Today, though, was a different story. He had played with Rae Ann in the middle of the day, so utilizing his typical method of disposal would be impossible. Even Milo recognized the danger inherent in carrying a human torso around the city surrounded by throngs of humanity. He would never get away with it.

So he left her taped to the torture chair in his living room. The duct-tape bindings had become moot, of course. It wasn't like she would be going anywhere now. But with other things on his mind, more important things, Milo didn't want to waste even a few minutes fussing with a cadaver. He would handle the cleanup when he returned, taking advantage of the soothing cloak of three a.m. darkness to transport Rae Ann the Schoolgirl Hooker to various suitable resting places.

Trash in life; trash in death. There was a certain symmetry there that Milo very much appreciated.

He understood full well he was taking a calculated risk. Leaving a dead body in his living space after hours of torture was hardly the best way to accomplish a long life span outside a jail cell.

It wasn't very bright.

In fact, it was more than just "not very bright," it was incredibly, unbelievably stupid and reckless, and those were two traits Milo Cain had gone to great lengths to avoid during his long and successful run as an amateur practitioner of torture. This foolishness was completely out of character for him.

He knew that. He also could not help himself. He was being driven by a compulsion beyond conscious thought. He *needed* to find the young woman who had been starring in his recent visions and he *needed* to destroy her, and he *needed* to do it in the most exceedingly painful manner possible.

The reasons why he needed to do it were beyond Milo's comprehension, but that did not make them any less real. The compulsion drove him relentlessly, and he knew that the risk he was taking was a worthwhile one, despite the fact he could not explain, even to himself, why that was the case.

So now he navigated the congested city streets in the middle of the day, driving away from the crowds in Boston and toward the crowds in Everett. He felt conspicuous, like a fish out of water, but hoped he looked like just another schmuck on his way to work to begin just another night shift at the factory.

No one paid the slightest attention to him, as far as he could tell, and the anonymity was reassuring. He would not get caught leaving Rae Ann the Schoolgirl Hooker's rotting corpse in his apartment because, well, because the rest of the people in the world were so caught up in their own little unimportant lives, with their own little unimportant problems, that he could probably walk down the street with a neon sign strapped to his chest flashing the words I KILLED A GIRL AND LEFT HER COOLING BODY IN MY LIVING ROOM! and no one would pay any more attention to him than they were paying right now.

The vehicle he had jacked was modern and comfortable, containing a built-in GPS unit that squawked out directions to 7 Granite Circle, Everett, providing precise turn-by-turn navigation, leading him inexorably to his destination. The Buick's silver-haired owner, a little old lady who had to be eighty if she was a day, hadn't put up a fight. In fact she had seemed almost resigned to losing her car, as if she had suspected sooner or later she was going to be car-jacked and today just happened to be the unlucky day.

And, Milo thought, that might well have been the case. An old lady driving a fancy new vehicle in stop-and-go traffic around a crowded city really should know better. All he had had to do was flag her down with a sheepish smile on his face—*Jeez, I'm a poor lost tourist and I need a little help!*—and yank her out of the car when she stopped. She rolled her window down a few inches and Milo grabbed a fistful of hair, yanking relentlessly until she popped the locks just to get a little relief from the pain. After that, he had simply slid into her place in the driver's seat and accelerated away while she stood in the middle of the street and watched, not screaming, not complaining, not saying anything at all. Just watching.

Milo felt a twinge of guilt about the whole thing. Carjacking was wrong and he had not been raised to be a common thief. But certain things in life were important and thus rendered minor issues like stealing some old bat's car irrelevant, and this was one of them. *Besides,* he told himself. *I'll dump the car somewhere when I'm finished and it will be returned undamaged to the old lady anyway. I'm just borrowing it for a couple of hours, that's all. No harm, no foul.*

He spun the wheel and listened to the radio—volume down low, so he could still hear the GPS—and followed the flow of traffic, not speeding, not driving recklessly, not doing anything to draw unwanted attention to himself. As anxious as he was to begin his new adventure, this was not the time to make a stupid mistake.

He sang along with Gladys Knight, riding on the Midnight Train to Georgia, pretending to be a Pip, daydreaming about what he would have done to Gladys some dark night in the back of the tour bus, and before he knew it the GPS informed him, "You have arrived at your destination."

Milo eased into the driveway and looked the house over and knew instantly that the electronic miracle worker had done its job. The number screwed into the weathered siding next to the front door was the right one, but even without the benefit of the brass "7" he would have known. He would recognize this house anywhere. He had memorized every detail of its exterior from his last vision.

Milo shut off the engine and smiled. He rubbed his hands together in anticipation. The girl from his visions wasn't here; he knew that. After all, he had seen her leave with his own eyes, or at least in his own mind, which was the same thing, practically speaking. But he wasn't worried. Getting her to return wouldn't be a problem. Not unless she had a soul as black and bitter as his own, and Milo Cain had never met anyone in his three decades on earth who could make that claim.

Gladys Knight serenaded him inside his head as he hurried toward the front door. He was anxious to get started. Time was wasting.

28

Franklin Marchand climbed the tenement's rickety back stairs as quietly as he could. He had no small amount of recent life experience in stealth, it being a necessary prerequisite to survival as a vagrant.

Early in his time on the streets, an older homeless man had taken Franklin under his wing and shown him the ropes—how to panhandle without frightening the mark away, how to pick a cheap lock to find shelter during the bitterly cold nights of winter, how to fade into the background of life to avoid drawing the attention of the police—so sneaking around this drafty old building presented little challenge.

Franklin had seen Strange Dude depart earlier, walking resolutely, with a spring in his step that indicated he had important business to attend to, so there was no danger the man would be inside his apartment when Franklin broke in. But he had no idea where Strange Dude had gone, and thus no idea *how long* he would be gone. Maybe the guy had only walked to the convenience store on the corner to buy booze and was even now on his way back, the spring in his step only because he was in a hurry to get home and start drinking.

The thought gave Franklin pause. He did not want to be caught by Strange Dude, especially not in his apartment going through his stuff. The guy gave Franklin the creeps, a serious case of the willies, and he had no interest in finding out how the guy would react if he walked into his place to find Franklin with his hands in the cookie jar.

But still, Franklin couldn't stop thinking about the unsettling situation with the girl last night—Strange Dude forcing her into the tenement building at knifepoint—and all of the other nights when similar things had happened. Something was going on, something bad, Franklin could just tell, and one of the few things he still cared about in this fucked-up world was his little girl. Samantha was twenty-two now, no longer little and not even a girl, she was a full-grown adult woman, but to Franklin she would always be that tiny whirlwind in blonde pigtails running around the house, her bare feet slapping the linoleum tiles of the kitchen floor.

If Strange Dude was raping girls Samantha's age, or, God forbid, raping and then *killing* them, Franklin knew he could no longer stand by and allow it to happen. Every young girl was someone's daughter. More to the point, who was to say the next young girl to be ushered up here at knifepoint wouldn't be *his* daughter?

That was assuming his suspicions were even correct. Maybe there was a perfectly reasonable explanation for the things Franklin had seen. For the life of him he couldn't imagine what that explanation might be, but that didn't mean there couldn't be one.

So he had waited across the street from Strange Dude's tenement building, sitting on the sidewalk with his back propped against the stained red brick façade of a long-abandoned dry-cleaning establishment, smoking cigarettes and watching, waiting for his morning hangover to subside.

Sometime after noon, Franklin wasn't sure exactly when—he didn't wear a watch anymore because time meant nothing when you had nowhere to go—Strange Dude had come out the tenement's battered front door like he owned the place and turned toward Government Center. Franklin watched him walk briskly away, his form growing smaller and smaller until he disappeared from sight. Then he waited a little while longer before tossing his cigarette into the gutter and rising unsteadily to his feet. He circled the building and entered through the long-abandoned service entrance in back.

Franklin arrived at the third-floor landing and slipped quietly down the shabby hallway. He expected to see no one and did not. A series of three doors lined each side of the narrow corridor and for a moment Franklin was stymied. It hadn't occurred to him that there might be more than one possible apartment up here. It seemed obvious now, but he hadn't given the situation much thought. Hell, he was just some homeless loser, not a fucking private detective.

He stood still, a couple of steps inside the hallway, unsure of how to proceed. Then he smiled. Strange Dude had provided a roadmap straight to his front door. The entire building was understandably in poor condition. After all, it had been deemed unlivable years ago by some anonymous building inspector. But dirt and dried mud caked a path straight to one door—the door roughly one-third of the way along the hallway on the left. It had to be the one.

Franklin reached it in a few steps and studied the cheap lock built into the punky wood above the tarnished brass knob. It was exactly what he had expected to find: worthless protection that would provide no challenge. He fished his lock-picking tools—he had liberated them from his mentor's coat one morning after discovering the man dead as a doornail on a park bench—and got to work.

Within seconds the tumblers clicked into place and the lock turned and Franklin was in.

29

Cait was not typically one to be bothered by crowds. She liked people, enjoyed being around them, interacting with them, even when they were all strangers. Today was a different story, though. Today she felt out of sorts, thrown off her game by the terrifying Flicker she had experienced back at the hotel room. Seeing the young girl die right in front of her—experiencing the awful torture in a way that was as real as if she had been standing next to the killer—was a completely new and unsettling experience.

The scene had been unlike any Flicker she had ever lived through, graphic and disturbing, and when she walked through the automatic sliding doors leading into the terminal at Logan Airport and saw the throngs of restless travelers she was thrown for a loop. She shrank against Kevin reflexively, covering her mouth with her hand and gasping.

"What is it, babe? What's wrong?" Kevin held her tightly and his eyes bored into hers. "Is it happening again?"

"No, I'm okay," she answered with a nervous laugh, making it perfectly clear she was anything but. "I just don't feel like myself. Everything seems a little...I don't know...off, I guess."

"Well, that's understandable. First you find your long-lost mother, then you discover you have a twin brother you never knew about, a man who, for reasons completely unknown, would like nothing better than to see you dead, then your newly located long-lost mother tells you she never wants to see you again. *Then,* to top it all off, you have to live through the worst Flicker ever—a horrific, bloody murder."

A young mother trudged past, pulling a wheeled suitcase behind her with one arm and holding a squalling infant with the other. She looked at them sharply as Kevin's voice bounced off the walls of the terminal, magnifying the words "horrific, bloody murder." She shook her head in disgust and leveled a withering stare at them.

"Sorry about that," Kevin said to the woman, lowering his voice to nearly a whisper. Then he turned to Cait. "But you get my point, right? Anyone would be feeling a little off after the kind of day you've had."

Cait started to giggle and a sound halfway between a laugh and a sob came out. "Yes, I get your point. So does everyone else here in Terminal B. We'd better buy our tickets back to Tampa before the TSA decides we're terrorists, discussing bloody murders and the like. Much more talk like that and we'll end up in a holding cell."

Kevin smiled and they walked to a row of uncomfortable-looking molded plastic chairs. He indicated she should sit and said, "Wait here. I'm assigning you the very important job of keeping an eye on our luggage. Just relax and I'll get us on the first flight back to sanity."

Cait slumped in her chair—it really was as uncomfortable as it looked—and wondered how in the hell she could even begin to relax. She decided the chances were pretty good that she would never relax again. She watched Kevin as he waited in line at the ticket counter, fidgeting and glancing back in concern every few seconds. He was big and strong and overprotective and she had never loved him more than she did right now.

Her eyes felt grainy and heavy and began to close, and then what seemed like a second later a hand clamped down on her shoulder and she was being shaken gently awake.

Kevin smiled down at her. "Hey, sleepyhead. Some watchdog you turned out to be. I turn my back for one minute and you fall asleep on the job. Fortunately for you our fancy, expensive luggage is still here, otherwise you'd be out on your ass looking for a new job."

Cait glanced at the two worn duffel bags, still on the floor at her feet where they had been placed. "Ha!" she said. "Fat chance this 'fancy, expensive luggage' would ever be stolen. No self-respecting thief would be caught dead stealing our crappy stuff."

She forced herself to her feet. Her body felt heavy and slow, filled with a bone-deep exhaustion. All she wanted to do was get on the airplane and go back to sleep. She had no doubt she would be unconscious all the way back to Tampa.

"How long was I out?" she asked, trying to stifle a yawn and mostly failing.

"Almost half an hour. That was the slowest-moving line outside of the DMV I've ever had the misfortune of waiting in." Cait could see the concern still etched in Kevin's eyes. He was trying to keep the conversation light for her benefit but was clearly worried about her and she loved him for it.

"Let's get moving," he said. "We have a date with two coach-class seats on the next flight out of this burg, but if we hurry, we might have enough time for a quick dinner first. Play your cards right and I might even buy you a drink."

"Ooh, big spender," she teased halfheartedly.

"If you've ever eaten in an airport restaurant, you know just how big."

"And you're going to spring for drinks too? What did I do to deserve this?"

"Drink, I said. Not drinks. I want you just buzzed enough to accept my advances but not so trashed you'll fall asleep before we're done. Again."

Cait burst out laughing, something she wouldn't have believed possible even ten minutes ago. "As if I could ever fall asleep with you at the controls, lover-boy."

She hooked her arm around his and he shrugged both duffel bags over his shoulder. They moved through the crowd, weaving and bobbing, making slow but steady progress through the terminal until spotting a franchise steak house.

Once again Cait thanked God for her boyfriend. She felt better already. Sure it had been a lousy day, one of the worst ever, but she was ready to put it all behind her. Things were going to be just fine.

30

The neighborhood appeared bleak and deserted. Milo took his time walking toward the house. He wasn't in any hurry, and as he meandered along the flagstone walkway he examined the homes flanking 7 Granite Circle. All of the yards were empty and so were most of the driveways, their pavement stained and discolored by leaking oil and other automotive fluids. This wasn't the type of upscale area where the homes had garages, so it was easy to tell that most residents were at work.

All in all, Milo was satisfied. The area was relatively secluded, given its location in densely packed Everett. There were fewer than a dozen homes on the cul-de-sac, all probably constructed at the same time and by the same builder using a cookie-cutter approach more than a half century ago. It had the feel of a solidly blue-collar neighborhood, the kind of place where the husbands and wives both worked full-time, struggling to earn enough money to avoid falling behind on the mortgage. Milo felt there was at least a decent chance that the older lady from his visions was the only person at home in the entire fucking development.

He climbed three chipped concrete steps to the tiny landing and rang the doorbell. He had no particular plan in mind, no elaborate ruse developed with which to gain the trust of the woman. The days were long past, if they had ever existed at all in a hardscrabble neighborhood like this, when an older woman, living alone, would ever allow a young man she didn't know into her home unless she had set up a service appointment and the man provided adequate identification, none of which was the case here, obviously.

So why waste the time and effort required to even try sweet-talking his way inside? Milo Cain believed in the straightforward approach. It had worked many times in the past and he had every confidence it would work again today.

He waited after ringing the bell. Nothing happened. He waited a little longer, tempted to ring it again, but the last thing he wanted was to frighten the woman so badly she refused even to open the door. He had visions of her retreating to her phone and calling the cops.

At last his patience was rewarded as the heavy storm door swung inward and an older, frail-looking woman regarded him suspiciously from behind her still-closed screen door. Milo recognized her instantly as the woman from his visions.

"Yes?" she said, clearly not inclined to proceed any further without good reason.

Milo put what he hoped was a harmless-looking smile on his face as he pondered how to proceed. The question he faced was a simple one: Was the screen door locked or not? If it was, getting inside was going to be a problem, maybe even an impossibility. He could break the door down, it was constructed only of flimsy aluminum, but he didn't think he could manage it quickly enough to prevent the woman from slamming the heavy storm door closed and then locking it.

But how likely was it that the screen door would even be locked? With the storm door closed and locked there would be no reason to lock the lighter screen door as well; it would accomplish nothing in terms of added safety and would be a pain in the ass for the homeowner when it came time to enter or exit. Milo tried to remember one single time his adoptive parents had locked the screen door in their home when he was growing up and could not.

He concluded it was extremely unlikely this door was locked.

All of this went through his mind in two or three seconds, but it was enough time that the woman's demeanor changed from mild city-dweller suspicion to growing alarm. She opened her mouth as if to say something else—Milo had still not uttered a word—and then seemed to think better of it and retreated back into her house, stepping clear of the storm door and swinging it closed in his face.

So the decision was made for him. It was now or never. Milo reached out and turned the handle and pulled on the screen door and thought, *open sesame,* and as he had hoped, it flew open, light as a feather and about as effective, security-wise. He slipped the steel toe of his left work boot inside the doorframe and the storm door rebounded like a basketball off an iron hoop, clipping the woman on the shoulder and knocking her to the floor where she fell with a surprised *"Oomph!"*

Milo's smile widened and he walked into the house, stepping over the body of his host, who lay sprawled on the floor, too surprised even to scream. Yet. He nudged her clear of the doorway with his foot and eased the storm door closed, making sure to lock it behind him.

"So, how are you?" he asked.

The woman came to her senses and began scuttling backward down her hallway, looking up at him with an expression of growing fear on her heavily lined face. And there was something else as well. It looked to Milo a little like resignation, as if she had been expecting his arrival but had been unsure exactly when he would show up. She moved surprisingly well for someone who appeared so frail.

She continued crab walking backward, apparently forgetting the hallway wall was behind her. She slammed into it with a loud crash and a small handgun toppled out of the right pocket of her sweater. It dropped to the floor next to her and her eyes instantly darted up to his, the fear that had already been etched on her face morphing into all-out panic.

Milo leapt forward. The woman grabbed her gun and flicked off the safety—Milo could see it, plain as day, right on the side of the handle—but before she could bring the weapon to bear on him, he wound up like a football placekicker and booted it right out of her hand. It sailed through the air and then bounced into the living room where it disappeared. A second later, Milo heard a muffled thud as it came to rest against something hard.

The fucking bitch was going to shoot me! Milo tried to wrap his brain around the thought that this old bat could have come so close to putting a bullet in his head. He would never have seen it coming.

This was unacceptable. She would have to be dealt with, and in the strongest possible manner. But first things first. He had a job to do.

"I already called the police," the woman said, interrupting his train of thought, her voice unwavering and stronger than he would have expected, given the situation.

"No you didn't. Only the most paranoid of crazy bitches calls the cops just because someone knocks on their front door. And you're not the *most* paranoid of crazy bitches, now, are you? You might be close, but you're not the *most* paranoid."

She said nothing, slumping to the floor, taking the weight of her body off her arms and legs. Milo took a step toward her and she flinched as if expecting to be hit. Her eyes were locked onto his hands, growing almost comically wide.

"I have no desire to hurt you," he said, wondering whether the lie sounded as transparent to the old bitch as it did to him. "In fact, you have to do just one thing to ensure your safety and if you do it, I promise you will not be harmed."

"Wh-what's that on your hands?" she asked as if he hadn't even spoken.

He glanced down at them and saw faded remnants of Rae Ann the Schoolgirl Hooker's blood. He had scrubbed them conscientiously at the Y, but with the kind of close work he had been doing back at the tenement, it was damned near impossible to wash all traces of the incriminating stains away. And he *had* been in a hurry. He thought he had done a fairly decent job removing the worst of the blood, but maybe he hadn't been that thorough after all, since it was the first thing the old lady had seen.

"What is it?" the gun-toting bitch repeated as he stared down at his hands as though they belonged to someone else.

"I'm a butcher," he said, pleased with his little private joke. "Occupational hazard."

Now the panic exploded in the woman's eyes, and Milo flashed back to his fun with Rae Ann. The expression on this old lady's face was remarkably similar to Rae Ann's. The bitch rose up as if to scuttle backward some more before clearly coming to the conclusion it was pointless.

"Anyway, as I was saying," Milo continued, "I want you to do one simple thing for me and then I'll leave you alone. I can't promise I'll let you go, but I can tell you that you won't be harmed. And that's a hell of a lot more than you deserve after what you were going to do to me with that little peashooter you had in your pocket. If you ask me, it's a pretty good deal. It's certainly the best offer you're going to get out of me."

"What do I have to do?" The woman's voice trembled as she spoke and Milo felt a surge of excitement, the kind he always got when he demonstrated his dominance. The old bag wasn't as tough as she seemed to think she was.

"You're going to call the young woman who visited you earlier—"

"I can't—"

"And you're going to tell her to get her pretty little ass back here," Milo finished, ignoring the interruption.

"I can't do that." The woman was shaking her head obstinately. It was as if Milo had asked her to negotiate world peace. Or change the oil in his fucking car. Did this dim bitch not understand that he was in charge?

"You can and you will."

Tears welled up in the woman's eyes. "I don't have her number."

"Don't lie to me."

"I don't have it."

"I SAW HER GIVE IT TO YOU!" Milo screamed, dropping to his knees next to her and shouting into her face, spittle spraying, rage bubbling up inside him.

The woman groaned and buried her face in her hands. "I can't do it." She began to cry, obviously expecting to be hit or kicked.

Milo nodded, saying nothing. This was ridiculous. Time was passing and he wasn't any closer now to getting that fucking little whore back here than he had been when he walked through the old bat's door. He shrugged his backpack off his shoulder and it fell to the floor with a metallic clank.

The woman cringed like a dog that had been beaten its whole life and peeked through her spread fingers. "What's in there?" she whispered.

It seemed to Milo as if she had a pretty good idea what was inside his backpack and was simply awaiting confirmation, although how she could know was beyond him, and in any event he wasn't going to play her little game.

"You need to stop asking so many fucking questions and start answering a few. I'm running out of patience and if we don't begin making some progress—and I mean NOW—I'm going to hurt you, and in ways you can't even begin to imagine."

The woman covered her face with her hands again like an ostrich burying its head in the sand. Milo almost laughed. The biddy was stupid as well as old if she thought that was going to make a damned bit of difference. He unzipped the main pocket of the backpack and retrieved one of his favorite tools. The pliers felt comfortable in his hand and he immediately began snapping them briskly, confident the staccato beat would get the woman's attention.

He was right. She dropped her hands and her eyes snapped open, focusing on the pliers like they had been focused on his hands a moment ago.

"Get the phone number," he said softly, his voice barely a whisper. It contained a menace that didn't need volume to be understood.

She shook her head mutely, terror in her eyes.

Milo reached out, the movement lightning-quick. He grabbed her hand and held it like this was some perverted May/December Hollywood love scene. Harold and Maude for the twenty-first century. He selected a finger at random, noting with amusement that her nails were short and stubby like a dude's. But it didn't matter. He wasn't concerned with aesthetics. Effectiveness was the goal.

He dug the nose of the pliers under the nail of her pointer finger, pushing hard, burrowing into the tender flesh, making sure there was plenty of nail to grip. The woman sucked in a shocked breath and began to scream as Milo yanked, ripping the nail from the tip of her finger in one smooth motion.

He clamped his hand over her mouth—he was pretty sure the neighborhood was empty, but why take chances?—and said again through gritted teeth, "I want that telephone number."

31

The knob turned and the door opened with a muted squeal, and Franklin Marchand stepped into the mess that constituted Strange Dude's "home." Trash was everywhere: fast-food burger boxes, crumpled-up candy wrappers, and empty cans and bottles were strewn over virtually every inch of the floor's surface. It was disgusting, enough to make even a homeless man used to sleeping in a garbage-strewn alleyway retch.

But it didn't make Franklin retch. In fact, he barely noticed the mess, his gaze passing over the trash in the blink of an eye, settling instead on a strange contraption erected in the middle of the room. It was a chair, big and blocky, and it had been bolted to the floor with steel bracing straps.

And secured to the chair was what looked like—

Oh, God, it looked like—

Oh good Lord, Franklin thought, because although he had stopped believing in a benevolent God just about the time he lost his job and his home and his family and his future, for the life of him he couldn't think of another phrase that fit the situation. *Oh good Lord,* he thought, *that's a girl, or at least it used to be a girl until she was stabbed and slashed and, oh good Lord, skinned alive,* but now she was not alive, no, she was quite obviously dead and had just as obviously died in a tremendous amount of pain, in gut-wrenching pain, in agony really, Franklin could see that as plain as day, and he took two staggering steps toward the chair without thinking because the girl, oh good Lord the girl, she was skinned alive and—

And Franklin's legs gave out. He collapsed to his knees and puked up an acidy yellow concoction of partly digested chicken sandwich and the burning remains of the Mad Dog he had drunk last night. The mixture erupted out of him in a chunky spray, splattering the fast-food cartons and the empty cans and bottles and the legs of his jeans.

He didn't notice.

And if he *had* noticed, he wouldn't have cared. Franklin Marchand had a daughter roughly the same age as this girl, this poor, suffering soul who was once a living, breathing being and was now barely recognizable as human. She was barely recognizable but not completely *un*recognizable, and Franklin knew she was the girl he had seen being forced into this piece of shit tenement building at knifepoint last night.

And how had he reacted? What had he done while this young victim was being marched to her terrible fate? He had made a solemn promise to investigate the situation later, because he had been tired and, let's face it, drunk off his ass and in no condition to investigate anything but his stolen wool blanket last night. And while he was working on his latest buzz, while he was busy drinking himself into a drunken stupor, this defenseless girl who could have been his daughter was being brutally tortured by Strange Dude inside the rotting building not fifty feet away.

And now she was dead.

Tortured.

She might have died this morning while Franklin sat smoking cigarettes and waiting for Strange Dude to leave. And he was *too late!* He was *too late,* and this girl had died and it was mostly Strange Dude's fault—he *had* tortured and killed her, after all—but it was also at least partly Franklin's fault because he had known something was wrong and had done nothing about it until it was too late to make a difference.

Franklin hung his head. He thought about Samantha and how this could have been her and almost puked again but swallowed hard and choked it back.

He stood shakily, suddenly very tired, and forced himself to look at the torture chair and the fresh human corpse fastened to it. Strips of skin hung off her body where they had been peeled, presumably while she was still alive, some of them eighteen inches or more in length. Bones were visible beneath the oozing pinkish mess, an ulna here, a kneecap there. A hint of pubic bone.

Veins and blood vessels and unidentifiable gore crisscrossed the areas where the strips of skin had been carved and peeled away. Blood still dripped obscenely off some of the longer strips of skin, pooling on the clear plastic tarp placed around and under the chair. The blood was beginning to congeal around the outermost edges of the puddles, appearing almost black in the dim light struggling through the filthy windows of the apartment, a ghoulish lake lapping at a horrifying shore.

Franklin stumbled to his feet, suddenly sure Strange Dude would return at any moment and find him here. And he now knew who Strange Dude really was. Mr. Midnight—Franklin had heard the name whispered hundreds of times over the last several months, all over the city and by all classes of people, and he knew immediately he was looking at Mr. Midnight's handiwork—would walk through the door and pull a knife, blood and gristle and human tissue still hanging off it, and he would hold Franklin at knifepoint while he unstrapped the dead girl from the chair. Then he would roll her mutilated corpse onto the floor, and he would replace her with Franklin and he would begin, oh good Lord he would begin peeling, and oh, good Lord he would—

Franklin forced himself to slow his breathing, to choke back the rising tide of panic like he had choked back the vomit a few moments ago. He had to get ahold of himself. If Mr. Midnight *did* come back right now, Franklin would rush him before he could get his knife out of his pocket or his scabbard or wherever the hell he kept it.

If Mr. Midnight came back, Franklin would deal, as Samantha would say. He would deal somehow.

Right now, the priority was getting to a telephone. He had to get the police here. The very same authorities Franklin had developed a serious mistrust and even hatred of since becoming homeless now looked to him like angels of mercy, like the very guardians of sanity.

He took one last look at the girl—he didn't want to, wanted nothing more than to drink the memory of the last few minutes out of his brain, to wash it into oblivion with a fifty-five-gallon drum of Mad Dog, and he promised himself he would do exactly that as soon as his task was complete—but he just couldn't help himself. He took one last look and then he turned and stumbled out of the killing room. He had to get to a phone, to call the police, and he certainly didn't own a cell phone anymore and there was no earthly way the telephone lines into *this* piece of shit building were still active.

He staggered into the dingy hallway and realized he was holding his breath. He breathed deeply and yanked the door closed behind him with much more force than was necessary. Then he moved blindly toward the stairs, determined to find someone, anyone, a passerby or maybe a fellow vagrant who had stolen a cell phone. He would grab it and use it to dial 911.

Franklin paused at the top of the stairs as another wave of nausea overtook him. He bent over, hands on his knees, and somehow managed to avoid losing what was left in his stomach, if anything even *was* left, and then he ran down the stairs, moving much too fast for a shaky homeless alcoholic who had just seen a mutilated dead girl, taking them three at a time, risking a violent fall and a broken neck.

He burst out of the cursed tenement at a dead run—*that's a good one,* he thought crazily, *a "dead run," I'll have to remember that the next time I stumble onto a carved-up human corpse*—and turned into the alleyway. It had never looked as inviting as it did right this minute. He sprinted the length of the crumbling pavement toward the front of the building, panting and gasping, trying desperately not to puke again.

32

Patience had never been one of Cait's strong points, and it was especially hard to maintain now. The crush of travelers waiting to board the plane was almost as massive as the line for the metal detectors had been. She was tired and dispirited and wanted nothing more than to be back in Tampa, where she could begin to resume a normal life, or at least what passed for a normal life for someone blessed—or cursed—with the ability to receive Flickers.

They had waited seemingly for hours, shuffling forward a couple of feet every few minutes, just for the opportunity to empty her pockets and step through a metal detector while some TSA drone leered at her underwear as her bag rolled through the X-ray machine. That humiliating experience would be followed by hours inside a crowded airplane with a bunch of other tired, dispirited people. The prospect seemed almost too much to bear.

She sighed and leaned against Kevin. "What's taking so long?" she said, not really expecting an answer.

His arm was draped over her shoulder and he hugged her tightly. He seemed immune to her mood and was making an obvious effort to raise her spirits. "I know you're vertically challenged, but I can see over the crowd and believe me, we're getting close to our goal. At least our short-term goal. Before you know it, we'll be snuggled up with a good in-flight magazine, chomping on our complimentary bag of stale peanuts, winging our way down the East Coast back to paradise. Or at least Tampa."

"Hmmph. Sounds so romantic."

Kevin laughed. "Maybe not romantic, exactly, but at least you'll be getting where you want to go."

"I suppose," she said morosely. Cait felt badly for raining on Kevin's parade, but she just didn't have the energy to put on a happy face. This trip had been a disaster from the get-go, and at the moment it felt like it was never going to end. Dinner at the airport steak house had been good, better than she had expected, but it had also been exorbitantly expensive, and Cait had felt extra guilty when Kevin picked up the check. She knew his salary as a Tampa police officer, knew what a strain this ill-fated trip had put on his wallet, and yet he refused to complain.

She tried to smile up at him and assumed she had failed when he took one look at her and burst out laughing. "What's the matter, suffering from gas?" he asked, and she giggled despite her foul mood. She just couldn't stay upset around Kevin no matter how crappy she felt. It was one of the many reasons she loved him.

"No, it's not gas," she said, elbowing him in the ribs. "I wouldn't dream of trying to compete in *your* area of expertise."

"Thanks. And now that you mention it..."

"Don't even think about it," Cait answered, wrinkling her nose. "None of these unsuspecting travelers ever did anything to you, there's no reason to put them through that kind of torture." She laughed now, her bad mood forgotten, at least temporarily. The line moved forward and they shoved their carry-on bags ahead with their feet.

Finally they arrived at the front of the line and trudged down the jetway into the Boeing 757. Their seats were located toward the back of the plane, the penalty for purchasing tickets only moments before a flight. Cait didn't give a damn where they had to sit. At least they were getting the hell out of there. They moved single-file down the narrow walkway, stopping next to every row to allow passengers to load their belongings into the overhead bins. Finally they reached their allotted seats, located just north of the lavatory.

Kevin hefted the two duffel bags up to the bin. They barely fit. He struggled with the plastic door, finally slamming it down, and they slid into their seats. Cait sighed wearily. She was still so exhausted she thought she might be asleep before the airplane reached the runway. She hoped the flight attendant wouldn't be too insulted when she slept through the entire preflight song and dance.

She squeezed Kevin's hand and closed her eyes. And that was when her cell phone rang.

33

Milo was astonished when it took more than one fingernail to convince the old bat to part with the information. That crap she tried to sling about not having the number was total bullshit, and he knew it, yet the first nail he ripped out with his trusty pliers accomplished nothing more than establishing that the bitch possessed one hell of a strong set of lungs.

He held the fingernail in front of the broad's eyes, dripping blood onto her lap, until she opened them and stared at it in horrified appreciation.

Then he said, "What's the number?" and to his utter amazement she shook her head again.

"I can't do it," she began, her voice thick with fear and pain, and before she had completed the sentence Milo grabbed her hand again, yanking it out from under her armpit where it had only recently taken up residence. He repeated the impromptu surgical procedure he had just performed on her pointer finger, this time taking the nail from her middle digit.

Again she offered up a lusty scream and again he slapped his free hand over her mouth until she lost her enthusiasm. It took even longer this time than it had the last.

"What's the number?"

The woman let out a groan of misery and this time just nodded.

Milo smiled. "Good girl. I'd like to remind you that this is your own fault. You could have saved yourself all that pain—not to mention saving me precious time—if you had only done what I asked at the beginning, but that's okay. We all need to learn the hard way sometimes." He took her by the elbow and helped her to her feet and she staggered to the trash can in the corner of the kitchen.

She reached into the bin and plucked a slip of paper off the top of the garbage with her good hand. Then she passed it to Milo, still without uttering a word besides the occasional soft moan.

He looked at it and handed it back to her. "Is this the number I asked for?"

"Yes." The woman bent over in agony, her face chalk-white, her injured hand once again tucked away in the folds of her armpit. She refused to look at Milo, not that he cared. He was finally getting what he wanted and that was all that mattered.

He placed a finger under her chin and lifted her face until she was forced to look into his eyes. "*I* don't need the fucking number," he said. "*You* do. Call the little bitch and get her back here."

Milo snapped his pliers open and shut in front of her face for effect. She reached for the telephone and began punching numbers awkwardly, holding the handset with her good hand and using her thumb to press the buttons. Her injured hand stayed out of sight.

Milo watched carefully. He didn't think this shriveled old bitch would dare pull something stupid, like calling 911 or the local police, but you could never be too careful, and taking care was what had enabled him to stay one step ahead of the authorities with over a dozen grisly murders under his belt.

She punched the numbers faithfully into the phone and when she finished, Milo said, "I don't care what you have to say to get that chick back here, but your life depends on your success. Don't fuck this up or what I did to your fingers will be just the beginning. You'll wish you were dead a hundred times before it actually happens. Do you understand me?"

The woman nodded and Milo told her to hold the telephone's handset at an angle so he could listen in. Seconds later a tinny voice came through the receiver. "Hello?"

"Hello, Cait," the woman began, her voice wavering and paper-thin from pain and barely controlled hysteria. "This is..." Milo held his pliers in front of her face and she continued. "This is your mother."

"I—I know who it is," the tinny voice said. "What's wrong?"

Milo narrowed his eyes at her. She hesitated and then said, "Why would you think something's wrong?"

"Well, I'm a little surprised to hear from you, given what you said earlier. You know, about never coming back and forgetting we ever met. Why are you calling me?"

"I'm so sorry." Tears began to fall as the woman's tenuous grip on her emotions loosened.

Milo shook his head, his eyes lasering into hers, and she took a deep breath and continued. "I—I think we have more to discuss. A lot more. Would you consider coming to see me again?"

"Of course," the little bitch replied. "I would love that. I may not be able to make it back up here for a while, though. Money's a little tight, you know."

"I don't mean some time in the future, I mean we need to talk now. Right now."

"But Kevin and I are on our way back to Tampa. We've bought our tickets and we're sitting on the airplane. We should be pushing back from the gate and taxiing for departure at any moment."

Milo covered the phone's mouthpiece with his hand and whispered fiercely, *"You do whatever you have to do to get her here!"* Then he released his grip and nodded toward the phone.

The woman's shoulders slumped and she began to cry again, but somehow she kept her voice relatively steady. Milo hoped the bitch on the other end of the conversation couldn't hear the pain and regret in the woman's words. He thought the poor quality of the connection might mask it enough to be successful.

"No," she said. "You can't leave. Please don't leave yet. Come here, just for the night. We'll talk and if you still want to leave right away, you can fly back to Florida tomorrow morning. I can pay for your tickets if that's a problem. Would that be all right?"

The young woman on the other end of the line hesitated, saying nothing. The silence continued for so long Milo began to fear the connection had been lost or that somehow she had sniffed out the danger.

At last she said, "I...uh...I suppose so."

The little bitch was clearly suspicious but Milo was certain that once she had agreed to return, she would follow through. He knew next to nothing about her, only what he had been able to glean through a couple of intense visions, but it had been more than enough to make him recognize her unusually strong will. "Um, we'll be there in just a little while."

The old biddy nodded at the telephone handset as if maybe the younger one could see her.

Milo spread his hands in a *go ahead* gesture, and she said, "All right. I'll see you soon. And I'm so sorry."

Milo ripped the telephone out of her hand and pressed the button to terminate the call. "Sorry?" he said to her. "You're so sorry? You'd better hope you didn't just blow it with that last little bit of stupidity, or you will be sorrier than you've ever been about anything in your entire miserable life."

He replaced the handset on its charger and led the old lady to a kitchen chair, where he pushed her roughly into it and took a seat next to her. "Let's get to know each other a bit while we wait for our guests to arrive, shall we?"

34

"That was the strangest conversation I think I've ever had." Cait held her cell phone at arm's length, staring at it like she thought it might sprout wings and attempt to fly away.

"Who was it?" Kevin asked as the big Boeing 757 jerked backward and began trundling away from the gate.

"Oh no!" Cait exclaimed, standing up in the aisle. "I'll explain it to you later. Right now, we have to get off this plane!"

A flight attendant rushed down the aisle. She was middle-aged and harried and looked as though her patience had reached the breaking point, despite the fact the flight hadn't even gotten off the ground yet. "Miss, you'll have to take your seat. We're ready for departure."

"No, you don't understand, you can't depart! We have to get off the plane right now!"

"Miss, please, I'll have to insist you sit back down. Do it now. Don't force me to call the captain."

Cait tried to squeeze past and the flight attendant leaned into her, grabbing her by the upper arm. Cait shook her arm free. The other passengers watched the developing altercation with a mixture of shock and resignation as it became increasingly clear the flight would not be departing anytime soon.

"That's it," the flight attendant snarled through gritted teeth. "I'm calling security."

"That won't be necessary," Kevin said.

Cait turned in surprise to see him standing behind her, his body half in the aisle, head lowered to avoid bumping it on the overhead storage bin.

"Is that so? And who are you?" All pretense of politeness and professional courtesy were gone. It was clear the flight attendant had bypassed "harried" and was now spoiling for a confrontation.

"My name is Kevin Shaw. Officer Kevin Shaw." He flashed his Tampa P.D. shield at the woman and continued. "This is my partner, Caitlyn Connelly. We've just received information critical to an ongoing investigation, and it is imperative this plane return to the gate immediately and we be permitted to disembark. I'm afraid I'll have to insist."

The flight attendant—her name was April, Cait could see the shiny nameplate pinned to her blouse—took a step back, clearly caught off guard by this unexpected development. By now the plane had pivoted away from the jetway and was bumping slowly along a taxiway. Cait wondered how much longer it would be before they reached the runway and accelerated smoothly into the air, forcing her to miss what might be her only chance to take advantage of her mother's unexpected change of heart.

"Please, miss," Kevin pushed, utilizing his authoritative law-enforcement voice, the one Cait rarely got to hear. "Every moment counts. Please advise the captain that we need to return to the gate."

The woman took a deep breath, blowing it out hard. Cait caught the scent of cinnamon. "Lemme see that badge again," she said.

Kevin retrieved it from his pocket and she studied it carefully. "It says Tampa police."

"That's right."

"What are you doing in Boston?"

"We're cooperating with the Boston Police Department on an investigation, and if we miss out on an arrest because you were too timid to make a decision, I'll be sure to let the D.A. know who to thank. Let's see..." He made a show of squinting at her name tag. "...your name is April. And your last name?"

The flight attendant gave him a frosty glare and marched down the aisle at double speed, stopping at the cockpit door and knocking. She stepped onto the flight deck and Cait could see her talking quickly, gesturing angrily back toward them.

A head swiveled around the door and looked back at them and when it did, Kevin held his badge up in response, although they were much too far away for it to be read. The captain shrugged and said something to the flight attendant and she returned, closing the door firmly behind her.

"The captain says *he* will be happy to return and allow you to disembark." She emphasized the word "he," doing her best to make it clear she disagreed with the decision. "Please take your seats and stay in them until we've come to a complete stop at the gate."

She turned her back on them without another word and marched back up the aisle, refusing to acknowledge the "Thank you" Cait lobbed at her as she retreated.

Moments later the plane made a left turn, followed a quickly by another left. Cait began to relax as it became clear they really were returning to the terminal.

Kevin whispered, "What the hell is going on here?"

Cait squeezed his arm and said softly, "Wow, you were awesome!"

"Let's see if you still think so when the TSA and the Boston police surround us and stick their guns up our asses when we get off this big tin can."

"Do you really think the police will be waiting for us?"

Kevin shrugged. "I don't know. They take airplane disturbances very seriously since 9/11, but the captain seemed pretty cool, and he's the one in charge, thank God. If it were April the Airline Nazi, we'd definitely be screwed. We'll just have to wait and see. Now, could you please explain to me why we're risking imprisonment to return to the very place you couldn't wait to leave not twenty minutes ago?"

"That was my mother on the phone before."

"Yeah, I figured that much out on my own. What did she say to you?"

"She wants to see me again."

"And?"

"And nothing. She changed her mind for some reason and wants to see me right away."

Kevin stared at her long and hard and she felt her face begin to redden. "What?" she asked defensively.

"Why would she do that?"

"What do you mean, 'why?' I'm her child and she wants to see me. Isn't that enough?"

"It would have been enough if we hadn't gone through one of the more painful meetings I've ever attended earlier today. The kiss-off she gave us as we were leaving sounded pretty clear—and pretty permanent—to me."

Cait said, "But you were the one who said she might change her mind given a little time."

"Sure I did, and I meant it. But by 'a little time,' I was talking about months or even years, not a few hours." Kevin glanced out the small window next to him. In the distance the Boston skyline moved slowly past.

Cait watched him without speaking as the airplane taxied slowly up to the same jetway they had left just a few minutes before. Finally she said, "Something's bothering you. What is it?"

He turned his attention back to her, his intense blue eyes clouded with concern. "I don't know, exactly," he answered. "But something's not right."

* * *

It seemed to take forever to get off the damn airplane once they had nosed into the terminal. Cait had expected to leap out of her seat and hurry out the door the moment they stopped moving. Their un-scheduled return to the gate had meant the flight would depart at least fifteen or twenty minutes late, so she assumed it would be in the airline's best interest to move things along.

Her assumption was wrong. The plane rolled to a stop and Cait rose immediately, but the harried flight attendant rushed down the aisle before she could take two steps. "There's no one available inside the terminal to operate the motorized jetway," the woman said, smug satisfaction written all over her face. "You'll just have to take your seat again until dispatch can send someone over."

The unscheduled detour had annoyed most of the passengers in addition to the now-maddeningly polite flight attendant, and the next few minutes passed uncomfortably slowly, as all around them people muttered under their breath, leveled hard stares, and shook their heads in frustration.

At last they were allowed to leave. They walked off the airplane and into the otherwise empty tunnel leading back into the terminal building, passing the flight crew without acknowledgment, not that Cait cared.

She could feel Kevin's body tensing as they approached the mouth of the jetway tunnel. He had put his career on the line to con-vince the captain to return to the gate by claiming to be working with Boston PD and identifying Cait as his partner. If the police really were waiting for them to exit, as he had said they might be, a call to Tampa would undoubtedly follow and the ruse would be discovered. What would happen then, Cait didn't know, but she suspected it would not be pleasant, particularly for Kevin.

But the boarding area was quiet. The only people at the gate were a youngish man and woman, college kids perhaps, dozing side by side on two of the hard plastic chairs, clearly waiting out a long layover. Cait turned left and began the long walk through the terminal building with Kevin a step behind. He was deep in thought, still clearly bothered by Virginia Ayers's sudden change of heart and the resulting strange phone call.

Cait didn't see the problem. People changed their minds all the time, especially where momentous, life-altering events were concerned. She had put herself in her mother's shoes for a moment while sitting on the airplane and quickly realized getting contacted out of the blue by your long-lost daughter after three full decades would certainly have to qualify as life-altering.

She slowed to allow Kevin to catch up and they walked side by side, not talking, each lost in their own thoughts. Outside the terminal they hailed a cab and climbed into the backseat, settling in for the ride back to Everett and their second meeting with Cait's mother in two days.

This one would go better than the first. Cait was sure of it.

35

This time when Cait rang the bell it was with a genuine smile of pleasure on her face rather than one of nervousness. She still had no idea what might have changed her mother's mind—Kevin was right about one thing, Virginia had been dead set against ever seeing her again the last time they talked—but at the same time, she didn't really care. The important thing was that the telephone call represented real progress.

The door swung open and Cait's mother stood on the other side, just as before. Something was wrong, Cait could see that immediately. Her mother's face was pasty-white, her lips set in a straight bloodless line. She looked even frailer than before, if that was possible. It seemed to be taking all of her willpower to...what? Avoid screaming? Look Cait in the eyes? Welcome them into her home again?

But it didn't make sense. *She* was the one who had called Cait and invited her here. *She* was the one who had pulled them off the airplane just as it was about to take off. Had she changed her mind again, and now didn't want to see her? Maybe the woman was just plain crazy; who the hell knew? It wasn't like Cait had any history to go on. They had just met twenty-four hours ago.

Cait wrinkled her forehead. "Are you all right?"

That was when she noticed the blood.

Virginia Ayers's right hand hung limply by her side, unmoving and apparently forgotten as the woman gazed at Cait with dead, empty eyes. A slow drip-drip-drip of thick maroon-black blood gathered at the tips of two of her fingers and fell to the floor in a steady rhythm, dropping first off one finger and then the other. It seemed to be a fair amount of blood. It wasn't a river, exactly, but it fell in a continuous pattern, like the beginning of a soft summer rain, and was gathering into an impressive little pool on the hardwood floor.

"Oh my God, what's wrong?" Cait asked as she stepped through the door, overcome by her natural impulse to help the elderly woman. She felt Kevin hang back, still concerned about whatever had been bothering him since the phone call on the airplane. He had stepped one foot through the door, resting it on the interior floor, but his body hovered half in and half out.

Kevin grabbed Cait by the elbow as she was reaching for her mother's injured hand, pulling her insistently backward, trying to drag her out the door and away from her mother, who clearly needed help! Cait resisted, struggling, pulling in the other direction, but she was no match for his superior size and strength. She opened her mouth to complain. What the hell did he think he was doing?

And then a man stepped out from behind the front door. He moved smoothly and quickly behind Virginia, wrapping one arm around her waist, gently, like a lover, and the other around her throat, a long knife pressed to her skin. The blade glittered and winked in the light, drawing Cait's attention. She froze, her anger at Kevin forgotten.

Her heart stuttered and her stomach flip-flopped. It took only a second to recognize the stranger; his face was burned indelibly into her brain. It was the man from the horrible Flickers of the last couple of days. The man who had tortured the poor girl strapped into the blocky wooden chair. The cold-blooded killer who had begun haunting her dreams.

This was the man.

And he was holding a knife to her mother's throat.

The intruder offered up an easy smile, the smile of a man comfortable in his surroundings. In control of the situation.

"Please, come in," he said, directing his attention at Kevin, who had stopped tugging on Cait's arm and now stood unmoving.

Cait tore her eyes from the intruder and glanced back at her boyfriend. She had known Kevin a long time and instantly recognized he was reverting to cop mode, sizing up the situation, trying to determine what action he might be able to take to neutralize this unexpected threat. He instinctively grabbed at his hip, but of course his gun wasn't there. His gun wasn't within a thousand miles of there. It was locked safely away in the closet of his apartment in Tampa.

The intruder watched Kevin with dead eyes and a smile flickered across his face and disappeared. "No, really, come in," he repeated. "I insist. *We* insist, isn't that right, dear?" He waved the knife theatrically in front of Virginia's face before replacing it against the wrinkled alabaster skin of her throat.

"Don't hurt anyone," Kevin answered, raising his hands in a calming gesture, his voice steady and reasonable. "If it's money you're after, I'm sure we can get some together for you, maybe not as much as you'd like—none of us is rich, as I'm sure you can tell—but we will all be happy to contribute to the cause."

The man laughed. The sound was unexpected, Cait thought, and blood-chilling. His knife jittered against Virginia's throat as he chuckled and she let out a gasp either of fear or pain, Cait could not tell which. So far there was no blood besides the droplets that continued to drip steadily off the ends of her fingers.

"This isn't about money," the man said coldly.

"Then what is it about?" Kevin asked. He eased his right foot inside the door and stepped fully into the house. As he did, the man pulled Virginia Ayers an equivalent distance back down the hallway. The intruder was being careful to maintain a safe distance from Kevin, a precaution that struck Cait as utterly unnecessary. As long as that razor-sharp blade remained pressed to Virginia's throat, there was nothing Kevin or anyone else could do. It would take but one flick of the man's wrist and Cait's mother would bleed out within minutes.

"What is it about? It's about *her*," he answered, directing the business end of the knife at Cait for just a second. At that moment she thought it looked more like a dagger than a knife.

"Cait?" Kevin answered in surprise. It was clearly not what he had expected to hear.

"That's her name? Cait? What a pretty name. A pretty name for a pretty girl. A pretty, bad girl. A pretty, bad girl who's going to suffer."

In that instant everything clicked in Cait's mind. The phone call on the plane. Her mother's sudden, unexpected change of heart. The plea to return immediately. The man had been here, brandishing his knife, injuring her fingers badly enough to make them bleed, forcing her to bring Cait and Kevin back here. What she didn't understand was why.

Kevin continued to move slowly and unthreateningly forward until he stood next to Cait. She knew he was trying to place his body between her and the lunatic with the knife, partly to put himself in a position to help Virginia, but mostly to remove Cait from as much of the danger as possible. "What has Cait done that requires her to suffer?" He kept his tone conversational, like two neighbors discussing the weekend's football matchups.

The man shook his head. "Step away from the door and close it behind you. There's no need for the entire neighborhood to witness our little get-together, not that anyone's out there to see it anyway."

Kevin once again took Cait's elbow, this time moving her one step to the left. He reached back with his foot and pushed the door shut. It closed with a *thunk* of finality and she knew this was going to be bad. This was going to be very bad.

36

Maizie Adams had lived in Everett her entire life, the last forty-five years of it right here on Granite Circle. She had moved in when the neighborhood was still nearly brand-new, buying the only house she would ever own with her husband Roger, a printing press operator at the *Boston Globe*.

Roger had worked long hours, doing the dirty, messy work of putting out a newspaper back in the days when each page was laid out by hand, decades before the process was simplified by the advent of computer programming. In those days it took a team of professionals hours to get it right. Roger would come home exhausted in the middle of the night while the rest of the city slept, his hands and arms stained with ink halfway up to the elbow, the day's edition ready to go.

Then he suffered a massive stroke and, unable to work, found himself relegated to the Barcalounger in the cramped living room, oxygen tank at his side, a once-proud man slipping farther and farther into depression, his life eventually flickering out one night while Maizie slept on the couch next to him.

"Natural causes," the doctor had called it, but Maizie recognized that diagnosis for what it was: a steaming pile of crap. Roger had given up on living, unable to do the job he loved, unable to provide for the woman he loved, unable to find the will to continue breathing.

Maizie buried her husband and then soldiered on alone, missing him but knowing he was better off now, wherever he was. She took a job for the first time in her life, working for a short while as a medical transcriptionist, eventually quitting when she came to the realization she had no real use for the money she was earning. Roger's pension from the *Globe*, along with the small annuity from some long-ago investments, was more than enough to heat the house and buy the groceries and pay the property taxes. Maizie didn't need any more than that.

Now in her early eighties, Maizie Adams's days were mostly spent puttering around her house, watching her soaps and cleaning. Rare was the day when the carpet wasn't vacuumed at least three times, the dishes weren't washed after every meal, and the furniture went undusted.

She also maintained a healthy interest in the comings and goings of her neighbors. None of the other houses were occupied by the same people who had lived in them back in 1968, when the Adamses had moved in; in fact, most of the homes in Granite Circle had been sold several times over as families moved into these starter homes, made their mortgage payments for a few years, and then moved up to bigger and more expensive places in bigger and safer neighborhoods.

But none of that mattered to Maizie. In fact, in some ways she thought it was good. New families meant new routines to observe, new quirks to discover, new people with whom to familiarize herself.

For example, Virginia Ayers, in Number Seven, the house located directly across the circle from Maizie's, had been living in her home since 1983, and she was a strange case. Her husband was long gone, having died in a suspicious manner—Maizie suspected he may have killed himself, but wasn't sure—close to a quarter-century ago, and Virginia was nearly as reclusive as Maizie herself, although somewhat younger. She didn't *look* younger, Maizie thought, but she was.

Maizie could count the number of times Virginia had received guests since her husband died on one hand, which made the last two days' flurry of activity so noteworthy. Yesterday a young couple had visited, arriving by taxicab and spending a couple of hours inside the house. Then they had left after a strained exchange on the front porch. Maizie's eyesight was failing rapidly, along with most of her other senses, but the awkwardness of their departure had been clear even to her, watching from her living room at least a hundred feet across Granite Circle.

Then, today, a young man had arrived, pulling into the driveway in his own car, knocking on the door and entering the house after a short conversation. Maizie had been watching closely and darned near called the police then. She would have sworn the young man had half forced his way in, sticking his shoe in the doorway and pushing his way inside like a bull in a china shop.

She had *almost* called the police, but not quite. The whole thing happened so quickly and was over so fast that she immediately began to question what she had seen. After all, her eyesight wasn't what it used to be and although Everett could be a dangerous city at times, especially if you didn't know where you were going and ended up in the wrong section of town, this neighborhood was pretty safe most of the time.

So Maizie had let it go, ignoring the feeling of unease worming its way through her intestines, blaming it on the undercooked chicken breast she had eaten for lunch. But then, just a few minutes ago, the couple from yesterday had shown up *again*. Three separate callers in two days!

One caller was practically unheard of for Virginia Ayers, but three? Never. Something was definitely going on.

And things had only gotten more perplexing. The front door swung open wide at their arrival and Maizie was certain she had seen the young man who had (maybe) forced his way inside standing behind the door, in the shadows of the hallway, like he was trying to stay out of sight. Then the young couple had stood at the door for a few seconds before beginning to back away. They had suddenly changed their minds and entered. Then the door had slammed closed.

The entire incident had taken place in just a few seconds, and Maizie was watching from pretty far away and sure, she was old and her eyesight wasn't what it used to be.

But Maizie Adams knew trouble when she saw it. And she had seen it.

She picked up the telephone and cursed herself for being such an old fool. Why hadn't she trusted her instincts earlier? Whatever was happening over there at 7 Granite Circle was bad and she should have notified the police the minute she suspected something was wrong.

It was too late to worry about her foolishness now, though. All she could do was try to correct her mistake.

She squinted at the laminated card taped to the wall next to her telephone. Damn, the thing was hard to read. Her daughter Jeannie had placed the card there months ago, concerned about what might happen in the event of a fire or attempted break-in. All of Everett's emergency response numbers were listed, but to Maizie's way of thinking you had to have the eyesight of a twenty-year-old just to read it. She punched in what she hoped was the number for the Everett Police Department and was rewarded when it was picked up on the second ring.

"Everett police." The voice was female, and sounded young and bored.

"Yes," Maizie said. "I'd like to report..." What? A break-in? A disturbance? What?

"Yes?" the voice prompted, now impatient as well as bored.

"Well, there's something strange going on in the house across the street from mine. The address is Seven Granite Circle."

"Something strange? Could you please be more specific?"

"A young man I've never seen before knocked on the door a little while ago. I can't swear to it, but I think he may have forced his way in. Now two other people have entered the house after visiting yesterday, and they seem to have entered reluctantly. Please send someone quickly, I'm afraid something is very wrong over there."

"What was the address again?"

"Number Seven Granite Circle, here in Everett."

"Seven Granite Circle. Okay, ma'am, we'll dispatch an officer to check on your neighbor."

"Thank you," Maizie answered, hanging up the phone numbly, hoping she hadn't waited too long.

37

"Let's move into the parlor and get comfortable, shall we?" The man gestured toward the end of the hallway with his knife and the group moved en masse, all four bodies shuffling in a kind of tense, loosely choreographed dance, the man with the knife sliding slowly backward, pulling Virginia along, Cait and Kevin matching him step for slow step.

Cait couldn't take her eyes off the blade. It was thin and shiny and long, with a bone-white handle clutched expertly by its owner, who maintained light but steady pressure on Virginia's throat. She glanced into her mother's eyes and saw not just fear, but also regret and sorrow and a kind of tired resignation.

She thought back to their earlier conversation in this very house and everything fell into place. The intruder with the knife was roughly her age, with the same wavy auburn hair and the same general build, thin and wiry. There had to be millions of men throughout the country fitting the same general description, tens of millions maybe.

But she knew, nevertheless.

The man with the knife was her brother.

They moved into the kitchen and the man with the knife kept going, shuffling backward on the balls of his feet like he was performing some demented slow-motion version of the moonwalk. He turned ninety degrees to his left, pulling Virginia through a large open doorway and into the living room. He continued backing up until they reached a point more or less in the middle of the room. Virginia's television loomed behind him, a gigantic old Sony with washed-out colors teetering atop a frail-looking TV table. On it, glamorous soap opera characters played out their glamorous fictional lives, babbling about love and loss and treachery.

Next to the television, positioned roughly halfway between the TV table and the kitchen doorway, an ornamental cactus sat in an enormous ceramic pot. The cactus was mammoth, reaching almost all the way to the ceiling, and looked as though it had occupied its space for decades. Along the opposite wall, behind the man with the knife, was an old couch, worn and faded but scrupulously clean. The room was otherwise bare.

The man with the knife—*my brother,* Cait thought with a numb fascination—focused his gaze on Cait and then inclined his head toward the TV. "You. Drag your ass next to the television set and don't fucking move."

Cait froze and glanced uncertainly at Kevin. He nodded almost imperceptibly. The intruder pulled his knife away from Virginia's throat and indicated that she should join Cait. Together the two of them took small, hesitant steps until they stood between the TV and the cactus plant. Cait felt like a junior-high wallflower at her first dance but was relieved her mother was no longer in immediate danger.

Kevin moved to follow them and the man snapped, "No, no, no, not you." He held his hand up like a traffic cop and Kevin stopped. "You look nice and strong; you can do some of the heavy lifting in preparation for our little party."

Kevin waited for instructions. He appeared completely at ease, didn't even seem afraid. Cait had never had the opportunity to observe him in his work as a police officer, but was starting to understand why he was so highly regarded on the Tampa force, despite his relative youth and short time on the job.

The man with the knife regarded Kevin with his cold eyes. "Go into the kitchen and bring two of those strong wooden chairs in here. Place them in front of your girlfriends, facing the couch."

Cait watched as Kevin walked into the kitchen. She wondered if he might be able to grab something and use it as a weapon but realized the man with the knife had positioned himself so he could monitor Kevin's progress the entire time. In less than a second, if he sensed a threat, he could slice Cait and Virginia both from head to toe.

Kevin returned a moment later, lugging one chair in his beefy hands, moving slowly. He set it down a few feet from the couch and then rotated it so that it was facing forward. Cait wondered why he hadn't grabbed both chairs at the same time; he was certainly strong enough. Then she realized he was stalling, dragging things out as long as possible, slowing everything down while searching for an opportunity to take the offensive.

Kevin turned, his right hand resting lightly on the chair back. "What's your name?" he asked.

The other man paused for a moment. "Milo," he said.

"Hi, Milo. I'm Kevin. What's this all about?"

"I don't care what your name is, and as for what's going on here, you'll find out soon enough. I think you'll find the upcoming spectacle to be very revealing. But for now, just do as you're told and keep your mouth shut."

"Okay," Kevin answered agreeably. "You're in control," he said. "We're all doing exactly as you say."

"You're right about that. You *will* do as I say, if you know what's good for you, that is. Now stop stalling." He knelt and reached into the backpack at his feet, rooting around for a moment while keeping his gaze fixed on his three prisoners.

He pulled out a roll of reinforced duct tape and tossed it to Kevin. "Secure the old bat in the chair, nice and snug. I want two strips around each wrist and two around each ankle, tight to the chair. No wiggle room."

Kevin turned to Virginia and nodded gently at the chair with a grim look on his face. It was obvious he didn't like the way things were playing out. Cait watched as her mother eased into the chair and placed her arms on the armrests, making it easy for Kevin to secure them. He muttered something Cait could not decipher and the man immediately shouted "Shut up!"

When the job had been completed to the man's satisfaction, he said, "Now slap a strip across her mouth."

Kevin complied and in a matter of seconds Virginia was trussed up tightly, completely helpless and unable to speak, facing the couch.

"Go get the second chair," the man continued. "Set it down right next to the first one. Think of it as stadium seating for the live show that's due to begin," he made an exaggerated display of looking at his watch, "any minute now."

Kevin disappeared into the kitchen again, returning moments later with another chair. He seemed to have abandoned his delaying strategy; it took only about half as long for him to carry the second chair into the room as it had taken to bring the first. He dropped it onto the floor in the prescribed spot with a thud, then turned and faced the man with the knife.

"Now, sit your ass down in it," Milo said. "That'll be where you enjoy your girlfriend's starring role in this little performance art exhibition."

Cait shifted her gaze back and forth between the two, her muscles clenched, tense and afraid. Amazingly, Kevin still seemed at ease, leaning with one hand on the back of the chair, while the man with the knife—Milo—appeared nervous and twitchy. Milo opened his mouth to say something and that was when Kevin flinched, startled, and glanced into the hallway in surprise before returning his attention quickly to Milo.

A suspicious look darkened Milo's face; it was as if a cloud passed in front of his eyes. He leaned forward and craned his neck, twisting his gaze to the left, determined to see what had caused Kevin to jump.

Cait reflexively glanced into the hallway at the same time. She wondered what Kevin had seen. Whatever it was, it had disappeared. The hallway was deserted.

Out of the corner of her eye, Cait saw Kevin's fingers flex once and then he straightened his body quickly, lifting the chair as he did so. He pivoted and took one long step toward Milo, uncoiling like a baseball pitcher striding toward home plate. He whipped the chair in a sideways arc, head-high, as Milo swiveled toward the oncoming danger.

Virginia cried out in surprise, her grunt muffled by the duct tape, and Milo flinched, leaning away from the makeshift weapon as it whistled through the air. Kevin seemed to have planned for that reaction, though, as the chair's trajectory was taking it to a point *behind* the monster with the knife. By reacting as he had, Milo was effectively backing directly into the danger.

Time seemed to slow from Cait's perspective. She watched for what felt like an eternity as the heavy wooden chair flew through the air, eventually crashing into Milo's body. His reflexes were surprisingly quick, and he ducked his head out of harm's way, lifting his shoulder and turning, taking most of the blow on his back. The chair shattered, the seat and legs falling to the floor where they thudded into the corner of the room, the seat-back exploding, sending dozens of wooden projectiles flying around the room.

Milo tumbled, falling in a shower of splinters. The force of the blow ripped the knife from his hand and it clattered across the varnished floor, sliding like a hockey puck on an ice rink. Cait screamed as Milo rolled, reaching for the knife, his hands and feet scrabbling for purchase on the slippery hardwood.

Kevin fell to the right, off-balance after striking the blow. He dropped to one knee, almost tumbling onto his side; then he put his right hand to the floor and pushed off hard, launching himself in the other direction. He took one long stride in an effort to leap over Milo's scuttling form, desperate to beat him to the knife, and his foot slid out from under him and he crashed in a heap in the exact spot Milo had occupied seconds ago.

He wasn't going to make it. Cait could see he wasn't going to make it. She realized only now that *she* should have been halfway to the knife already. She swore at herself and stood, far too late to make a difference now but wanting to do something to help her fiancé, although she had no idea *what* to do.

Kevin lunged, crawling over Milo and diving for the knife. His fingertips grazed the handle but then Milo snatched it away as Kevin crashed again to the floor. Then the lunatic rose to his knees and half turned. He raised his arm sideways and in a slashing motion, buried the knife up to the handle in Kevin's chest.

Blood gushed thickly, soaking Kevin's shirt. Cait heard another scream and she realized it was coming from her. She took a step toward her injured boyfriend and Milo yanked the knife out of Kevin's body, sensing the approaching danger. He took a backhanded slash at her without even looking and she pulled up short as the deadly blade whizzed past, droplets of Kevin's fresh blood splattering her blouse in a delicate pattern.

"Sit down!" Milo screamed. "Sit down!"

Cait did as he said. She had no idea what else to do. She backed toward the couch, watching Kevin, desperate to help him, wondering how badly he was hurt. She was still screaming. She thought she might never stop screaming. The backs of her calves struck the upholstered cushions and she fell heavily onto her butt.

Kevin rolled onto his side, clutching his injured chest, and then, incredibly, pushed off the floor to take another shot at Milo. The moment he removed his hands from the deep wound, blood pulsed out. It was bright red, running like a river, and Cait realized with horrifying clarity that there was a very real chance she was watching her boyfriend die.

Milo turned back toward Kevin, raising the knife and slashing at him again in a quick, panicked motion, before relaxing as he took in the sight of the badly injured man. Kevin stopped and clamped his hand over the knife wound in a vain attempt to stanch the bleeding but succeeded only in soaking his palms with his own blood. He swayed on his feet and began moving again, shuffling grimly toward Milo.

Milo laughed, the sound grating and unexpected after the events of the last few seconds. He stepped forward and shoved Kevin backward and Kevin pinwheeled his arms weakly, the blood once again welling up and out of his chest the moment he removed his hand from the wound. Kevin stumbled once, tripping over the smashed chair seat, then crashed heavily to the floor, the back of his head bouncing off the polished hardwood with a loud *Crack!*

Kevin blinked once, twice, three times. He shook his head. He rolled onto his stomach, gravity increasing the effect of the stab wound, causing the blood to flow even more heavily. He pushed himself onto his knees, eyes glazed from pain and shock. Then they rolled up into his head and he tumbled face-first onto the floor and lay still.

And Cait screamed again.

38

Boredom was the part of police work that Hollywood never seemed able to capture in their silver screen portrayals of law-enforcement officers. Or, more likely, they *could* capture it, they just didn't want to. Rico Petralli figured that was probably it. After all, who wanted to pay twelve bucks a ticket, not including highway robbery charges for snacks and drinks, just to watch bored cops drive around all day in their cruisers busting teenage punk gangbangers and rousting smelly homeless guys from park benches? Moviegoers wanted to see car chases and flinty-eyed detectives and gun battles, Rico figured. *He* certainly did when he went to the movies.

But the fact of the matter was real police work involved mind-numbing boredom, hours of it, day after day, much more often than it involved car chases or flinty-eyed detectives doing anything besides sipping bitter coffee on stakeouts. Certainly more than it involved gun battles. Rico had been an Everett cop going on four years now and had never once fired his weapon in anger.

So when the Granite Circle call came in—an old lady worried about her neighbor—he shook his head wearily. He was only a quarter-mile away, closer than anyone else, which meant that he had no choice but to respond.

He hated these types of calls—"Is everything all right, ma'am? Are you sure, ma'am?"—even more than most. They represented not just boredom, but awkwardness as well.

Rico knew he would have to explain that the next-door neighbor—who had undoubtedly been peeping out her bedroom window—was concerned and had been sticking her nose into business that wasn't hers. The "intruder" would end up being a visiting relative who had shown up unexpectedly or something. Rico sighed and shook his head wearily.

Boredom.

Rico's day hadn't been all that great to begin with, and was undoubtedly about to get just a little worse. He pulled into Granite Circle, struck by the absolute stillness of the neighborhood. There didn't seem to be a single person around, which was silly. There had to be at least one—the citizen who had gotten a glimpse of something that had made her nervous and called it in.

He scanned the numbers on the fronts of the houses and eased to a stop behind a Buick parked in the driveway at Seven Granite Circle. He reached down and picked his hat off the seat next to him and placed it on his head, turning off the cruiser's engine and climbing out of the vehicle reluctantly. Something was not right. Something was...off. It took a moment for him to figure out what that might be, and then it struck him like a sledgehammer.

The place was quiet. Too quiet, as the cliché went.

The house was graveyard-still. The silence was unnerving. It was deathly.

Rico climbed the stairs and pressed the doorbell and waited, his right hand resting on the butt of his service revolver. For a long time nothing happened, and he began to wonder if he had gotten the address wrong. He looked around. The neighborhood remained quiet and still.

Then the door swung open and a man filled the doorway. He was young—around Rico's age—and appeared preoccupied. And he was sweating, as if he had just been involved in some form of heavy physical activity. Like beating his wife, maybe?

"Yeah? What is it?" he said, an edge to his voice.

Rico tried to look past the man and into the house and found he couldn't. The dude's body was blocking his view and besides, the hallway behind him was filled with shadows, too dark to make out much of anything. "Everything all right, sir?"

"Sure it is. Why wouldn't it be?"

Rico ignored the question. "What's your name, sir?"

The man hesitated and then answered. "Milo Cain."

"Anyone else home with you, Mr. Cain?"

"Nope. I'm here all by myself."

"Really. Because we received a call from a neighbor concerned about the resident at this address. A resident who happens to be a lady. Can you shed any light on that for me, Mr. Cain?"

"I sure can't. Sorry. Like I said, no one else is even here. Now if you'll excuse me, I'm kinda busy..." He began closing the door in Rico's face and Rico reached out with his left hand to block it. His right hand stayed where it was, on the butt of his weapon.

"May I come in for just a moment, sir?"

A shadow of something—annoyance, impatience, fear?—flickered across the man's face and Rico thought for a moment the guy might actually try to force the door closed in his face despite his efforts at holding it open. It had happened before.

And then the man shrugged and said, "Whatever. Can you make it quick? I'm trying to prepare for a little party I'll be hosting later." He smiled and the sight chilled Rico. The man's eyes were cold and calculating and distant.

Rico stepped through the door and as he did a moan floated on the air, coming from somewhere inside the house. He hesitated for a half second, confused. It sounded like a man's voice, not a woman's, and the dispatcher had specifically stated the complainant was concerned about a *woman* being in danger.

The screen door slammed behind Rico. The face of the man standing in front of him gave away nothing. Then Rico heard the sound again—definitely a moan, definitely a man's voice—and in one smooth motion unholstered his Glock. He reached out to grab the man, whom he expected to retreat.

But the man didn't retreat. He stepped forward, rattlesnake-quick, reaching behind his back and producing a knife he had hidden in the waistband of his trousers. His hand was a blur as he slashed at Rico and Rico squeezed off a shot and the gun bucked in his hand and a loud roar filled his ears and fire flew from the end of the barrel and a massive hole appeared like magic in the hallway wall behind the man and Rico realized he had missed—

—and he felt a stinging pain in his throat, like someone had taken their fingernail and dragged it across the skin. Suddenly his uniform shirt was wet. It felt as though he had stepped into the path of a fire hose. He could feel the wetness flowing down his chest and his belly like a wave.

He reached up reflexively with his left hand and covered the damage to his throat as he pulled the trigger again with his right. By now the man had sidestepped to *his* right and even though Rico's aim was better this time, the man was no longer there. The same roar filled the little house and the same fire flew from the barrel of Rico's gun, but this time the bullet disappeared somewhere past the end of the hallway. Rico registered screaming now, loud screaming, coming from a room off the end of the hall.

He stumbled forward, aware of the man approaching him from the left. He pulled his hand away from his throat and saw that it was drenched in blood, his blood, lots of blood. It flowed like a tiny river, splattering his shoes as it struck the hallway floor. Rico knew he was in big trouble and he slapped his left hand back on the gash in his throat and incredibly he splashed blood into his eyes and he heard a desperate keening moan and dimly realized it was coming from him.

Rico lurched backward toward the front door. He had to get out and regroup, had to call for backup. And an ambulance. Then he felt a sting in his side, just under his ribs, and he turned his head and saw the man pulling the knife out of his side and that was when he heard the sirens in the distance and he knew everything would be okay. Backup was coming.

Rico fumbled with his gun, trying to turn to his left and bring it to bear on his attacker, but his fingers were starting to feel numb and the gun seemed like it was getting heavier by the second. It no longer felt like a 9mm Glock sidearm, instead it felt to Rico like he was trying to maneuver a five-gallon bucket of water.

He fell to his knees and slipped in the blood on the floor, rolling onto his side as he worked on getting off another shot. But the man had moved again, he was like a fucking magician. He had somehow gotten behind Rico and the gun was now pointing in the wrong direction. Rico twisted his weapon and realized he couldn't shoot now or he would likely put a bullet into his own head.

And where were those fucking cruisers and ambulances? He could hear them, why hadn't they arrived yet? The sound of the sirens had grown much louder, except now it didn't resemble sirens as much as it did the buzzing noise his mother's clothes dryer used to make when a load of laundry had finished drying. It sounded like his mother's dryer, only the noise didn't stop; it just kept buzzing and buzzing, getting louder and louder like the dryer was moving down the hall.

Rico realized through his mounting fuzzy confusion that he wasn't hearing sirens at all. Nor was he hearing a clothes dryer. The noise was coming from inside his own head.

And that made sense. He had never had a chance to call for backup. Had never had a chance, period. The guy had suckered him and

Rico had made it easy for him. Out of nowhere, the old cliché, "Don't bring a knife to a gunfight" popped into his head and it occurred to him in retrospect that the saying wasn't entirely accurate. Sometimes bringing a gun to a knife fight can be just a bad an idea.

The blood continued to gush from his neck, casting the scene in a bright-red pulsing glow, and Rico realized the knife-wielding motherfucker had severed his carotid artery. He was fucked. The buzzing noise had continued to increase in volume and now it was more of a roar, like a helicopter was hovering out of sight just overhead. Dark clouds roiled at the edges of his vision, which was beginning to flicker, and he struggled to breathe, gasping vainly, and he knew he would lose consciousness soon.

He looked around for the man with the knife to blow him to hell—if Rico was going to die, he would make goddamned sure he took the fucker with him—but the man had disappeared.

Then someone turned out the lights and Rico Petralli felt an instant of heartache and regret. Then he was gone.

39

Cait barely registered the sound of the ringing doorbell. She barely registered anything besides the sight of Kevin lying motionless on the floor. Then the man who called himself Milo cursed and hurried out of the room. He paused in the doorway and turned. He reached one long arm toward her and pointed the bloodstained knife blade. "Stay perfectly quiet or everyone dies," he said, his voice low and soft and menacing. Then he disappeared.

Cait didn't know who was at the door. Didn't care, either. It wasn't like the cavalry was going to come riding in on their white horses and save everyone; no one even knew they were here. And her top priority, her *only* priority, was Kevin.

She rushed across the floor, sidestepping pieces of broken chair, and knelt next to him. His face was white, his lips a frightening shade of pale blue. His eyes were closed and he lay unmoving and for a horrible moment Cait feared he might already be dead. If that were the case, she would rush the maniac, knife or no knife, and inflict as much damage on his murdering soul as she could before she went down.

But then Kevin coughed and moaned. His eyes remained closed and his face was still sheet-white but he was alive! Cait steeled herself and turned him over onto his back. She had to examine his wound. She had no idea how long their captor would be gone and doubted she would be allowed to care for Kevin once he returned, so speed was critical.

She lifted his shirt, now soaked and matted with his own blood, and when she did, a sickening gush of it bubbled up and out of his chest. The shirt was acting as a kind of rudimentary bandage, partially restricting blood flow, and it occurred to Cait that Kevin's loss of consciousness might be the only thing keeping him alive. His heart rate had dropped and was no longer forcing the blood out of his body at such an alarming rate.

But something had to be done. Quickly. She needed to improvise a more effective compress than a piece of cotton resting against the gash. Cait ripped his shirt down the front, scattering buttons across the floor. They bounced around like little rubber balls. She worked his arms out of the sleeves and lifted his upper body as gently as she could off the floor, sliding the shirt out from under his back. His blood dripped down her hands.

She eased Kevin back to the floor and then twisted the shirt into a long, thin bundle of material, wringing the blood out of it like a sponge. She looped it across his chest, pressing it over the wound, and then began to tie the sleeves into a knot.

As she worked, she began to feel a gentle pressure in her brain, like a Flicker trying to gain a foothold, and she slowed down and forced herself to ignore it, to push it away. She had far too much to worry about right now to indulge a fucking mind-movie.

The Flicker was insistent but so was she. She closed her eyes, angry at the waste of precious time, but felt certain that losing a few seconds to fight off a Flicker was far preferable to losing who knew how many minutes if she were to let it in.

Finally the pressure eased and Cait was able to continue. She breathed a sigh of relief, having been uncertain she could actually fight it off. She strained to tie the sleeves together as tightly as possible, hoping sufficient pressure would be applied to the wound to prevent Kevin from bleeding out right here on the floor. But it was a temporary fix at best. He needed medical care and he needed it quickly.

Again the gentle pressure of a Flicker pressed into her brain and again she shut it out, her annoyance growing along with her terror.

Dammit!

This was the worst time to have to deal with this. Out of her peripheral vision she could see Virginia straining against her bonds, her muffled voice soft, clearly trying to pass along some kind of message. It was quiet and low and completely unintelligible thanks to the duct-tape gag. Cait felt badly for her but her priority at the moment had to be Kevin.

Besides, Milo would undoubtedly be back soon—Cait was surprised he hadn't already gotten rid of whoever was at the front door. He seemed awfully anxious to get started with whatever torture he had planned for her.

Cait's head was turned to look at Virginia, willing her to stop twisting and grunting in her chair, fearing Milo's threat to come back and kill them all. And then Kevin groaned. He remained unconscious, but let loose a long groan, certainly loud enough to be heard around the corner in the hallway.

Kevin groaned again and Cait slapped a hand over his mouth and prayed he would stop. His skin felt clammy and his eyes remained closed. She whispered into his ear, "I'm here, baby, it's okay, everything's going to be okay," knowing she was doing it for herself more than for Kevin, knowing also it was most likely a lie, but she had to do something; it was either this or break down and cry. So she whispered to him.

She whispered again and her voice was drowned out by the impossibly loud roar of a gunshot. Cait had never heard one before—she hated guns and wished every day that there was a way Kevin could do his job without having to carry one—but she recognized the sound immediately, nevertheless. The gunshot was followed by the sound of an intense struggle taking place around the corner and down the hall.

Another shot.

More struggling.

Cait realized she was screaming again but she couldn't stop herself. Oh, God, she couldn't stop. This day had turned into a living nightmare and she knew that whatever was taking place out by the front door had only resulted in more horror, more pain and more fear.

She removed her hand from Kevin's mouth and clamped it over her own, finally stopping the scream, sobbing uncontrollably instead. It seemed suddenly unlikely that silence mattered, but she still worked to get herself under control. She felt like she might puke and swallowed hard, forcing the contents of her stomach back down.

A sliding/scraping/slithering noise came from the hallway.

Cait told herself not to look. She refused to look.

Then she looked. She couldn't help herself. She glanced up as Milo turned the corner, hunched over, dragging...he was dragging...oh, God, it was a body. He was dragging a body, and the body was dressed in a policeman's uniform very similar to the one Kevin wore every day when he went to work. And the body was bloody and unmoving.

Then Milo dropped the policeman's body with a thud. He turned and straightened. He looked at her and smiled.

40

Boston Police Officer Gina Knowlin eyed the tenement building suspiciously from the front seat of her cruiser. She hated these sorts of calls. Some nutcase had reported a dead body on the third floor—anonymously, no surprise there—and, equally unsurprisingly, had not bothered to offer his name or any other information to the dispatcher who fielded the call.

The discovery of dead bodies was not particularly unusual, especially in this neighborhood, where vagrants, drug dealers, users, gang members, hookers and their johns combined to form a rich stew of potentially deadly violence. But what made this call different, according to dispatch, was the condition of the victim—a young female who had been, if the frantic report was to be believed, "skinned alive by Mr. Midnight," whatever the hell that was supposed to mean.

The call was bogus, that much was obvious. The police had been getting flooded with Mr. Midnight sightings for months, and they were almost always bogus.

And there was another factor to consider, particularly in this area. Gina had been a Boston patrol officer for over half a decade and had responded to dozens of calls exactly like this one. Some loser with a hard-on for the cops would call in a phony report just to see the authorities run around like chickens with their heads cut off, often using the distraction provided by the response as cover to commit some other felony nearby.

Gina stepped out of the vehicle, scanning up and down the street for the second responder. This was just about the worst place in the entire city to have to investigate a call alone. The building was abandoned, condemned, which meant that anywhere from a couple to maybe as many as a dozen fucking vagrants were using the piece of shit as their home base. And vagrants didn't like cops, for obvious reasons.

After a couple of instances last year where officers responding to calls exactly like this one had been ambushed, set up to be attacked and then badly injured, the administrative geniuses who hadn't walked a beat in decades had come to the conclusion—prompted by the patrolmen's union, of course—that it was too dangerous for officers to answer these types of calls in neighborhoods like this alone.

Now, the revised procedure called for a minimum response team of two officers, which was why Gina stood cooling her heels with one foot on the front bumper of her cruiser, scanning the area, waiting for Tommy Mitchell to join the party. So far, no one seemed to be paying any attention to her, but experience had taught her that could change in an instant.

Finally Mitchell's cruiser rolled slowly down the nearly deserted street and Gina felt the tension ease, if only slightly. Tommy was not what even the most generous observer would consider a self-motivated officer—he was a thirty-year veteran who had never risen above the rank of patrolman—but standing alone in this neighborhood had begun to make Gina feel conspicuous and uneasy. Like a target.

Tommy eased to a stop behind Gina and worked his way laboriously out of his vehicle. She figured he had to be two hundred eighty pounds if he was an ounce, and what might once have been muscle had years ago turned mostly to flab. If ever a cop fit the stereotype of the donut-eating flatfoot, it was Tommy Mitchell. Gina watched the left side of the cruiser rise on its suspension as he exited and tried to suppress a smile, more or less succeeding.

She wondered why she had been so tense just a moment ago. This was just another bullshit call phoned in by just another crank with an axe to grind. She would be treated to the sight of Tommy Mitchell trying to avoid a heart attack as he trundled up the three stories only to discover an empty apartment; then she would get to listen to his colorful language on the way back down. Then she would return to her vehicle and get on with her day.

No big deal.

Except something felt wrong. The crank calls involving fictional dead bodies designed to fuck with the police were almost always the same—very non-specific as to gender, age or cause of death, they were uniformly stunning in their lack of creativity. But this one was different. According to dispatch, the caller had been panicked and agitated, practically babbling in his haste to relate the information.

And he had been extremely specific: A young woman, probably early twenties, naked, tied up in a dentist's chair—that was a new one—and brutally tortured, tiny stab wounds all over her body and—this was the most disturbing—long strips of skin peeled completely away from her bones.

"Mr. Midnight," the caller had said.

Thinking about the report made Gina shiver and she wondered if Tommy felt any more nervous about this call than usual. He hitched his belt up under his massive belly and glanced at her, his face scrunched into a scowl.

"Let's get this shit over with," he said, and Gina decided Mr. Midnight would have to be standing in front of Tommy Mitchell with a loaded gun in one hand and a surgeon's scalpel in the other to arouse his suspicions, and even then he might not notice anything was wrong until he took a bullet in the forehead.

Tommy stalked across the cracked concrete walkway and up the dilapidated stairs into the building, not looking back or waiting, simply assuming she would follow. She sighed deeply and trotted to catch up. The lock had been broken off the front door—years ago by the look of the rusted mechanism—and never replaced. Undoubtedly any replacement would have been hacksawed off as well, so what would be the point?

Gina entered the gloomy building and followed the sound of Tommy Mitchell's boots clomping up the stairway to the right of the foyer. It was obvious he wanted nothing more than to clear the call so he could get back to whatever he had been doing before—sitting in his cruiser reading a book, most likely.

By the time she reached the second-floor landing, the sound of Tommy's footsteps was already receding as he proceeded down the third-floor hallway over her head. *Jesus,* Gina thought, *for a fat slob this guy can really move when he's properly motivated.* She sprinted up the final set of steps, cognizant of the shadowy stairwell, pissed off that Mitchell had left her behind when the whole point of having a pair of officers respond to the call was for their protection, not to split up so they could be picked off by any lunatic with a grudge and a weapon.

Hurrying down the hallway, Gina turned right and entered the only open doorway, crashing into Tommy and falling to her butt as she bounced off his massive bulk. He stood just inside the apartment's entrance, invisible from the hallway, frozen to the spot in shock.

Gina picked herself up off the floor, ready to tear into the stupid asshole. She considered herself a patient person, but enough was enough. "What the hell are you..."

She stopped in midsentence, taken completely by surprise as Tommy Mitchell unsnapped his holster and removed his service weapon. He turned and stepped nimbly over her, checking behind them both in the hallway, swiveling the gun left and right. Then he edged cautiously into the apartment.

A creeping sense of horror overtook Gina. Her instincts had been right. This was no ordinary crank call from a disturbed crackpot. She rose to her feet and followed Tommy, stopping in the exact spot he had moments ago, chilled by the sight in front of her.

Whoever had called in this mess had been spot on. Blood was everywhere, congealing on the floor atop a clear plastic tarp laid out with care around the base of what did indeed look like a gigantic dentist's chair. Secured to the chair with duct tape was a young girl, naked, unmoving and clearly dead, with wounds exactly as had been described to dispatch.

Gina slapped at her holster and removed her gun as Tommy had. She took three steps into the room and Tommy came around the corner. "This shithole's clear," he muttered. "There's nobody here. We need to call this in," as if expecting Gina to argue. She didn't argue.

While Tommy made the call, using his cell phone instead of the radio transmitter clipped to his shirt in the hopes of keeping the inevitable lookie-loos away for as long as possible, Gina moved deeper into the room, drawn toward the young woman immobilized on the chair. It was clear the victim was dead—no one could survive such massive blood loss, not to mention the terrible wounds that had caused it—but she went through the motions anyway, checking for a pulse on the woman's neck. Tommy hadn't bothered to do that and it should have been their first priority after ensuring the apartment was clear.

The mistake didn't matter, though. There was no pulse, as she had known there wouldn't be, and the victim's skin was cool and sticky with dried blood.

Gina turned away, angry with herself and Tommy Mitchell, unable to put her finger on exactly why. She glared at Tommy, an act that seemed to have no effect on him but made her feel marginally better, and then stepped back to the front door and checked the hallway once more. It would be very bad form to have the killer return and get the drop on them as she and Tommy were busy inside, and securing the apartment from the outside would be the first piece of business to accomplish while waiting for the homicide detectives to arrive.

The hallway was still empty.

She began to pace, waiting for the homicide dicks and the crime scene techs to begin arriving. She hoped it wouldn't take too long; the prospect of cooling her heels here for longer than a few minutes with nobody to talk to but Tommy Mitchell was almost as depressing as finding the body of the victim had been.

41

Milo used the dead cop's uniform shirt as a towel, pinching material between his fingers and sliding the knife blade through the gap. Blood sluiced off the stainless steel and ran down his fingers. The shirt's cotton wasn't terribly absorbent, but beggars couldn't be choosers, as the old saying went, and besides, after a moment the blade was nearly as good as new. A little blood on his hands didn't bother Milo Cain.

He reached behind his back and placed the knife carefully between his belt and his jeans, leaving it hanging down off his ass like a razor-sharp tail, exactly as he had done when the doorbell rang.

Then he knelt down and hooked his arms through the armpits of the dead cop. He rose to a semi-crouch and dragged the still-warm corpse around the corner and into the living room, turning the body sideways and dropping it across the doorway like a fallen log. Its head struck the floor with a teeth-rattling thud, hard enough to cause a concussion had the man been alive. Milo felt confident the interfering flatfoot was beyond such concerns now.

He flashed a bright smile at the younger woman, the one he was going to have so much fun with in a couple of minutes, and then glanced at the old hag to make sure she was still tightly secured in her chair. She was. The duct tape appeared intact.

He had taken a chance dealing with the knock at the door before securing the younger bitch to a chair. Had she been thinking clearly—and quickly—everything could easily have gone to shit for Milo in a matter of seconds. But based on the dynamics he had observed during his disturbing visions of these three people and the short time he had spent here in person, he had anticipated that when he went around the corner and answered the front door, the rattled younger woman would be so concerned about her injured boyfriend she would run to his aid, not even giving a thought to releasing the older woman or rushing to the kitchen for a weapon or to grab the phone.

And he had been right. The pretty young thing was even now crouched over the man Milo had stabbed, thus blowing any chance she might have had to get away.

Because now it was too late.

And she wouldn't get another chance.

And the best part of all—the delicious cherry on top of this exciting dessert—was that her desperate efforts to assist the man were clearly going to be futile. The boyfriend was still breathing but it was obvious to Milo, who had plenty of experience in this particular arena, that the guy was well on his way to checking out. His skin was bedsheet-white and his lips were turning blue and his breathing was shallow and ragged.

Milo nodded to himself, impressed with his handiwork. All that damage from one knife wound! Granted it was accidental, the result more of luck than skill, but the end result was all that mattered, and this was something to be proud of in any event.

Now that he had a moment to catch his breath, he thought back to what the cop had said at the front door, and how it might affect his plans. *A call from a neighbor concerned about the resident at this address. A resident who happens to be a lady.*

Apparently the neighborhood wasn't quite as deserted as he had originally thought. Someone had seen him enter the house and had alerted the police. And killing a cop, although every bit as satisfying as he had always dreamt it would be, had ensured that he would receive a visit by more of the fucking cockroaches before long.

A lot more. And they would be angry.

But Milo wasn't concerned. He had three hostages with which to bargain. Well, two, once you eliminated the chair-smashing hero, who was clearly not long for this world. One, actually, now that he thought about it, because after he finished with the pretty young thing currently blubbering over the unmoving body of the chair-smashing hero, she wouldn't be worth a damned thing as a bargaining chip. She was the reason he had come here in the first place and he had every intention of finishing what he started, law-enforcement cockroaches or no law-enforcement cockroaches.

But one hostage was plenty, anyway, and if it turned out that the authorities weren't in a bargaining mood, so be it. It wasn't like he had never considered the possibility of taking a bullet to the head. People with his...unusual...interests were universally misunderstood, and Milo had always accepted the possibility he would one day go out in a blaze of glory. If that day happened to be today, he was ready. He wasn't particularly enamored of the idea, didn't consider himself suicidal, wasn't looking *forward* to dying, but found that the idea of going out in a dramatic showdown didn't bother him all that much, either.

The woman crouching next to her boyfriend looked up at the sound of the cop's head striking the floor. She had removed the injured man's shirt and used it as a makeshift bandage, rolling it up and fastening it around the injury, then closing the gash by tying the sleeves together. It was clever, Milo had to admit, and seemed to have done a pretty good job of slowing the bleeding.

It wasn't going to make any difference.

"Well, ladies, that was exciting, wasn't it?" He turned his smile in the direction of the trussed-up old bitch in the wooden chair, but she had screwed her eyes shut. She sat rigid and unmoving, seemingly trying to disappear into thin air through sheer force of will. He shrugged. *Oh well.* It would have been nice to get a reaction, but she wasn't the reason he was here, anyway.

"Your boyfriend is one brave motherfucker," he said to the younger one, whose eyes were fearful but also watchful and wary as she gazed up at him. "Stupid as all get-out, there's no denying that, but he's brave. Unfortunately for him, his pain will be emotional as well as physical when he sees what I have in store for you."

"He can't see anything," she spat back. "He's unconscious, you stupid bastard."

Milo narrowed his eyes and glared at her. The hatred he had felt the moment he saw her in the first vision ratcheted up a little higher. He was used to commanding submission and fear, but while this one was clearly afraid, she didn't seem to understand her place in this hierarchy. She would find out soon enough.

He held her stare for a moment, then turned and stalked into the kitchen. He grabbed another chair to replace the one the unconscious hero wannabe had broken over his back, and returned to the living room where he set it down next to the old biddie. Then he nodded at the man on the floor. "Put him in this," he said.

"He's too big, I can't move him."

"Shut up and do it," Milo said, taking one step forward, reaching for his knife.

The pretty bitch had stopped crying, but her eyes were red-rimmed and puffy, and now they widened with his approach. "I'm afraid if I move him the wound will start bleeding again. I don't think he can afford to lose much more blood," she said, her voice a raspy whisper.

"Well, he should have thought about that before he *attacked me with a fucking chair!*" Milo was trying to control his temper, but the very sight of this little bitch pissed him off to no end, and her back-talking and sassy attitude were making it immeasurably harder to do. "So I don't give a fuck about his little razor-nick. If it bleeds, it bleeds. Now drag his ass over here and dump him in the chair."

"No."

Before he even realized what he was doing, Milo had taken three long steps across the room. He yanked the knife out from behind his back and knelt down next to the dim bitch. She leaned away from him but otherwise held her ground. Milo waved the knife in front of her face, then placed it against the unconscious man's throat and smiled at her.

"Your choice," he said, speaking slowly. "Put him in that god-damn chair or I'll finish him off right here and now."

"Oh, God," she whispered, and got to her feet, then leaned down and hooked her arms under her boyfriend's armpits, much as Milo had done with the dead cop a few minutes ago. With a grunt she began dragging the slack body of the much-larger man across the room.

Milo nodded his approval. "Good choice," he said, and observed the blood, indeed, begin once again to bubble through the already-soaked shirt. The process of the young woman pulling the body to the chair was resulting in a gush of blood every time she yanked. It was like watching an EMT doing chest compressions on a patient with a hole in his chest. It was almost dreamily hypnotic. Pull, bubble, rest. Pull, bubble, rest.

Finally the chick reached the empty chair. Milo looked at the older one again and now her eyes were open wide. She stared in horror at the scene being played out just inches away. Milo felt a surge of savage excitement and almost laughed out loud.

The younger woman leaned her boyfriend onto the chair. His bloody chest was laid across the seat and his head flopped down on his arms. The girl was breathing heavily, almost panting from the energy she had expended moving him. He probably weighed close to two hundred thirty pounds and she was a tiny thing, probably no more than one-ten, so obviously it had taken all of her strength to drag him across the room.

"I can't get him up there by myself," she said, looking at Milo pleadingly. "Just let me lie him on the floor on his back to minimize the bleeding and I'll do whatever you say, I promise."

"Let me get this straight. You'll do whatever I tell you to do, as long as I don't make you put him in the chair?"

"That's right. I promise," she whispered.

"Well," Milo replied. "That's quite the generous offer. Let me see..." He crossed his arms and cupped his chin in his hand, pretending to be deep in thought. He knew he should be hurrying things along thanks to the complications that were bound to arise from the dead cop lying on the floor, but this was just too much fun to pass up.

"Uhhh...no," he said after a satisfying pause.

"Please."

"Here's the problem," Milo answered. "In order to bargain, you need leverage, and you have none. You say you'll do whatever I want if I only let your dying boyfriend stay on the floor, prolonging his suffering, but the fact of the matter, missy, is that you're going to do whatever I want, anyway. I have all the leverage.

"So drag his ass into that chair and tape him in. He's probably not going to regain consciousness and that's a damned shame, but just on the off chance he *does* suddenly pop his eyes open, I want to be sure he has a prime view of the display of performance art to come.

"However. Just to show you I'm not unreasonable, I'll help you. Hold this," he said, flipping the knife into the air and catching it by the blade in the fingers of his bare hand. It was an impressive trick, one he had mastered years ago. He offered it, handle-first, to the young woman.

Her eyes grew wide and she froze, confused, then reached hesitantly for it. At the last moment, Milo yanked it away like Lucy pulling the football away from Charlie Brown. He had always thought that comic-strip gag was stupid, that there was no way in real life Charlie Brown would actually fall for it, but apparently the guy drawing the cartoon had known a little bit about human nature.

The dumb bitch moaned and Milo laughed companionably. This was too much fun. "I guess I'll just hold on to this for now," he said. "You don't mind, do you?"

She looked away and didn't answer.

"Now, let's get on with it. I'm afraid our time will be cut short thanks to *this guy.*" Milo nodded toward the body of the dead cop. "Once he fails to check in at headquarters on his hourly donut run, they may send someone to look for him."

He grabbed the unconscious hero wannabe by the shoulder with both hands, holding the knife handle nimbly in the fingers of his right. Then he flipped the man over so that his back was leaning against the chair seat. A great swell of blood bubbled out of his chest and the young woman gasped and quickly reached for him as well. Together they lifted him—she wasn't kidding, he really was quite solid—head lolling, into the chair.

The girlfriend held him steady while Milo reached for the duct tape, expertly rolling it around his ankles and wrists, taping them to the chair. He added a couple of long swaths, securing the man's waist to the chair-back and the tops of his legs to the seat for support. His head still rested on his right shoulder, but Milo supposed there was nothing he could do about that. This would have to suffice. The odds against the hero wannabe ever regaining consciousness were astronomically long anyway, especially after his eventful trip across the floor. Besides, the clock really *was* ticking.

He clapped his hands together and smiled at his two other companions.

The conscious ones.

"What do you say we get started?"

42

Holland Montvale had been a homicide investigator for longer than he cared to remember, and over the course of his career had seen the bodies of hundreds of murder victims, all suffering various desecrations and all in varying stages of decomposition. One thing they all had in common—maybe the *only* thing—was the ugliness of the crime's aftermath.

Gruesome injuries, tissue breakdown, a stricken look etched on the victim's face, the stench of bowels and bladder being voided, all served to make the act of leaving the world via violence even messier than entering it had been. Learning to compartmentalize the reaction to that messiness was essential for any homicide dick and Holland Montvale had long since become accustomed to doing so.

But Holland had to admit this scene was worse than most. The young woman had suffered, and terribly, from the wounds inflicted upon her small frame, and it was clear, even this early in the investigation, that death had come slowly. His gaze lingered over the ravaged body and he said a fervent prayer that when his time came, it would be over quickly.

The CSI techs were busy doing their CSI tech stuff. Holland tried his best to stay out of the way until their work was done. He stood off to one side of the room, waiting patiently, watching the flurry of familiar activity with a professional detachment as he tried to put himself inside the killer's head while the crime was taking place. It was awful to contemplate.

A full complement of BPD officers had descended on the tenement building and fanned out in all directions, canvassing the area, searching out potential witnesses and, as unlikely as it seemed, hoping to get lucky and retrieve the murder weapon. Holland knew he would have to wait for the coroner's report to be sure, but he felt confident the wounds had been caused by a common kitchen knife. What else would someone use to strip skin from bone?

Assuming it *was* a knife, maybe it had been thrown or dropped by the killer in his haste to escape the scene.

It seemed unlikely, but based on the condition of the victim's body and the damage that had been done to her, Holland felt there was at least some chance the patrol officers might uncover something useful. He was no psychologist, but as a longtime homicide dick he felt he could reasonably make a few assumptions based on both the condition of the victim and of the apartment itself.

The nature of the wounds on the body suggested that the suspect possessed, in addition to a terrifying level of psychosis, a meticulous personality and high intelligence, as evidenced by his preplanning skills. It couldn't have been easy to set up the torture device and to lure the young victim here without being discovered.

But the sloppiness of the execution—blood splattered everywhere, the corpse still strapped into the chair, the crime scene not even the subject of the most perfunctory cleanup—gave Holland pause.

He had worked similar scenes before. If his theory was correct, the man—it was almost always a man when the crime was this vicious—was dissembling. He was being overtaken by his psychosis. He was becoming even more dangerous and unpredictable than he clearly already had been. The thought gave Holland a sinking feeling in his gut.

He wandered around the tiny shell of abandoned apartment, concentrating mostly on the room where the young girl had been butchered. The living room. He thought about the irony of such a vicious murder occurring in the "living room" and a chuckle that sounded suspiciously like a choked-off sob escaped before he was able to stop it. He looked around to see if anyone had noticed and was relieved to see no one had.

He considered the murder weapon. Or, more accurately, the absence of a murder weapon. What did it mean that the knife was gone? In most cases, it would simply mean the killer had maintained the presence of mind to take it with him when he left and had disposed of it elsewhere.

But in this case, Holland wasn't so sure. The perpetrator had not made any attempt to hide the mutilated body of his victim or in any way clean up his mess. Would it be consistent with the apparently mindless, frenzied nature of this attack to assume the man had regained enough logic and preplanning skill after committing this horrifying crime to take the murder weapon with him and get rid of it somewhere?

Holland didn't think so. He thought maybe it meant something else. Maybe it meant the killer wasn't quite done yet. Maybe he planned on using the knife again.

Holland had moved to the entryway between the living room and the kitchen in an attempt to stay out the way of the evidence techs, whose work he hoped would be finished soon. He shook his head slowly, thinking about Mr. Midnight running around the city, and when he did, his eyes fell on a piece of trash, no great surprise since the entire apartment was filled with trash.

But this particular piece of trash appeared to have been *placed*, not scattered haphazardly like everything else, on a small, uncluttered portion of the scarred kitchen counter. Something about it bothered Holland. He bent down and examined it without touching it. It looked like the back of a cardboard insert to a snack cake package. Written on it in messy, spidery script, was "7 Granite Circle."

Holland felt his pulse quicken. It was a long shot, but maybe this "7 Granite Circle" was where the killer had gone. Maybe he had tortured this information out of his victim and was even now either at this address or on his way there. That the person who had planned and executed a crime of this magnitude would leave a handwritten note leading investigators to his current whereabouts seemed unlikely in the extreme, but if Holland's theory about the killer dissembling was correct, it was at least a possibility.

He reached into his pocket and pulled out his cell phone. Holland Montvale had no idea how many towns and cities in the surrounding area had an address of 7 Granite Circle within their boundaries, but that information could be accessed easily enough. And it needed to be accessed right now.

Before it was too late.

43

When the disgusting murdering psycho had offered his knife to her, flipping it into the air and then holding it out like a proud teen offering flowers to his date on prom night, Cait had known immediately he was screwing with her; she wasn't stupid and he wasn't nearly as clever as he thought he was. But she still could have grabbed for it. She had just been so concerned with Kevin and the awful blood bubbling out of his chest that she was just a little too slow on the uptake.

If she had only whipped her hand up and grabbed it out of his slimy paw! She pictured herself plucking it cleanly from his palm and stabbing him in the heart, puncturing his chest like he had punctured Kevin's, blood pouring out of the wound as he stared disbelievingly at the tiny woman he had so badly misjudged, at the knife handle sticking out of his own body, quivering to the pulsing beat of his dying heart.

Cait considered herself a pacifist and not so long ago would never have imagined herself capable of the sort of black fantasy she was currently experiencing. But the world she had known her entire life, a world where people treated each other with dignity and respect and where things proceeded along a rational and understandable arc, that world was gone, at least for now.

It was gone and it had been replaced by a world of madness and hate and unimaginable brutality and violence, a world where an armed police officer is no match for a madman with a knife.

Cait was so wrapped up in the vision—not a Flicker, just a regular, garden-variety daydream—she didn't realize the murdering bastard was talking to her until he leaned down into her face and shouted, *"Hey!"*

She recoiled in surprise. "What?" she whispered.

"I said it's time to get this production rolling. Are you ready for Act One?"

"What is that supposed to mean?"

"It means you're to get your pretty little ass over to that couch and lie down on it."

Oh, God.

This was worse than she thought. The idea of that horrible, nasty man raping her, sticking any part of his disgusting body inside her, was too much to bear.

As if he could read her mind, the man snickered. "It's not what you're thinking," he said. "Although, if you don't get moving, I might fuck you just to make a point."

Cait knew she should shut her mouth and do what the man said, but she couldn't help herself. "What point would that be?" she said, half wondering when the breakdown she was expecting any moment would strike and she would be reduced to a blubbering, sniveling idiot. So far it hadn't happened, but how far off could it be? She felt her sanity warping, being stretched to its limits.

"The point," he answered, baring his teeth, his hate for her radiating off him like a force field, "is that you think getting raped is the worst thing I could do to you, but you have no fucking idea how wrong you are. But if you don't do as you're instructed, and I mean *right fucking now*, I *will* rape you just for the fun of it and then we'll take things from there."

Cait began moving in a confused daze toward the couch. She wondered why he wanted her to lie down if he didn't plan on raping her. She wondered what she had ever done to this man to warrant the kind of hatred he clearly felt for her.

She couldn't recall having ever met him—and she was certain she would remember a man this evil if their paths ever had crossed—but everything he was saying seemed to indicate this was personal, that everything he was doing was about her, and her alone.

She wracked her brain, trying desperately to think, but her brain wouldn't cooperate. It felt like mush. The panic that threatened to overwhelm her made concentrating difficult. She knew this was her long-lost brother, the twin she had not even been aware existed until yesterday; that much she had already deduced, even without the benefit of a Flicker.

Could it be he was aware of their relationship? If so, could his barely controlled rage be somehow related to that knowledge? And more importantly, could she figure out a way to use that knowledge to her advantage? *Dammit, think!*

She reached the couch and turned to sit on the dingy material but Milo stopped her with a hand on her shoulder. "No," he said. "We can't very well put on this performance with you still in your street clothes, can we?"

The panic threatened to mushroom again. What the hell did he mean by that? The situation was bad enough without this madman speaking in riddles.

"I don't understand," she said, a lump forming in her throat, tears on the verge of returning.

Cait longed to be wrapped in Kevin's arms, his muscular body pressed to hers. It was an almost visceral need. She glanced at him, still unconscious, duct-taped to the chair, and forced herself to focus. He was dying and he needed her, and falling to pieces from terror and confusion would do nothing to help him.

"So I need to change my clothes?" she asked, amazed at the steadiness of in her voice. She had no idea where *that* was coming from.

"Well, not change, exactly," he said with a smile. It made him look like a shark about to strike.

"May I undress in the bathroom?"

The crazy bastard actually laughed at that one. "Oh, sure," he said. "No problem. You go right ahead into the bathroom, where there are probably no more than a couple of *dozen* potential weapons you could use against me! Scissors, tweezers, nail files, maybe a toothbrush to jab into my eye. How fucking stupid do you think I am?"

Cait dropped her head. Her eyes swept the floor, taking in the damage from the smashed chair. She sighed. She knew where this was going. She raised her head resolutely and began unbuttoning her blouse. She hesitated only a moment before shrugging it off her shoulders and down her arms. She shook it onto the floor where it fell, inside out, atop a jagged splinter of broken chair. Then she unsnapped her jeans.

Another moment's hesitation and then she pushed them over her hips and down her legs, stepping out of them, and then they joined her blouse on the floor and Cait Connelly was standing in front of her assailant—her *brother!*—in just her matching black panties and bra and socks.

She reached behind her back to unhook her bra and to her surprise, Milo shook his head. "That's enough," he said, his voice husky, "at least for now."

Cait let her hands drop to her sides and the two of them faced each other and Cait waited for the next awful instruction from this awful man and suddenly she felt it again—that little *push* she had first noticed when she was kneeling over Kevin's body trying to stanch the bleeding while the lunatic with the knife was preoccupied with carving up the police officer.

The little *push* was familiar. It was the sensation of an image being forced into her brain without any effort on her part to accomplish it. Cait had tried to describe the sensation to Kevin once and had likened it to an inflation needle being inserted into a basketball—the air that was already inside the ball stayed there, but once the needle forced its way inside, more air could be pushed into the ball.

There was one very significant difference, though. She had never been able to stop a Flicker. Once that little *push* started, the Flicker was coming and there was not a damned thing she could do about it. But when she had experienced what she believed to be the onset of a Flicker a few minutes ago—twice—while occupied with trying to stop Kevin's bleeding, she had managed to successfully block it out.

At the time she had not given it too much thought; things were happening fast and she was in a panic and there were other, more critical issues to consider. Now, though, as she felt the relentless *push* in her brain, she wondered if she could do it again. It was absolutely imperative that she keep her wits about her. The last thing she wanted was to disappear insider her mind under the influence of a Flicker and allow this maniac even more control over her than he already enjoyed.

Kevin needed her, he was dying because he had tried to protect *her*, and she represented his only chance at survival. She willed herself to ward off the Flicker, concentrating with everything she had, rejecting the *push*. The lunatic with the knife—her brother—was talking to her, he was saying something, she could hear him and knew she should answer him, but her concentration was focused entirely on rejecting the Flicker and so for the second time in just a few minutes she risked everything by ignoring him.

And it worked.

After a few seconds the *push* eased off, started pulling away, made a last-ditch final effort to invade her mind and then was gone. Cait felt a trickle of sweat roll down her cheek and brushed it away with her hand. She was exhausted but thankful she had been able to repel the ill-timed Flicker.

She glanced at Kevin—he was still unconscious and seemed to have gotten even paler—and noticed her mother staring at her with a look of intense concentration, she seemed almost to be pleading with her expressive eyes.

Then she shrugged her shoulders and returned her attention to the crazy man named Milo. She waited to see what was coming next.

44

Everett Police Captain Lynn Talmadge punched the flashing yellow button on the ancient console phone taking up an almost comically large portion of her desk. An audible *clunk* told her she was now connected with the outside caller, Lieutenant Bruce Miller of the Boston Police Department. Miller had insisted to the dispatcher that he be connected immediately with the watch commander at the Everett station, that he had critical information to pass along regarding potentially a life-and-death situation.

"This is Talmadge. How can I help you, Lieutenant?"

"Hello, Captain. Thanks for taking my call."

"Well, you made it sound pretty important. What's going on?"

"We're investigating a homicide here, a very bad one. Another 'Mr. Midnight' killing. The victim has been dead just a few hours. It's a young woman, probably a prostitute. She was stabbed, slashed, had her fingers broken and..."

Miller hesitated on the other end of the line and Talmadge prompted him. "Yes?"

The lieutenant took a deep breath and it sounded like he was working to keep a tremble out of his voice, but that seemed absurdly unlikely. The Boston Police Department investigated murders routinely. Bruce Miller had probably seen hundreds of victims during his career and had undoubtedly become detached and clinical when investigating murders years ago.

Finally he continued, his voice subdued: "...and she had entire sections of skin stripped off her body. She was literally peeled like an apple. Someone's into some seriously weird shit with a knife."

"Oh, God," Talmadge muttered, not saying what she was thinking—that she was glad the nutcase had chosen Boston to go off in rather than Everett.

"You and me both," Miller agreed, a little more vigor returning to his voice. "But there's more."

"I was afraid of that."

"You should be. The suspect's in the wind and our lead homicide investigator uncovered evidence that may indicate he isn't finished yet."

"And?"

"And he's possibly headed in your direction."

Talmadge sighed and closed her eyes. "What sort of evidence?"

"It's a hastily written note that looks as though it may have been jotted down by our killer. It was found next to the body."

"And what does the note say?" Talmadge asked, a trace of frustration creeping into her voice. This Miller character couldn't just come out with it, he had to string her along, make her ask a million questions. Officious prick.

"It doesn't really say anything. There's just an address jotted down on the back of a piece of scrap paper—Seven Granite Circle."

"Ooookay..." Talmadge hesitated. Why did that street name sound familiar? She shrugged and continued, "I guess the obvious question would be, why did 'Seven Granite Circle' make you think of Everett and not somewhere else?"

"Because there are only two communities in the entire Commonwealth of Massachusetts containing Granite streets, and—"

"—and one of them is Everett," Talmadge finished. She felt her stomach tighten as she suddenly remembered why the Granite Circle address rang a bell. One of her officers had been dispatched to that address a short while ago. A report from a neighbor concerned about a possible break-in.

At 7 Granite Circle.

Suddenly it became very important to get Lieutenant Miller off the phone and talk to dispatch. Her officer had walked straight into a nightmare.

45

Milo frowned in frustration. What the hell was it with this bitch? She should have been nearly out of her mind with fear, crying and blubbering and begging for her life. He had had extensive experience torturing pretty young women—there weren't many things in this life he was good at, but torture was definitely one of them—and the cycle of emotions undergone by his playthings was virtually always the same.

First would come surprise. More like shock, really, as the realization struck them that this man was not the harmless person they thought he was. Surprise would be followed immediately by fear. It wasn't quite terror; that would come later. Rather, it was more of a realization that things were spinning out of control and they knew everything was going wrong but did not yet realize just *how* wrong.

After that would come resistance and a stubborn belief that if they worked hard enough at convincing him to let them go, he might change his plans and target a different girl. This was always the most entertaining part of the whole experience for Milo until the actual torture started. Some of the girls would beg and plead, others would act tough, putting up a brave front, displaying a belligerence they could not possibly feel. Some would sweet-talk him, coming on to him like a lover, as if maybe he was too stupid to see through the obvious ruse. He hated that, being treated like an idiot by a common streetwalker.

Eventually, though, the girls always reached the breaking point. Often it was not until he started in on them with his knives and his pliers, but it always happened. They would break down and begin screaming (hence the all-important duct-tape gag) and babbling incoherently, unable due to fear and pain to manage a coherent sentence or even an intelligible word.

The cycle was as regular as the tides in Boston Harbor. But this girl was different, which of course made him hate her even more but also—if he was being honest with himself, which he always tried to be—fear her just a little bit. It wasn't a fear that she might overpower him and somehow escape. That was a complete impossibility, so unlikely as to be laughable.

Rather, it was a twinge of concern, a vague notion that he might be unable to gauge her reactions properly and thus be ineffective in controlling her. With everything that had happened over the last few minutes, this clean-cut, innocent All-American beauty should have been well on her way to her inevitable nervous breakdown. And yet there she stood, clad only in bra and panties, clearly uncomfortable about her near-nakedness but standing ramrod-straight and looking him in the eye, determined not to let him get the upper hand.

It was a ridiculous notion, of course. He already had the upper hand and was not about to relinquish it. But it did throw him off his game for just a moment. He reached behind his back, stroked the knife handle, comforted by its presence, excited he would be getting an opportunity to use it, and very soon now.

He said, "Lie down on the couch," and she stood there, gazing into the distance, as if just now realizing she had left the iron on or forgotten to put in the roast beef for dinner. Jesus, this bitch was annoying!

"I said, get your pretty little ass onto the couch." He raised his voice for emphasis and the woman came back from wherever she had gone, blinking hard and looking at him in surprise, almost like she had forgotten he was there. Again, annoying as hell.

A tiny flicker of fear passed across her eyes and then she seemed to regain her composure and it disappeared. *Not for long*, Milo thought. *Pretty soon it will be back for good.* She eased into a sitting position on the threadbare couch, crossing her legs and folding her arms across her chest. She looked good, had a great figure, well-toned abs, smallish tits but very proportional, and long, lean, athletic legs. For a moment Milo wished he was like most men. He could have had a field day with this girl.

But he *wasn't* like most men. An attractive female form did nothing for him unless he was working it over with a knife or pliers, stabbing and slashing and ripping. Then, and only then, would he find himself getting hard. Then, and only then, would he be able to achieve sexual release.

Of course, he had no intention of letting this girl in on that little secret. It had been his experience that the longer a playmate thought she was managing to avoid being raped, the easier she was to control and the longer she would remain compliant.

He eyed her, seated demurely like a virgin on prom night. "That's a good start," he sneered. "Now, lie across the couch on your back."

The fear returned to her eyes, this time not just flickering across them but thundering into them like a runaway freight train. Milo felt a twinge in his groin as his body reacted to this demonstration of the power he held over his victim.

The girl hesitated, just as she had done when instructed to strip, but after a moment she seemed to acknowledge the helplessness of her situation. She lifted her feet, knees still locked together, and swung them onto the plush cushions. Then she slid her upper body down along the couch-back, never taking her eyes off Milo's, until finally arriving at the position he had intended, fully horizontal with her head propped up on the armrest.

A smile spread across his face and he pulled the long knife out of its makeshift scabbard at his back. He studied his victim like an artist pondering a blank canvas. An electric tension hung in the air. Milo could not see the older broad—she was behind him, still trussed up on her chair next to the unconscious hero who had tried to save the day—but nevertheless he knew she was trying to avert her eyes and failing. She didn't want to watch but she had to, which added a nice little charge to the excitement he was already feeling.

At last he stepped forward, knife held firmly in his right hand.

And the girl said, "There's something you should know."

46

Cait thought she had done a pretty good job of keeping herself together until the crazy bastard told her to lie down on the couch. That was when she thought the tenuous grip she had managed to maintain over her emotions might come crashing apart, like water rushing out of a smashed drinking glass.

The thought of lying nearly naked, utterly exposed in front of this monster, was terrifying. It made no logical sense, of course. Realistically, she should have been just as frightened sitting on the couch with her legs crossed and her arms folded. None of that would provide her with the slightest protection if Milo decided to begin wielding his blade.

But then, nothing that had happened since leaving Tampa made sense anyway. A simple trip up the East Coast to reunite with a long-lost parent had turned into a nightmare of the highest order. This whole experience was a tumble down the rabbit hole, a field trip to hell, an inexplicable descent into madness.

So in a matter of seconds, when the lunatic grinned his greasy, terrible grin and told her that sitting on the couch wasn't good enough, that she would have to uncurl her limbs and stretch out on her back, her body almost completely unclothed, Cait Connelly fully and unforgettably discovered the meaning of the phrase, "the last straw." A roaring that only she could hear filled her ears and puffy black clouds bloomed in her vision and she thought for one awful moment that she was suffering a stroke and that she would either pass out from the debilitating fear or just freeze up and turn into a gibbering, drooling mental case.

But again the thought of Kevin kept her going. His condition had not improved, he was still unconscious and taped to a chair, hanging on to life by a thread, blood slowly seeping out of him, still depending on her resourcefulness for whatever slim chance at survival he might have.

She clamped down on her fear and forced the clouds away.

Forced the roaring freight train out of her ears as well.

Did the only thing she could think of that might buy her a little more time, although what good could possibly come from it, she had no idea.

She started talking as he moved toward her, the bloodstained knife held in front of him in both hands like some religious icon. "There's something you should know," she said, and he stopped dead in his tracks and stood unmoving. He stared at her, seemingly flummoxed by this unexpected development. It was clearly not the reaction he had been expecting.

"What are you talking about?" he said.

Cait knew his indecision would not last long, so she pressed on, willing her voice to remain steady, making up her strategy as she went. "I'm your sister."

Milo shook his head and Cait wondered whether he was disagreeing with her statement or simply trying to process it. Maybe he was doing both. "What the fuck are you talking about, bitch?" he finally managed. "I don't have a sister. I'm an only child, and thank God for that."

Cait wondered what he meant by the last part of that statement but continued on quickly, while she still had his attention and before he came to the conclusion talking was pointless.

"You were adopted as a baby, weren't you?" She was grasping at straws, trying desperately to recall the incredible story her mother had related to her, putting things together as she went, wondering as she talked whether she hoped it was all true or all a lie.

Milo eyed her suspiciously. "Yes, I was adopted, so what? And how did you know that?"

"I knew it," Cait answered, her voice growing stronger and more confident, "because I was adopted, too. And I just learned the story of my history yesterday. I learned it from my real mother. The same woman who is *your* real mother. The woman sitting right over there." She risked lifting her arm and pointing across the room at Virginia, hoping he wouldn't interpret the movement as a threat and slash at her with the knife.

He didn't. He followed her motion dumbly, making a slow half-turn toward the frail older woman duct-taped to her own kitchen chair, her mangled hand still dripping blood slowly onto the floor. Virginia closed her eyes and hung her head before nodding slowly, a mute affirmation of Cait's story.

"You see things, don't you?" she continued. "In your mind, I mean. You see things in your mind from other people's perspective. You know things you couldn't possibly know and it's always been that way, ever since you were a very young boy. Am I right?"

The man's jaw had gone slack and his eyes glazed over. He still clung to the knife but it seemed to have been forgotten, at least for the time being.

"I've always seen things," he whispered. "I never understood it but I've always been able to see pictures, like mental movies, of things happening in other people's lives. Sometimes it's overwhelming, sometimes the visions just keep coming, one after another, they won't stop for hours sometimes, and it's just so fucking...exhausting..."

Cait nodded, hoping to keep him talking, hoping against all reasonable hope that by beginning to forge a connection with him, however fragile and tenuous, he might see her as a human being rather than simply as a potential victim, and that in so doing she—and, hopefully, Virginia and Kevin as well—might somehow have a chance to escape this nightmare with their lives.

"I've always had the ability as well," she said gently. "I call those visions 'Flickers,' because they are like those old-time black-and-white movies that flicker up on the screen when you watch them.

"Our mother didn't want to give us up," she continued. "I just found that out yesterday. It was the hardest decision she ever had to make; it literally tore her family apart. But she had no choice in the matter—" Cait stopped talking, suddenly realizing she had gone too far, remembering what Virginia had said about the history of fratricide among twins going back centuries in her family's history, remembering what Virginia had said about *her* becoming a target should she ever be reunited with her brother.

Suddenly she understood that he didn't comprehend his burning hatred for her any better than she did.

But the problem with making things up as you went was that you didn't have time to plan ahead, and Cait immediately regretted her words, knowing they could logically lead only to one question in her brother's psychotic mind: Why? Why had his mother cast him away? And the answer to that question would likely lead to a knife in the heart, not just for her but for Virginia as well and probably Kevin, just to round things out.

She hurriedly tried to steer the conversation in another direction, desperate to get onto safer ground. "But it doesn't matter," she said. "Adoptive parents can be wonderful; they can treat you with love and respect just like biological parents. In fact, you could argue that if they were unable to have children of their own, they may appreciate the opportunity to raise kids even *more* than biological parents would."

Milo's face hardened, and as he tightened his grip on the knife, Cait realized immediately she had said something wrong, had blundered into a taboo area.

"Or," he answered, "they might treat you like an object, a slave, an animal to be beaten and abused and tortured."

Milo took a menacing step forward and Cait shrank back, wishing she could disappear into the couch cushions.

"How nice that you were given parents who treated you with *'love and respect'*"—he spoke in a falsetto voice filled with sugary sweetness, the anger behind the words spilling out despite his tone, or maybe because of it.

"*My* parents never gave me a chance. They were well-respected in the community, but at home my father was a monster, using his belt as a motivational tool, flaying my back until it bled for the smallest transgression, using a fork to gouge ridges into my skin if I took too long bringing the trash out to the curb."

Cait's eyes widened in horror now as well as in fear. Milo's anger seemed to be building on itself as he spoke, gaining momentum, taking on a life of its own. He was working himself into a rage, exactly what she was trying to avoid, and there was nothing she could do about it.

"You want to see the *'love and respect'* you seem to value so highly?"

She stayed silent, afraid of saying the wrong thing again, and he continued. "Here's an example of *'love and respect.'*"

He pivoted suddenly, showing his back to Cait, and raised his shirttail. He was not wearing an undershirt, and Cait clamped a hand to her mouth in horror at the sight of his skin. Puckered scars crisscrossed his back, raised and angry, hundreds of them, tiny ridged welts, remnants of the torture he claimed to have received as a child.

"My entire body is like this," he said, "practically every square inch of skin that could be covered up to hide the evidence. My father was an animal, but he was also very careful.

"So don't sit there and try to tell me how wonderful it is that I was given up for adoption. I have no idea whether what you're saying is true, whether that dried-up old bitch back there is my mother, but if she is, I consider her just as responsible for what happened to me as a child as my adoptive parents.

"Now," he said, dropping his shirt into place and turning slowly back toward the couch. "Any more bright ideas about how you're going to soften me up so I won't carve you like a Thanksgiving turkey?"

Cait closed her eyes, breathing in short gasps, trying to control her burgeoning terror and mostly failing. There was nothing she could say to save them. Family meant nothing to this man. He had been broken beyond saving, maybe by his adoptive parents, maybe by genetics, but any connection she had hoped to forge with this lost but terrifyingly dangerous soul was turning out to be a pipe dream.

It was over.

She was going to die and so was Kevin, and if there had been any chance, no matter how unlikely, that Virginia would survive what was about to happen here, that was likely gone as well.

47

Milo could not believe how the fucking little bitch had tried to manipulate him. Her efforts had been transparent and pointless, and, if anything, served only to increase the black rage coursing through his system. He had never heard a more bullshit story in his entire life. She was his sister? It was the most ridiculous thing he had ever heard.

Then again, she *had* known about the visions he had been cursed with his entire life, and she *had* known he was adopted. It seemed highly unlikely that could be a mere coincidence.

But still, suppose she was telling the truth and she really was his sister, and the old hag taped to the kitchen chair really was his mother. Say for just a second that it was all true. What did that change?

Nothing.

It changed nothing, except, as he had informed his "sister," it now became all the more critical that he complete what he had set out to do here today.

Now, though, instead of skinning one victim, he would do two. His intention from the very beginning had been to kill everyone when he was done with the young bitch, despite what he had told his "mother" earlier about not hurting her. It only made sense. It would serve no good purpose to leave any eyewitnesses.

So in reality, his plans only required some minor tinkering. Rather than making it quick with the old broad, if there was any time left after finishing off the girl, he would take his time and have a little fun with Mommy Dearest as well. It seemed only appropriate, just on the off chance the younger one was telling the truth about the familial relationship. He had meant it when he said his biological mother was responsible for his horrific upbringing. If she hadn't thrown him out like yesterday's trash, he wouldn't have been adopted by his psychopathic father and willfully unseeing mother and permanently damaged.

It made perfect sense.

The young girl had stopped trying to soften him up. It was obvious she had finally reached the conclusion that there was nothing she could say to change his mind about what was going to happen here. Her eyes were closed and she seemed terrified but resigned to her fate.

In some ways, that was a bit of a disappointment. Milo liked it when his victims struggled. It increased his arousal because it demonstrated his dominance over them, thereby making the experience even more enjoyable.

At least for him.

There was one advantage to this new development, though. Less struggling meant the process would take less time, and although he would normally have preferred to go slowly and do the torture right, the dead cop cooling in the doorway changed everything. He would soon have lots of company.

In fact, he was a little surprised more pigs weren't here already. With all that had happened since his arrival here in Everett, Milo realized he had completely lost track of the time. It seemed as though it was moving simultaneously fast and slow.

He picked up his duct tape and unrolled a decent-sized strip, then wound it around his "sister's" ankles. She barely struggled and didn't utter a word, and for a moment Milo wondered why. It seemed this goddamned girl was keeping him constantly off-balance and he hated that.

Then he realized she was still half expecting to be raped, and the act of tying her legs *together* rather than apart had come as such a relief that she wasn't sure how to react.

Whatever.

She would find out soon enough that being raped would have been a walk in the park compared to what she was about to experience.

He ripped off another even longer strip of tape and secured her ankles to one end of the couch, winding it over her legs and around the armrest. He slapped the silver surface to ensure proper adhesion and allowed himself a moment to soak in the sight of his next, and arguably greatest, triumph.

She was a good-looking piece of meat, much more desirable than Rae Ann the Schoolgirl Hooker. More desirable than any of his previous playthings. For one thing, she appeared fresh and girlish, rather than used-up and cynical as all the prostitutes did, no matter how young or new to the game they were. And while his college girl victims weren't hardened and cold like hookers, none of them had ever possessed the kind of worldly self-assurance and dignity this girl seemed to. It was a real turn-on.

As an added bonus, she was perfectly proportioned; he could see that now with her body stretched out in front of him, her attributes barely concealed by her bra and tiny black panties.

He ran his eyes up and down his "sister's" form and licked his lips slowly, not because he felt any sexual arousal from the sight of her near-nakedness, but because he knew it would confuse and terrify her. It was all part of the game, designed to keep her off-balance, and even though she had been the one keeping *him* off-balance so far, things were about to change.

Winking at her with a sly smile, he rose from the couch and strolled to the window to check on the scene outside the house. He knew he should be rushing to get the job completed and get the hell out while he still could, but he was just having so much fucking fun that he couldn't bring himself to hurry.

He pulled the heavy blue crushed-velvet curtain to the side—Milo had always thought his adoptive mother had horrendous taste in home furnishings but this broad's house put her to shame—and sucked in a breath reflexively. Police cars were scattered all over the development, parked haphazardly, and cops were scurrying around like ants at a fucking picnic. A big, armored SWAT van was idling at the curb halfway up the street.

The moment he appeared at the window a couple of the blue-uniformed motherfuckers did a double take and raised their weapons. They seemed so surprised by his appearance they were temporarily frozen in indecision. He let go of the curtain and it slid closed with a thick swish of material.

This was not good.

48

It happened again as the crazy bastard with the knife—Cait couldn't bring herself to think of him as her brother no matter how hard she tried—stalked across the room to look out the front widow. That little *push,* the signal that a Flicker was about to start, tried to nudge its way inside Cait's head once again.

She closed her eyes and concentrated, and as she had done previously, repelled the Flicker before it could begin. She had bigger issues to worry about right now than dealing with a mind-movie.

But something had been bothering her, unspoken but felt, hanging around the edges of her consciousness. She had been so busy trying to stay alive she hadn't been able to pin down what it was, but now that Milo had stepped away for a moment, it crystallized in her mind: why the hell was she suddenly manifesting abilities concerning the Flickers that had never existed before? Did it have something to do with the proximity of her mother, who had similar abilities? Was it somehow related to the sudden appearance of her brother, the Human Psychotic Break himself?

Either way, Cait succeeded in blocking the Flicker, an important consideration since Milo's mood seemed suddenly to have changed. He raced across the room toward her, his hurried steps in stark contrast to the almost languid way he had approached the window.

Something was happening, and it was happening outside.

The police!

The police were here!

What else could it be?

It made sense. The murdered officer had been out of contact for a while now, and the Everett police must have figured out that something was wrong. Cait's heart skipped a beat and she began to allow herself to hope that maybe, just maybe, they could still escape this nightmare alive.

Then Milo passed by the couch, not even glancing at her. He strode hurriedly into the kitchen and grabbed the last of Virginia's kitchen chairs, then turned and dragged it across the floor, placing it next to the couch. He held the knife tightly in his right hand as he eased into the chair, a look of grim determination on his face, immediately dashing Cait's irrational hope of rescue. He was still in control, and it was clear he intended to stay in control until he finished whatever he came here to do.

She forced herself back against the cushions, levering her body into the V where the couch-back met the seat, pushing with her bound ankles against the armrest, trying to escape him.

It was stupid even to try, she knew that. There was no way she could simply disappear into the couch like the magician's helper in some third-rate Vegas floor show, but rationality was beginning to slip away. The knife was big and long and razor-sharp, and the glittering deadly blade appeared mammoth as he displayed it mere inches from her face. Sickening smears of blackish maroon blood still stained it, left over from the butchering of the police officer. The killer had wiped the blade but had done so hurriedly and incompletely.

Cait strained against the back of the couch and Milo laughed, the sound simultaneously brutal and mocking. "Going somewhere?" he said.

She didn't answer. She couldn't answer. She couldn't form the words. All she could think about was that big knife and the human being it had been used to kill, and the dreadful knowledge that she was moments away from suffering a similar fate.

Milo grabbed her right wrist, pulling it roughly toward him and plunking it onto his lap. Cait struggled and bucked and yanked her arm away and without warning her brother clubbed her in the side of the head with the knife handle.

"Knock it off," he rasped, veins sticking out on his forehead, his lips pressed in a bloodless line across his teeth. "If you struggle, I'll make this much, much worse for you. And that's something you don't want, believe me."

Cait believed him.

He returned her wrist to its previous location on his lap, staring into her eyes as he did so. Then he reached down and *slashed* it quickly across her skin and she screamed and he clamped his hand over her mouth and she looked down at her arm expecting to see blood gushing from the gash and there was nothing there and he laughed, long and loud.

"I used the dull end of the knife," he said, still chuckling. "This time."

And at that moment Cait realized she hated him. He was inhuman. Any sympathy she might have had for his horrible upbringing, any consideration she might have given him for being her brother, was gone. She saw him for what he was, a playground bully, a little boy burning ants in a field with a magnifying glass, a psychopathic monster without any shred of humanity.

Milo's forehead wrinkled in concentration as he placed her arm in his lap one more time and Cait knew this time there would be no sick jokes, no fake cutting of skin. This time he was really going to slice her.

She whimpered, sounding pathetic, knowing it and hating herself for it but unable to stop. Almost as if on cue, across the room Kevin moaned, the first sound he had made since before the cop's murder. As one, Cait and Milo glanced over at the interruption, Cait thankful not just for the few extra seconds it afforded her before the butchering began but also for the first real evidence in quite some time that Kevin was alive.

She watched as his head lolled, moving from his right shoulder to his left, his eyes still closed. Blood bubbled in a thick wad out of the knife wound in his chest, squeezing out around Cait's makeshift bandage. His eyelids fluttered open and he seemed to take a look around the room. They passed over Cait unseeingly and then closed again and all movement stopped.

"That was interesting," Milo said with a ghastly smile, and then he reached down and instead of slicing her arm as Cait had been expecting, he turned the knife blade sideways and peeled the skin of her arm back like he was peeling an apple. The shock was so great she gave no reaction at all. Not a scream, not a cry of pain, nothing.

And then Virginia's telephone rang.

49

Milo was annoyed but unsurprised when the phone jangled, the old broad's ringtone set to sound just like the ancient black rotary phone his psycho parents had had in their kitchen in Amesbury.

It figured. This was just his luck. No sooner did he finally get down to business with the cute little bitch than the cops would pick the worst possible moment to stick their fucking pig noses into his business. He had no doubt it was the police calling. The old bitty who owned the house obviously didn't have many friends, who else would it be?

The phone rang again and he ignored it. The little bitch's eyes widened, then filled with water, and as her brain finally deciphered the distress signals being sent to it by the nerve endings in her injured arm, she let loose a jagged, panicked scream and Milo clapped his hand once more over her mouth.

He had not gagged her because he wanted to fully enjoy her re-actions, but that had been a mistake on his part. The police were tak-ing things slowly for now, but if they heard screaming coming from inside the house, they would undoubtedly be prompted to act more swiftly than he wanted them to.

The strip of skin he had peeled hung back from her arm, red and raw, flapping against her elbow as a surprisingly small amount of blood flowed. Milo had been doing this a long time and he was very skilled with a knife. In another life he thought he may have been a surgeon, not that he had any desire whatsoever to save people. The knife-play every day would have been a real charge, though.

He sighed. In the kitchen the phone rang and rang and he knew that in order to buy himself the time he would need to finish up here he would have to answer it. An unanswered call would prompt too many questions in the heads of the pigs and they would be tempted to storm the house. They would launch concussion grenades through the windows and smash down the door and overpower him and everything would be over.

Goddamn it! Why couldn't they just have left him alone?

Milo swore under his breath. He eased the strip of skin gently back onto the lucky little bitch's arm and she instantly covered it up with her left hand, whimpering and panting like the sweet little victim he wanted. Unfortunately he had no time to enjoy it.

Yet.

He leaned over and grabbed his roll of duct tape off the floor. He peeled off a generous strip and slapped it over the bitch's mouth, taking the time to ensure it was tightly sealed in place. He didn't need her working it off and then screaming while he was on the phone with the pigs.

The telephone continued to ring.

Once he was satisfied with his handiwork, he ripped off more tape and used it to secure her arms to her bare belly, allowing her to keep her left hand covered over her damaged right arm. He wasn't an unreasonable man, after all.

Then he stood and took one step toward the phone just as it stopped ringing.

He turned back to the girl and said, "Doesn't that just figure? The minute you make the dentist appointment, the damned tooth stops aching, you know what I mean?"

She stared back at him uncomprehendingly. The tears that had filled her eyes were now leaking out of them, rolling down her pretty cheeks in twin tracks. She continued whimpering and panting into her duct-tape gag and Milo knew she was going to be even more fun to torture than he had anticipated.

First things first, though. He would have to deal with the pigs. He needed to buy himself enough time to enjoy his adventure with the nearly naked girl on the couch. He still hoped to do Dear Old Mom, too, but only time would tell on that one. At the very least, he wanted to make sure the girl suffered long and hard before he snuffed the life out of her. He had come here to do his thing with the young woman and he was going to make damned sure he did it before he left. Whether he was in handcuffs or in a body bag when that happened didn't really make much difference to Milo Cain. He had always possessed a single-minded sense of purpose, and it was coming in mighty handy right now.

In the kitchen the phone began to ring again, the bell shrill and harsh and penetrating. Milo smiled. He had known they would call again immediately and he was right, as always. He was filled with confidence. He knew he could pull this off. He was smarter than the police and more motivated, to boot.

He strolled into the kitchen and picked up the receiver. "Yellow." The key was to sound as in-control and carefree as possible. The closer the cops felt he was to snapping, the more likely they would be to do something counterproductive, like storm the building before he had a chance to do what he needed to do.

"Hey there," came the response. "You're a tough guy to get ahold of."

Milo was silent. He hadn't heard a question, so volunteering information was pointless.

"My name is Lieutenant Sanders," the voice continued. "I'd like it if you would call me Bob. To whom am I speaking?"

"My name is not important," Milo answered.

"Okay, then, let me ask you this: are you the man in charge in there?"

Milo laughed and looked around the room. The dead cop lay in the doorway, the hero boyfriend lolled unconscious on his chair, the dried-up old hag sat next to him pleading with her eyes for her life, and the stupid little bitch who had started all of this lay in her underwear on the couch, clasping her wounded arm and moaning softly into her gag.

"You could say that."

"Okay, how about if you just give me a first name, nothing that could be used to identify you, just something I can call you so we can get to know each other a bit, how does that sound?"

Milo thought about it for a second. What the hell; it wasn't like he was going to get out alive, anyway, his only goal was to delay the inevitable long enough to finish skinning the little bitch and maybe her mother, too.

"Fair enough," he said. "My name is Milo."

"Excellent. Well, Milo, first things first. I need to know what the situation is in there. Is everyone alive? Does anybody need medical attention?"

Milo didn't even hesitate. He knew if the negotiator realized his pig brother was cooling on the floor, it would only be a matter of minutes before he was either on his way out of the house in handcuffs or lying dead next to him. There was no way he would have the time to finish the little bitch on the couch unless the cops thought there was at least a chance everyone was going to exit the building still breathing.

"Or course everyone's alive," he said.

"That's wonderful. Next question, Milo: One of the neighbors saw an Everett police officer enter the house a little while ago and he has not come back out. May I speak with him, please?"

"Gee, Bob, I don't see any reason for that, at least not at this point. You'll have to take my word that he's doing just fine. He's decided to take a little break in here and join the party."

"You never answered my question regarding injuries. Does anyone in the house require medical attention?"

Milo glanced at the hero boyfriend, wondering whether he was even still alive. His face was pale and his lips were purple and he appeared either dead or knocking at the door.

"You know," he said casually, "everyone in here has been pretty cooperative. Aside from a minor bruise or two, we're all doing just peachy."

"I'm glad to hear that. Since that's the case, let me tell you a little bit about myself. I've been a law-enforcement professional for almost seventeen years and a member of the Everett Hostage Negotiation Team for the last ten years. I've seen these things end well and I've seen them end badly, and I very much want this particular situation to end well.

"My question to you, Milo, is this: What do we need to do to ensure a happy ending to this scenario?"

"A happy ending," Milo repeated into the phone. "Well, let's see. You need to understand that I am in control here. The first time I see someone sneaking along the side of the house, everyone dies. The first time you people try to storm the house, everyone dies. The first time a flash-bang comes through a window, anywhere in the house, everyone dies. Do you see where this conversation is going?"

"You've made yourself very clear. Thank you for that. It's important everyone know where they stand. And that includes you, Milo. I'm sure you realize that as long as all the people in that house stay alive and unharmed, things are much more likely to end well. Now, let's get down to the heart of the matter—"

Milo almost laughed out loud. *The heart of the matter.* That was a good one, considering he had come so close to stabbing the hero boyfriend right in the heart. The pig cop negotiator continued droning on and Milo had to force himself to concentrate. All he wanted was to get back to the couch and resume his work with the little bitch lying there so invitingly.

"So, really," the pig cop negotiator was saying, "what it all boils down to is this: what do you want? If you tell us why you're doing this, maybe we can take some action to resolve whatever is bothering you and we can all go home."

Except me, Milo thought. *Me, you would just as soon shoot in the head as not. That little nugget you're keeping to yourself, though, aren't you?* He forced himself to calm down and focus. All he needed was to buy enough time to finish what he had started.

"What's bothering me?" he answered. "Tell you what, let's get into that later. First things first, as you so aptly stated a moment ago. We've been having so much fucking fun in here that everyone is famished. How about you send out for a couple of pizzas for us?"

He partially covered the telephone's mouthpiece with his hand, making sure he could be heard through the line. "What kind of pizza do you guys like?" he said, getting dull stares in return, at least from the two other conscious people in the room. They didn't seem to care about pizza. Neither did the dead guy or the unconscious one.

"Pepperoni? Sounds good," he pretended to answer.

"Did you hear that?" he said into the line. "We've reached a consensus that pepperoni is the way to go. I'm more of a veggie man myself, but in the interest of demonstrating that I can play well with others, I've decided to toe the company line. So you go ahead and work on getting that food for us, and when you've done that, you call back and we'll discuss the next step. How does that sound?"

There was a short pause on the other end of the line. Finally Lieutenant Sanders—Bob—said, "Of course we can get some pizza for you. But I'm sure you realize we will need something in return, some gesture of good faith on your part. Perhaps you could release one of the people inside the house in exchange for the food?"

"We'll talk about that when the pizza actually arrives. It's been a pleasure working with you, Bob. Remember, no stupid moves. Let's all try to row in the same direction. Talk to you soon, Bob."

He placed the handset gently down on the receiver and turned toward the little bitch on the couch, happy he had gained some time and excited he could now get back to work.

50

The pain in Cait's arm was excruciating. It felt as though she had jammed the entire limb into a roaring fire in Virginia's fireplace. She had anchored the long flap of skin in place with her left hand before the crazy bastard Milo duct-taped her arms to her belly, and as soon as he walked away to answer the telephone, she lifted her body into a sitting position.

She was able to protect the injury a bit, at least for the time being, huddling as much of her body around it as possible. She knew it wasn't going to matter, that the moment he returned he would force her back into a horizontal position and resume his ghoulish work, but it was a reflexive reaction to the trauma inflicted on her body and one she could not have prevented even if she wanted to.

In the kitchen, Milo replaced the phone on its cradle and hurried back, looking a bit preoccupied but smiling down at her like a doctor who had been called away on an emergency. "I'm sorry for the interruption," he said sweetly. "Those people can be real pests. Now, where were we? Do you remember?"

The terror returned with a vengeance and Cait babbled into her gag, trying to beg for her life, trying to tell him she would do whatever he wanted if only he would stop peeling the skin from her body, but of course it was no use. She could not make herself understood and knew it wouldn't matter even if she could. She began hyperventilating, panting into her gag, feeling faint and light-headed, almost wishing she would pass out so the pain and fear would just go away.

No such luck.

Milo reached out and placed his strong hands on her shoulders and forced her back down on the couch. The moment he let go, her body sprang back up into the sitting position in a desperate attempt to protect her arm.

He made a disappointed *tsk-tsk* sound with his tongue and said, "Apparently you've decided not to cooperate. That's unfortunate, as you'll soon discover. Normally, your reticence would translate into just that much more fun for me, but since we're under a mounting time crunch, I'll have to handle things a bit differently than I'd like." Then he ripped the duct tape off Cait's bare belly without so much as a word of warning. Tiny flecks of skin came with the tape, bonded to the super-sticky surface like flies to flypaper but Cait barely noticed. All she could think about was what was to come.

She lifted her injured arm over her head, left hand still clamped over the awful injury, in a desperate attempt to remove it from Milo's reach. He fumbled on the floor for his duct tape and ripped off another long strip, holding it in front of Cait's eyes with an evil smile.

She knew he was waiting for a reaction and willed herself not to give it to him, but she simply couldn't stop herself. She whimpered and moaned into her gag and he watched for a moment, eyes glazed. Cait noted dispassionately in a dusty corner of her brain that he was getting off on her fear and was disgusted by the knowledge.

He sat and watched her, doing nothing, lost in his reverie, stupid smile creasing his face, and then something seemed to click in his head and he pushed her roughly onto her back once more. He grabbed her left arm and slammed it against the back of the couch, then wound the duct tape over it and around the couch's wooden frame, effectively immobilizing her.

The flap of skin he had created with his knife before the telephone rang hung loosely off her arm now, wet blood dripping onto her belly. The flap was maybe eight inches long and a couple of inches wide—a tiny landing strip carved into her arm—and Cait stared at it with renewed horror as the pain re-intensified, the nerve endings in her arm screaming and complaining and begging for relief.

She panted and moaned and cried into her gag and watched her captor with wild eyes, praying for Kevin to leap out of his chair, miraculously healed, duct-tape bindings flying off him like in a Hollywood movie, or for the dead police officer to spring suddenly back to life and save the day.

But none of that happened. Kevin lay unmoving and pale next to Virginia, and the police officer remained just as dead as he had been since Milo dropped him in the doorway like so much cordwood.

Then the determined psychotic got to work, muttering something about time pressure and pizza deliveries, of all things, and how it was so unfair. Cait didn't understand what the hell he was talking about, but forgot all about it a second later, because that was when he placed the blade of his knife against her skin next to the landing strip he had already made and began carving another.

He drew deftly back on the blade and lifted another strip of skin right off her arm, maybe a half-inch thinner than the first but just as long, and the pain ratcheted up again, she hadn't thought it possible, but God help her, it was. Cait wailed into her gag and bucked against her bindings and she felt the knife dig into the meat of her arm as a result but she continued to struggle as she lost what little remained of her self-control. Her arm burned and throbbed in fiery agony and she forgot all about Virginia and Kevin and even Milo the Butcher himself, as her entire being was fixed on the damage being done to her right arm.

The room turned red around the edges of her vision and a buzzing began in her ears—it sounded as though an airliner was taking off right in the living room—and somewhere deep inside her head Cait knew she was about to lose consciousness. She was going to pass out from the intense pain and she welcomed the relief. She willed herself to lose consciousness, to escape this torture. Whether she lived or died was irrelevant, the only thing that mattered was somehow putting an end to this terrible burning agony consuming her right forearm.

But she didn't pass out.

She wasn't so lucky.

Through the pounding red pain she watched her torturer do his gruesome work. He completed his second pass with the knife, finishing the second tiny runway right next to the first, and examined his handiwork with a critical eye. He was breathing heavily, sweat dotting his skin just above his upper lip.

He glanced at her face and smiled when he noticed her watching him. "Looks good," he said, as though they were discussing tomorrow's weather forecast or the chances of the Tampa Bay Buccaneers reaching the playoffs.

And then he spoke and sent a chill through Cait's overtaxed brain. She hadn't thought things could get any worse. Surely this was it. Surely he was done. Surely he would get up and walk away and leave her alone now.

But this wasn't it. He wasn't done. He didn't get up and walk away.

Instead he smiled that devil's smile and said, "What do you say we work on the other arm now?"

Cait began screaming anew as he reached up and pulled off the strip of tape anchoring her left arm to the back of the couch. He held her arm firmly with both hands as she tried to yank it away, anticipating her actions. He was incredibly strong, or maybe she was just so weakened by now that it wasn't a fair fight. Either way, her struggle was short and it was over quickly and within seconds he had secured her arm—a fresh new canvas for his sick sculpture-work—over his lap.

Cait felt the knife blade sink into her flesh once again as the telephone began to ring in the background and someone cranked the volume of the buzzing in her ears to the max and the pain increased exponentially and Cait screamed into her gag and it felt like her head was going to blast right off her body and—

—and finally, mercifully, Cait Connelly lost consciousness.

51

Milo had known the telephone would ring again and had likewise suspected it would happen at precisely the wrong time. After all, how long did it take to order a couple of fucking pizzas? On the bright side, his little torture toy had just passed out—he must be losing his touch; normally he could keep girls conscious for much longer—so it wasn't like he was being forced to stop in the middle of his fun to answer the damned thing.

"What is it?" he barked into the phone, not bothering with the silly gamesmanship of the last call.

"Hello, Milo, this is Bob. Remember me?"

"Of course I remember you, *Bob,* we just spoke a few minutes ago, for chrissakes. Is there a point to this call? We're all pretty busy in here enjoying ourselves and I'd like to get back to the party."

"Of course, I understand. I just thought you might like to know the pizzas are on their way and will be here in the next few minutes. Is there anything else you think you might need?"

Jesus, Milo thought. *Just my luck to get stuck with some fucking Martha Stewart party-planner-in-training.* "No," he said, trying to keep his voice calm. "The pizza will be plenty."

"Okay, fine. Maybe now would be a good time to discuss how we're going to get it into the house. I can have one of my men deliver it to the door, but I'll need your assurance that you won't take any action to harm him when he does. It would be a real career-ender for me to have a man killed delivering pizza, you know what I mean?"

Milo shook his head. Was this guy for real? "Don't worry," he said. "I promise I won't hurt your precious police officer. I certainly don't want to be responsible for ending your car—"

BOOM!

The entire house shook on its decades-old foundation as the front door was blown off its hinges. Instantly Milo knew he had been played for a sucker. There was no pizza, there was never going to be any pizza, the pig cops had been playing him just as he thought he had been playing them. *Goddammit!*

He rushed from the kitchen back into the living room, vaguely aware as he crossed the end of the hallway of the ruined door lying flat on the floor and a cluster of SWAT team members, suited up and armed for bear, gathered on the small front landing in the process of storming the house.

This sucked. He was not going to get to finish skinning the little bitch alive, but if he was going down, he would make good and goddamned sure he took her with him. Undoubtedly the rescue pigs would exercise at least a modicum of caution; hopefully that would give him the few seconds he would need to finish the girl.

She wouldn't go in the way he wanted, slowly and in excruciating pain, but at least he would still have the opportunity to end her miserable life. With any luck, perhaps they would meet up again in hell and he could properly finish what he had started.

Milo rushed into the living room, knife clutched securely in his right hand. The little bitch lay half on the couch and half off it, her feet still securely taped to the armrest, her body flopped off the cushions, her bare shoulders, arms, and head lying on the floor. She was still unconscious, which represented another disappointment because Milo had hoped that he would at least get the satisfaction of knowing the bitch had seen it coming: terrifying a sweet, innocent little thing beyond her endurance as he pulled the knife blade across her throat from ear to ear, severing the jugular, would have been the perfect way to spend his last few seconds on earth.

No matter. It was time to get to it. He could hear the heavy *clomp clomp clomp* of SWAT Team boots on the bloodstained hardwood floor as they came to get him. He smiled. They would be too late. Maybe he could even finish off the little bitch and then leap across the room and dispatch Dear Old Mom before they came around the corner with guns blazing.

Mr. Midnight skidded to a stop in front of the prone body of his greatest conquest. She still hadn't moved. Her head rested on her mutilated right arm, her left hand curled under her chest. A strip of bloody skin lay on the floor surrounded by tiny flecks of the bitch's blood, apparently the result of her falling off the couch. It served the annoying pain-in-the-ass right.

He leaned over the motionless body and lowered his knife. It would take just a fraction of a second to draw the blade across her throat and end her life. He couldn't wait.

52

There it was again, that relentless *push,* the feeling of a Flicker trying to force its way into her head, the very same sensation she had fought off time after time over the course of the last couple of hours.

Cait's eyes fluttered open and she tried desperately to focus, but she just couldn't manage it, and then her eyes closed again of their own accord. She felt groggy and woozy and somehow oddly disconnected from her body. From somewhere far away came the sensation of millions of pins and needles being shot into her arm at the same time out of some hellish weapon.

Or maybe her arm was on fire. Yes, that was it, her arm was on fire. She was so very tired and all she wanted to do was sleep but she couldn't because her arm was on fire, it was burning and blistering and the extreme unrelenting pain was keeping her awake.

And now came that infernal *push* and at first she tried to repel it one more time. But why? Why bother trying to resist it? What would be the point? Why had she tried to keep it out in the first place? There must have been a reason, maybe even a good one, but for the life of her she couldn't remember now what it might have been.

So her eyes fluttered and her vision wavered and her arm burned horribly and finally she relented. She stopped trying to resist the *push.* She was too exhausted to concentrate that hard, anyway.

The moment she gave in, the Flicker flooded her brain, filling her senses with the sights and sounds and smells of a confrontation. It felt hyper-real. She could smell the stale pungent odor of sweat and adrenaline and fear; especially fear. Cait was inside Virginia's body, she was inside her long-lost mother's body, and her mother was trying to escape from...she was trying to escape from...oh, God, she was trying to escape from *Milo!*

She was on the floor, she was flat on her back on the floor and she began scrabbling backward down the hallway in an attempt to buy some time, she needed to buy enough time to reach into the pocket of her sweater and pull out her gun, the one she had hidden away in her pocket. It was a little Smith & Wesson Model 40 handgun that she had owned for decades and had never used but had kept for protection because sometimes Everett could get a little dangerous and you could never tell when you might need to defend yourself.

She scuttled backward, trying to open up a little room between herself and this young man who had barged into her home with bad intent written all over his face. He wanted to hurt her, she could tell he wanted to hurt her and somehow she knew he wanted more than that. He wanted to hurt the daughter she had just met for the first time in thirty years, she knew that, too, and she was not going to allow it to happen. She would crab-walk away from him and then she would pull the gun out of her pocket and hold it on him, she would hold it on him to stop him from doing whatever he was planning on doing and then she would call the police and—

—and she slammed into the hallway wall with her back. She slammed into the wall because after all it had been half a century since she had crab-walked and what had seemed natural and easy when she was ten years old wasn't quite so natural or easy anymore. She slammed into the wall and the impact jarred the little S&W out of her pocket and the intruder saw it on the floor and his eyes widened in surprise.

She reached down and grabbed the gun and flicked off the safety
and prepared to blast him to hell, but he wound up and *kicked* it before she had a chance to pull the trigger. He *kicked* it and it skittered
away across the floor and into the living room where it disappeared
under...it disappeared under...it disappeared under...

And then Cait understood.

Despite her near-unconsciousness and her wooziness and the fire
burning in her arm and her fear of Milo and what he was doing to
her, despite all of it, she finally understood. The Flicker disappeared,
vanishing from her head like the popping of a soap bubble in bathwa-
ter.

She understood it all with a clarity that bordered on mystical. It
wasn't a typical Flicker she had been fighting off all afternoon. Typical Flickers were random and held absolutely no meaning most of the
time. They were pointless snippets of people's lives.

This had been different. Cait realized now that this Flicker had
come from Virginia purposely, it was something she had been trying
desperately to force into her daughter's brain because it was something she needed her to see, but in Cait's determination to concentrate fully on fighting off the monster that was her brother Milo, she
had forced it away, time after time.

But now she understood. She understood Virginia's desperation.
Because when the monster had seen the gun fall out of Virginia's
sweater pocket and had kicked it away, it had sailed down the hallway
and skittered into the living room, eventually coming to rest under
the couch.

This couch.

The couch currently serving as Cait Connelly's combination
prison/torture chamber.

And Virginia had remembered.

Far off in the distance, Cait heard an explosion and felt the house
shake. She wondered if it had been hit by lightning, or whether per-

haps an airplane bound for nearby Logan International Airport had fallen out of the sky and crash-landed on it. She waited for her life to be snuffed out like some insignificant bug's from the airplane explosion but when nothing happened, she snaked her left hand underneath the couch, feeling around on the floor with the back of her hand for the gun, for the little Smith & Wesson revolver waiting patiently to be found.

And against all odds she found it. Her knuckles brushed the cold steel plating of the gun and pushed it a little farther away on the varnished floor and Cait, incredibly, chuckled. It would be the very definition of irony, she thought, to find the gun, the object of her salvation, only to push it out of reach before being able to use it.

But it wasn't out of reach. She strained and stretched, doing her best to ignore the horrible fiery pain in her right arm, the arm Milo had skinned from wrist to elbow, and when her hand brushed that cold steel plating again she wrapped her long, delicate fingers around it like a drowning swimmer grasping a life vest.

She secured the gun in her hand and then, with the advancing form of her attacker approaching rapidly in her peripheral vision, pulled it out from under the couch and curled her hand under her breast and closed her eyes just as he skidded to a stop in front of her. She hoped the pistol was hidden from his view by the angle of her body but could not be sure.

There was noise and what sounded like an approaching army and Cait realized the crash that had jarred her awake moments ago was not an airplane falling from the sky onto Virginia's house, it was the police breaching the door and coming, finally coming, to rescue her and Virginia and Kevin.

But they were too late, despite the fact that they were in the house, or at least *about* to be in the house. She risked opening an eye and when she did, she saw Milo, the man who had begun torturing her and was going to continue torturing her until she was dead—it was all true, everything her mother had told her this morning about Flickers and her bloody family history of twin murdering twin was all true—standing right above her, not two feet away.

In his hand he held the knife he had used to peel her skin from her bones, only this time he was not going to use it merely to torture her and cause intense pain. This time he was going to use it to slit her throat. He leaned down, thinking she was unconscious, and swiveled his wrist and brought the knife blade forward and—

—and Cait swiveled her own hand, her left hand, the hand holding her mother's snub-nosed Smith & Wesson revolver. She pulled the weapon out from under her body and she pointed it at Milo's face and suddenly everything ground to a halt. The sounds of the police forcing their way into the house faded away to nothing and somehow Cait's fear did the same. She was no longer a helpless victim, no longer cowering in fear against an attacker with intentions she could not comprehend.

Milo froze, the lethal knife poised inches away from the delicate, tender skin of Cait's throat. And for seconds that seemed to stretch into hours, nothing happened and nobody moved. This nightmare day had come down to a deadly standoff.

Cait spoke, her voice somehow strong and steady despite the pain hammering her right arm and the adrenaline coursing through her body. "It doesn't have to end like this. It doesn't have to end at all," she said, and for an instant she saw regret and longing share space with the madness in her twin's eyes.

But only for an instant. Then it was gone, replaced by a cold hard calculating shrewdness, and Cait knew it was over.

He opened his mouth as if to speak but no words came out. And then he half-smiled and lunged with the knife and Cait felt the tip of the blade gash the side of her neck just under her ear, and she expected more white-hot pain, but there was no pain, there was nothing at all, just an emptiness she knew she would never be able to fill.

And she pulled the trigger.

The Smith & Wesson roared in her hand and she watched with a kind of numb, horrified fascination as a gaping wound opened on the side of her brother's head. A red mist appeared like a halo around his skull and she wanted to close her eyes but could not.

Mr. Midnight wavered over her, swaying like a skyscraper in a hurricane, his hand still grasping the knife he had used to carve and slice her flesh. His eyes were absurdly large and he furrowed his brow as if he could not quite comprehend what had just happened.

He lifted the knife again in his now-trembling hand and began to lunge forward and she pulled the trigger a second time. More blood spurted from her brother's head and this time he fell. The knife clattered to the floor and her brother's eyes glazed over and then he dropped straight down and lay still.

Cait dropped the gun like it had given her an electric shock and it thudded to the floor next to her injured arm.

And of course at that moment the police rescue team flew around the corner, four men dressed in fatigues and body armor, guns drawn, entering the room prepared to do battle. The men skidded to a stop directly in front of the murdered police officer's prone body. Their weapons swept side to side as they covered the room, alert for any threat.

Cait's eyes began to blur, either from pain or shock or the tears welling up in her eyes as a result of the horrible knowledge she had just killed a man. And not just any man, a blood relative. And not just any blood relative, her own brother. Her own twin.

Her vision wavered and she fought to stay awake.

Her arm burned and she fought to stay awake.

The law-enforcement team stood motionless in the doorway, taking in the scene, seemingly shocked into inaction by the devastation in the room. One of the officers spied Cait's mangled arm, a strip of skin stretching outward from her elbow across the floor, and retched. He clapped a hand to his mouth and looked away.

Cait tried to tell them to get help for Kevin, that he was gravely injured and needed medical attention immediately, and all that came out was a pathetic little croak. She swallowed. Tried unsuccessfully to force some saliva into her throat. Opened her mouth to try again.

At that moment the men in the fatigues and body armor sprang into action, one of them moving quickly to secure the Smith & Wesson, another stepping over the dead cop to assess the condition of Kevin and Virginia, and a third to check Milo's unmoving body for a pulse. Cait wondered why he would do that; she couldn't imagine anyone being alive with two bullets fired from almost point-blank range into his head.

The officer who had picked up the gun bent over her. It was the same man who had nearly thrown up at the sight of her arm, and he trained his eyes on hers, steadfastly avoiding looking at the oozing red mess that used to be her forearm.

Cait opened her mouth to say something to him and without warning he disappeared. Everything disappeared. She fell away into a warm, dark hole where it was safe and comfortable and no one tried to peel the skin from her bones with a knife.

53

The water of Tampa Bay shimmered in the distance, a deep teal blue as sunlight glinted off the tops of the waves. Salsa music drifted across the beach from a radio playing somewhere to Cait's right, lively and enthusiastic but soft as an afterthought. Cait's eyes were closed and she felt warm and drowsy, but still she caught bits and pieces of conversations, some in English and some in Spanish, as groups of people passed her beach chair, all chattering and laughing and enjoying the tropical Florida heat.

Her right arm sweated and itched incessantly. Surgeons had performed skin grafts to repair the damage done to the arm and had then covered it in antibiotic dressing before wrapping the whole thing in swaths of bandages, all of which needed to be cleaned and changed daily.

Cait wasn't about to complain, though. The doctors had said there was no structural damage and thus every reason to believe she would regain full use of the arm, although it would always look a little...off, with discolored skin from the grafts and small scars crisscrossing it like a road map. She considered herself incredibly, unbelievably fortunate not to have died an agonizing death in that tiny house in Everett, Massachusetts.

Every few seconds she opened her eyes, squinting against the hazy brightness, reassuring herself she really was still sitting on the beach in Florida. She reached out to touch her mother's arm. Received a comforting squeeze in return.

She sighed tiredly. The worst part, now that the ordeal had ended, was her inability to get anything close to a good night's sleep. Every night was the same: she would begin drifting off and the crippling fear would strike, the terrifying certainty that Milo Cain was lurking at the foot of her bed, knife in hand, waiting to begin peeling back her skin once more.

The psychologist said it was a natural reaction; that it was to be expected and would begin to fade over time—the trauma was only a couple of weeks old, after all—but Cait wondered whether that was true. The psychologist hadn't been in that house, hadn't gone under the knife with no anesthesia. The psychologist didn't understand. Not really.

But Virginia understood, and that was why, no matter how many times Cait reached over in the warm Tampa sunshine to make physical contact, no matter how many times she started a seemingly normal conversation about the weather, or where to eat lunch, only to dissolve into tears for no apparent reason, her mother never complained. She never told Cait to buck up, or to be strong, or to tough it out because tomorrow was another day; she never once said any of those things.

Because Virginia understood.

Virginia told Cait that watching while her newfound daughter, her own flesh and blood, was carved up by her newfound son, also her own flesh and blood, while bound and helpless, tied to a chair in her own living room, was the worst thing she had ever experienced in a life that had seen more than its share of trauma.

Cait reached over once again and stroked her mother's arm and mumbled, "Tell me again."

And Virginia understood.

"Well, let's see," she said amiably, as if sharing her recipe for lemon meringue pie. "You were conscious when the police SWAT team came charging into the room. That was right after you shot Milo."

She said it matter-of-factly, like it was no big deal. But Cait knew better.

She swallowed hard and nodded. She did not look at her mother or even open her eyes aside from her almost unconscious little blinking motion every few seconds to assure herself she was still on the beach. She didn't like thinking about that afternoon two weeks ago but couldn't stop. And hearing her mother tell the story was cathartic. She had asked Virginia to tell it dozens of times over the past two weeks.

"After you passed out," Virginia continued, "the policemen split up, one checking Milo to be sure he was no longer a threat—as if there could be any doubt, after taking two .38 slugs in the head, one of them through his eye—another freeing me from the chair, and an officer each tending to you and Kevin."

"Tell me about Kevin," Cait said, certain Virginia had known the request was coming. It was the same every time.

"Kevin had lost a lot of blood and the stab wound had punctured a lung, the blade passing ever-so-close to his heart. In fact, the young man who checked him out couldn't find a pulse and told his partners that Kevin was already dead. Needless to say, the medical personnel were inside the house the second the SWAT team radioed that it was clear. They stabilized you and then wheeled everyone out to waiting ambulances. That was the last time I saw Kevin."

Tears filled Cait's eyes as they always did at this point in the story. It was like she was watching a horror movie where she knew every plot twist and every line of dialogue by heart, but still could not keep from screaming when the boogeyman jumped out of the closet. She hadn't even managed to stay conscious to see her fiancé wheeled out on a stretcher after he had sacrificed everything in his failed attempt to save them.

"The last time you saw him," Cait repeated wonderingly.

"You mean the last time until after the surgery," a voice boomed from behind them, startling Cait and causing her to jump. She swiveled in her beach chair and drank in the sight of her boyfriend, his chest still swaddled in bandages covered by a light T-shirt. He looked ridiculous among all the tanned, shirtless surfer dudes dotting the beach, but also looked more desirable to Cait than all of them put together.

Kevin took in the look on her face and chuckled. He handed Virginia a lavender-colored frozen drink in a big plastic cup with a tiny umbrella sticking out the top before easing into a beach chair next to Cait with a satisfied sigh.

"I'm telling you," he said to her, "you really need to try these frozen pina coladas. They're unbelievable."

"I'll pass," she said. "I don't want to get drunk. I want to stay sober so I can look at you with clear eyes."

Kevin laughed. "To each his own. But I think Virginia is being a little overdramatic. It's not like I was *that* close to death. I just chose an inopportune time to take a little nap, that's all."

"Yeah, right," Cait shot back. "I've heard this story a hundred times *and* I've talked to the doctors. They said if the rescue had taken five minutes longer, you would have died right there in the chair, so don't give me that macho male crap!" She smiled as she said it, still amazed at their incredible good fortune.

Cait knew she had lost a lot on that couch—shooting her brother less than twenty-four hours after learning of his existence had opened a hole in her heart that would never completely heal—but she knew also she had had no choice in the matter, that Milo Cain had been irreparably broken and would not have stopped until everyone inside the house was dead, and that made all the difference in the world.

She felt sadness for what she had done but no guilt.

And while the sadness of losing her brother might never disappear, Cait understood she had gained something as well: a mother who would now be in her life forever. Virginia had already made plans to sell the house in Everett and move to Tampa permanently, and was on her way to becoming friends not just with Kevin, but with Cait's adoptive mother as well.

Milo had miraculously survived the shooting despite the delay in receiving medical attention, but was presently hospitalized and in a coma, and would require months of convalescence, maybe years.

In any event, according to the Suffolk County district attorney, he would never see the outside of a prison again. The full extent of Mr. Midnight's crimes, of his horrific brutality, was only beginning to be uncovered, and the D.A. assured Virginia and Cait that there was already more than enough evidence to keep Milo under lock and key for the rest of his life.

Cait blinked and smiled at Kevin.

She squeezed her mother's hand.

"You know what? I've changed my mind. Maybe I'll have that drink after all."

EPILOGUE

Footsteps echoed as the nurse moved away, waddling down the shadowy corridor of the prison infirmary like an overweight duck. Still in a coma two months after being shot in the face, Milo was unable to move a muscle, not even to open his one remaining eye.

What the others didn't realize, however, what they failed to understand, was that he could still hear and comprehend. In fact, although it had changed, he still possessed an acute awareness of his surroundings.

Milo paid particular attention to the doctors, who proclaimed, with their stuffy country-club Ivy-League medical school wisdom, that he would likely never regain consciousness, and even if he did, would remain forever in a vegetative state, paralyzed from the neck down, the result of a broken vertebra suffered from falling to the floor after being shot. It seemed a dismal future, and in those first agonizing days and weeks after the ill-fated confrontation in Everett, Milo had wallowed in utter solitary despair. He was unable to talk or to communicate in any way, a situation that left him desperate to bring an end to his misery, through death if necessary.

Not that he had any way of making that happen.

And then something strange and wonderful had occurred, almost mystical in its revelatory significance.

About three weeks after the Everett fiasco, a nurse had been bustling around his lonely hospital room, changing his bed linens. She was ignoring him completely, of course, not that Milo minded. What would she possibly be expected to say to an unresponsive lump of human tissue huddled under threadbare prison hospital blankets, especially when that lump of tissue had been "Mr. Midnight," one of Boston's most notorious serial killers?

Milo knew he would remember the following moment with the fondness and clarity other people reserved for their weddings, or the birth of their children. The coma and brain damage the gunshot wound had caused hadn't eliminated the mental movies he'd been subjected to his entire life; if anything, their frequency and severity had grown steadily stronger and more vivid, and as the nurse worked, he felt one blast into his head.

The nurse was daydreaming about her boyfriend, recalling their previous night's sexual encounter with what Milo considered admirable enthusiasm. He joined her in recalling the intensity of her climax, and then, without so much as a single conscious thought on his part, *pushed* a suggestion into her unsuspecting brain.

The nurse dropped immediately to the floor, panting and moaning and thrashing in a thirty-second orgasm. Afterward, she lay still for a moment. Then she rose, embarrassed and confused, but thankful no one besides the inanimate lump of tissue had been present to witness her carnal display. The nurse had hurriedly finished changing the sheets and then departed.

Just like that, Milo realized he had not lost everything. He had not come close to losing everything. In fact, it seemed he had *gained* something of extreme significance. He immediately stopped yearning for death and began testing his newfound ability.

And the more Milo tested the limits of his power, the more he discovered there weren't many. Maybe there weren't any.

What had once seemed like the ultimate prison sentence—the solitary confinement of his coma—now struck Milo Cain as nothing more than an opportunity to expand his consciousness...and his gift. Because he was free—*truly* free—in all the ways that mattered.

And now he was unstoppable.

———

To be the first to learn about new releases, and for the opportunity to win free ebooks, signed copies of print books, and other swag, take a moment to sign up for Allan Leverone's email newsletter at AllanLeverone.com.

Reader reviews are hugely important to authors looking to set their work apart from the competition. If you have a moment to spare, please consider taking a moment to leave a brief, honest review of *Mr. Midnight* at your point of purchase, at Goodreads, or at your favorite review site, and thank you.

———

About the author

Allan Leverone is the *New York Times* and *USA Today* bestselling author of nearly twenty novels, as well as a 2012 Derringer Award winner for excellence in short mystery fiction and a 2011 Pushcart Prize nominee. He lives in Londonderry, New Hampshire with his wife Sue, and has three grown children and two beautiful grandchildren. He loves to hear from readers and other authors; connect on Facebook, Twitter @AllanLeverone, and at AllanLeverone.com

———————

Also by Allan Leverone
Dark Fiction

After Midnight
The Lupin Project
Paskagankee
Revenant
Wellspring
Grimoire
Covenant
Linger: Mark of the Beast (Co-written with Edward Fallon)

Thrillers

The Lonely Mile
Final Vector
Parallax View: A Tracie Tanner Thriller
All Enemies: A Tracie Tanner Thriller
The Omega Connection: A Tracie Tanner Thriller
The Hitler Deception: A Tracie Tanner Thriller
The Kremlyov Infection: A Tracie Tanner Thriller
The Organization: A Jack Sheridan Pulp Thriller
Trigger Warning: A Jack Sheridan Pulp Thriller

Novellas

The Becoming
Flight 12: A Kristin Cunningham Thriller

Story Collections

Postcards from the Apocalypse
Letters from the Asylum
Uncle Brick and the Four Novelettes
The Tracie Tanner Collection: Three Complete Thriller Novels